Mystery at Lockley Grange

BOOKS BY CLARE CHASE

Mystery at Lockley Grange

CLARE CHASE

bookouture

Published by Bookouture in 2024

An imprint of Storyfire Ltd.
Carmelite House
50 Victoria Embankment
London EC4Y 0DZ

www.bookouture.com

Storyfire Ltd's authorised representative in the EEA is Hachette Ireland
8 Castlecourt Centre
Castleknock Road
Castleknock
Dublin 15 D15 YF6A
Ireland

ISBN: 978-1-83525-727-2
eBook ISBN: 978-1-83525-726-5

For Chris

PROLOGUE

Lance Hale floated in the warm water of his indoor pool, staring through the picture window across the dark grounds towards his house, Lockley Grange. Good grief, he'd had too much to eat and drink. Sonia kept telling him to cut back, especially when they had company, and she was right of course. She might not understand his work, but you could trust her on basic, practical things like that, including how to plan a party. She'd done it to perfection, and it had been much easier than hiring someone. If there was any justice in this world, things would go on like this... Anger gripped him as he realised how impossible that was now. He'd have to take action, one way or another.

He turned his mind to pleasanter thoughts of his many guests who'd arrived that night. The crowds had almost banished Lockley's shadowy corners and the dark corridors which echoed with memories. He'd stood up to give his speech acknowledging the Belford-Christie award. He was excelling in academia, just as he had as a diplomat. He visualised the sea of faces as he'd talked, lit by the glow from the sconces on the walls. The memory of the warm laughter as he'd made his opening remarks. The hush as he'd talked about his work in-depth had been gratifying too. So many people had come all the way to the wilds of Suffolk, just for him. That was what mattered in the long run, but why should he have to give up anything at all? He pondered his options, leaning back in the water, letting his legs float towards the surface.

He was pulled out of his reverie by a sharp pain, tugging in his chest. His feet were down on the pool's floor again in moments, and he waited, but the twinge was gone. Indigestion. That's all. And no wonder he'd got it. The evening hadn't been without tensions.

His mood soured as he remembered glancing down at the lectern to find the notes for his speech out of order, one page missing entirely. The pain came back and intensified. It had been sabotage, pure and simple. His assistant knew he'd had plenty to drink and hoped he'd struggle. But Lance had been practising the speech for days: in the bath, while walking the grounds, and in front of the mirror. Not because he was nervous – he simply enjoyed performing. So after a moment's surprise and a slightly awkward pause he'd rescued the situation like the professional he was.

It hadn't been the only challenge that night. On top of the ongoing background threat, there'd been arguments and that ridiculous message. Still, he'd met the problems head-on and, in the end, everything had gone smoothly. Swimmingly. He took a stroke along the length of the pool. But perhaps not. He felt odd again. Definitely too much to eat and drink. He shouldn't have started on the whisky so early in the day.

As he turned, instinctively making for the safety of the side, he saw a shadow beyond the window. Who was it? Someone coming to join him?

He felt worse now and hauled himself out of the water, but when he tried to stand, he couldn't manage it. Agony gripped him like a vice and he raised a hand in a plea for help, only to drag it down again and press it against his chest. He heard the door to the pool room creak and turned, but the figure was in shadow.

He tried to speak but the pain was intolerable. He only managed a groan. The figure rushed at him, and he was filled with fear. He curled into a ball but lost his balance and tumbled onto his side.

His last conscious thought was of that message he'd received. Why hadn't he taken it literally?

1

ONE DAY EARLIER

Eve Mallow and Viv Montague were rattling up the rutted driveway to Lockley Grange in the van belonging to Monty's, the teashop Viv owned. Viv treated the vehicle like a favourite pet, so Eve tried not to criticise it. All the same, she wished she hadn't eaten a cake before they'd begun the journey. Lockley Grange wasn't far from their home village of Saxford St Peter, but the van was a boneshaker. She found it impossible not to tense her stomach muscles, especially when Viv was driving. At least they were off public roads now.

The day was dark and dreary and the Grange looked grim and forbidding against the lowering sky. It didn't help that the place had a tragic history.

'You'd think the Hales would do something about the drive,' Viv said.

Eve fought the urge to grab the steering wheel as they approached a particularly large pothole. 'Things fell into disrepair years ago. The family didn't visit for a long time after Sir Lance's first wife died.' Eve hadn't shared the full details with Viv. She was worried she'd say something tactless when they arrived.

Viv shook her head. 'And I remember you saying his mind was always on his work anyway, not practical stuff.'

'That's right.' Eve had nannied for him and his late wife briefly, when she was just twenty-four and between jobs. Their kids had been four, three and one. Quite a handful. 'He was working for the Foreign and Commonwealth Office when I knew him, already well up the career ladder, and his wife was a high-flyer too. Household arrangements were chaotic.' She'd enjoyed the challenge.

Eve had heard that Sir Lance had begun to visit the Grange again when he wanted to focus on his work. These days he came down quite often. It must hurt, but she guessed he believed in facing his demons, and the place was relatively remote. If he wanted quiet, he couldn't do better.

After retiring from the civil service, he'd moved into academia, which had led to his current visit. He'd been awarded the Belford-Christie Prize for research into international relations and was hosting a party to celebrate, though after the death of his elder daughter three months earlier, the do was being billed as a tribute to her as well. Lance had insisted it was still a celebration – both of her life and his achievements. He didn't want anyone turning up in black.

'Tell me more about him,' Viv said, looking earnestly at Eve, not at where she was going. 'Why have you never looked him up?'

For Eve the more natural question would be, why would she? 'It's thirty years since we last met. I doubt he'd want some former nanny dropping in for tea.'

'Snob, is he?' Viv bumped the van into another pothole.

'I wouldn't say that. He was generous and jolly when I worked for him. He lent me one of his cars once, when a friend and I needed transport to a gig.'

'That was brave of him!'

Eve tried not to react. Her driving was considerably better

than Viv's. 'Anyway, I'm sure he'd forgotten all about me, but I reminded him when he hired us to cater for his party.'

It had come about via one of those small-world coincidences that sometimes happened. A neighbour of Eve's who knew Sir Lance's second wife had recommended Monty's as caterers, and Eve worked there part-time, so she and Lance had reconnected.

Viv was looking up at the Grange now. 'Must cost a fortune to keep up a house like this anyway. Perhaps he's given up trying.'

'I don't think it'll be that holding him back. He always had lots of money. Inherited mostly, from what I picked up back in the day.'

Whatever its state of repair, the Grange was impressive. She'd read up on it ages ago, when she'd realised it belonged to her old employer. Some of it dated back seven hundred years and most of the rest was mid-sixteenth century. The drive led directly towards the centre of the house, and to its left was the only modern touch: an annexe with huge glass windows. Eve could just see the luxurious swimming pool inside.

Robin, Eve's gardener fiancé who'd been hired to help tidy the grounds, had discovered the background to the new building from a member of staff. Sir Lance had installed it after his doctor told him he should take more care of his health. The Hales couldn't be hurting financially if that was the solution he'd chosen. It wasn't as though the Grange was even his main residence, though he'd been here for the past week, working and preparing for his guests.

'I saw an article about the Hales' London house in one of the Sunday colour supplements,' Viv said. 'Talk about immaculate. I suppose his second wife must have had some influence there.'

It would explain the media featuring the place too; Sonia Welton-Hale was a model and a household name. 'I'm surprised Sir Lance has chosen to host his celebration here, not in the capital.' Suffolk was the most beautiful county, but London would be easier for the dignitaries to reach.

'Less space there, probably.'

Lockley Grange was certainly cavernous. 'They could have hired a venue though.' Lance had always been extravagant when it came to parties.

'I'm surprised the prize committee didn't organise the event anyway.' Viv's hair, holly-berry red this Christmas season, gleamed in the Grange's outside light.

Eve cast Viv a sidelong glance and smiled. 'They did, I gather. A small, dry affair in the afternoon with a handful of top academics in attendance and no alcohol. If I know Lance, this will be a very different event with a much larger audience. The surroundings might be rough around the edges, but I expect the attendees will be dressed to the nines.' If it had been a celebration pure and simple, Lance would have lapped it up, but how must he be feeling when it was also a memorial to his daughter? Eve thought of the little girl she'd looked after all those years ago, and then of her own adult twins and the unimaginable pain of losing one of them. It was just like Lance to insist the occasion was still a celebration though – he was all about making sure the show went on.

'I can't wait.' Viv sounded excited. She and Eve had been invited to attend. 'I'm going to wear my pink and purple printed mini dress.'

'The one with the seventies flower-power design?' That would be interesting. Especially with the berry-red hair.

'Absolutely. I don't get out in it enough.'

Eve was still worrying over her own outfit and her mind was preoccupied with the food too.

They were supplying fine pastries for the event, both sweet, which they were used to, and savoury, which they weren't. It was an exciting new sideline and the samples Viv had produced were sumptuous, but Eve still couldn't help feeling nervous. They couldn't control how the food would be presented; hired staff would transfer it onto Lance's plates. Given the state of the drive, Eve wondered what the crockery would be like. She hoped it wasn't covered with chips and dirty-looking cracks.

'It's generous of Sir Lance to include so many of the villagers on the guest list,' Viv said. 'And he clearly wants to catch up with you; he wouldn't have invited you otherwise.'

Eve just smiled. She suspected he wanted to fill the place to the gills. He'd always loved a houseful and an audience. The fact that she worked as a freelance journalist when she wasn't helping at Monty's might appeal too. He wasn't averse to publicity, though he hadn't actually asked her to write anything. Eve hoped he wouldn't. Obituaries were her speciality. She'd occasionally dabbled in articles about the living but subjects that answered back tended to cause trouble. Eve always wrote honestly, which could be unpopular. She'd be happy to stick to producing pastries on this occasion.

Tonight, she and Viv were visiting the Grange to work out logistics: what could be put where, how much fridge space there was and so on. The following day they'd be back for the party itself, armed with everything they'd prepared.

Viv pulled up in the sweeping forecourt of the Grange and the van's engine juddered to a halt. She shuddered as she looked up at the house. 'I wonder if it's haunted.'

Eve could see where her unease had come from. The tall chimneys and the great walls of old brick were dark against the gathering dusk and the blank, curtainless windows were disconcerting. Anyone could be watching them; they'd never know. The grounds were the same: dotted with dark evergreen bushes and woods, beyond which anything might lurk. Her mind was dragged towards what had happened in the grounds many years earlier and her stomach tensed further.

'Let's get inside.' She needed to focus on the here and now

and see what they were presented with. Meeting Lance again would feel strange too – so far they'd only talked on the phone.

Eve pulled on a bell as they reached the huge oak front door but after waiting a full two minutes, no one came. The door was ajar, despite the frigid weather, and she glanced at Viv. 'Shall we?'

Viv shivered and nodded as Eve pushed it open, then shut it after them. If a house as vast as Lockley Grange stood any chance of staying warm, closed doors would be a must.

The entrance hall was dark and starkly lit by a chandelier in the centre, leaving its four corners in shadow. The walls were painted a depressing bottle green and dotted with paintings and a fox's head, its glass eyes staring down accusingly at them. To one side was a large, free-standing coat rack.

Eve was distracted by approaching voices.

'Of course, we haven't done what she suggested yet. What do you think? Worth the upheaval?' A deferential-sounding woman.

'Yes.' That was Lance's rich, melodious voice. 'She knows style, Lucy. It's her thing. Everyone has a talent.' He sounded entirely at ease with the woman called Lucy. Eve knew of her by reputation though they hadn't ever met. She guessed the 'she' they were talking about might be Lance's second wife, the model. She was an unknown quantity, though Eve had read articles about her.

'Right.' That was Lucy again. 'Six plug-in lamps for the entrance hall, then. I only hope the electrics can take it.'

Eve was pleased to know she'd get the before-and-after experience. The lamps sounded like a good idea. The place certainly needed something.

The pair still hadn't reached the hall but their voices were getting louder.

'I was thinking earlier that the fox head looks rather moth-eaten.' Eve wasn't surprised it had stuck in Lucy's mind.

Lance grunted. 'I agree, but she's right about that too. The less-faded paint behind it will show if we take it down. She suggests swapping out one of the darker paintings instead and putting that photograph of the bronze palm tree in the gilt frame in its place.'

'The palm tree?' The woman's voice took on a tone of surprise and slight disapproval. 'But you hate it!'

'I know.' The man laughed. 'I can't believe I haven't got round to chucking it out of the London house. But she says the photo of it will be perfect. The lamplight will make the bronze gleam and distract from the wall behind.'

It sounded like a smart move.

'She needs to think she's appreciated,' the man went on. 'As she is, of course,' he added, as though it was an afterthought.

'Of course she is.' The woman sounded as though she was assuaging any guilt Lance might feel. 'As I said when you asked me at the time, you made a fine choice for your second wife.'

Eve and Viv's eyes met. This was weird. Eve knew the history between Lance and Lucy. They'd been bound together by Lance's first wife's horrific death. Lucy had worked for him ever since. All the same, the importance he seemed to place in her opinion sounded like a recipe for trouble. How must his second wife feel about it?

2

A moment later, Lance stepped into the hall. 'Ah, who have we here?'

Eve was sure she'd have recognised him immediately, even without the recent press coverage. He was a handsome man in his sixties now with thick, greying hair swept back from his forehead and dark intense eyes. They seemed to flash as he looked from her to Viv.

She'd thought he might not recognise *her* but he rushed up to her immediately.

'Eve! How wonderful to see you again!' He gave her a hug and in seconds he'd turned to Viv and was pumping her hand. 'And you must be Viv! Thank you for helping us. We thought your samples were the best things we'd ever tasted.'

He'd found the short-cut to Viv's heart without any trouble, though he was probably being honest. Eve had been impressed when they'd tried some before dropping them off with a member of staff.

Eve felt the warmth of his welcome too, but the patronising way he'd spoken about his second wife still bothered her. *It's her thing. Everyone has a talent. She needs to think she's appreci-*

ated. She was glad she wouldn't hear what Lance said about her and Viv behind their backs.

'Lance, I'm so sorry about all you've been through since we last met.' Eve had written to him after both tragedies but it felt important to say it face to face.

He put a hand on her arm, nodded and blinked. 'Thank you.'

Behind Lance stood the woman who must be Lucy, wearing a chocolate-brown polo neck jumper and a tartan pencil skirt.

'Lucy, this is Eve, who I told you about. She once looked after the children for us in London. And here's Viv too, her talented colleague from Monty's teashop. We need to show them the kitchen, so they're clued up for tomorrow.' He turned to Eve and Viv. 'This is Lucy Garton. She's been my right-hand woman since time began. Without her, nothing I do would be possible. She's a genius and by rights she'd never have come to work for me.' He heaved a sigh. 'But life is unpredictable.'

Eve knew Lucy had been tipped for a prestigious job in academia, before Lance's first wife's death.

Lance put a hand on Lucy's arm, squeezing it for just a moment as their eyes met.

Their closeness was striking. Eve might have guessed they were lovers, had it not been for Lucy's tone when they'd talked about Lance's second wife. There'd been no jealousy there.

Lance turned back to her and Viv. 'Let me show you the kitchen while poor Lucy sorts out umpteen lights to brighten up this hall.'

It was good to see him treating her like an equal and relieving her of a job. He swept ahead of them down a dark corridor lined with heavy old paintings that needed cleaning. Once again, he moved with energy, as though he couldn't wait to get on to the next task. 'The children are looking forward to talking to you tomorrow, Eve,' he said, smiling at her rather tightly over his shoulder. 'Not that they're children any more.'

'I'm keen to see them too.' It must be harrowing for Lance that there were only two of them now. Poor man, losing a wife and an adult child. The knot of sadness at Eve's core tightened. As for the remaining two, it would be strange to fuse the impressions she'd formed thirty years ago with their adult selves. They were in high-powered roles now; they seemed to have taken after their parents.

'Here's the kitchen, for better or worse!' Lance waved a hand around the huge room. 'I'm down here at Lockley quite often now of course, but I'm afraid I only bothered updating the rooms I needed, and I'm not much of a cook.'

The fridge looked around fifty years old but it was a decent size. When Eve opened it, she wasn't sure if it was colder inside or in the room.

Lance met her eye and laughed suddenly. 'The house will come to life tomorrow, you'll see. It feels odd to throw it open after so many years, but it's time. We've had truckloads of wood delivered. We'll have fires going in every room and everything will sparkle.'

Eve hoped she wasn't blushing. She could have done without being so transparent. 'I'm sure it will. It's an amazing place.'

'Ah, yes. "Amazing" covers a multitude of sins, doesn't it?' He was laughing again. 'We're lucky to have half of Saxford St Peter helping us to get ready. I'll leave you so you can plan without me breathing down your necks but when you've finished, I hope you'll join me for a drink before you go.'

'He's a lot warmer than the house,' Viv said loudly, the instant he'd left the room.

'*Please* keep your voice down!' Eve whispered.

'What are you worried about? It was a compliment.'

They turned to work out where to store their pastries for maximum freshness and convenience, though unless the fire at one end of the kitchen worked miracles, they needn't worry about anything spoiling in the heat. Eve found some stackable racks which would help them cope with the quantities they needed to bring.

Ten minutes later, they retraced their steps down the corridor, listening for voices to guide them to Sir Lance and the drinks he'd mentioned. They were nearing the front entrance when they heard him and Lucy talking again.

'It's lucky that the other guests were prepared to come to Suffolk when you changed the venue,' Lucy said. 'It's been quite a scramble to get it all sorted but I know it's what you wanted.'

'It seemed essential at the time,' Lance replied. 'With the four of us in the same room the truth was bound to come out and it would only upset Sonia. I never thought I'd entertain here again, but Suffolk was the obvious answer at short notice. Though now it might all be pointless...' His voice turned irritable before it trailed off.

'What do you mean?' Lucy's tone was sharp.

'It doesn't matter.'

Eve had two seconds to ponder their words as she entered the room. So Lance hadn't come to Suffolk for the space Lockley Grange offered then. It seemed he and Lucy had rearranged the entire event to keep his second wife, Sonia, apart from someone who might hurt her. Eve's mind was full of questions: who was it, and why couldn't they travel outside London? What made them a threat, and why were Lance and Lucy keeping Sonia in the dark about it? Perhaps she was vulnerable in some way. Otherwise, it seemed downright peculiar that they knew about it and she wasn't involved.

3

The weather was bitter that evening, with rain turning to sleet outside the Cross Keys pub. Eve and Viv were holed up inside, close to the blazing logs in the inglenook fireplace. Viv looked very festive, her hair toning nicely with the berries of the holly which had been put up for decoration. It was just under a month until Christmas.

Sharing their table were Eve's fiancé Robin and her neighbours, Sylvia and Daphne. Sylvia was involved in Sir Lance's party too, thanks to her career as a professional photographer. She described herself as 'semi-retired', but Eve suspected that simply provided an excuse to reject any job she didn't fancy; she was always busy.

She was laughing now, eyes sparkling, her long grey plait hanging forward over one shoulder. 'I'm looking forward to recording the event. Lance says he wants lots of informal shots so I've got carte blanche to catch people unawares. The guests will be forewarned of course, but I'm hoping they'll forget all about me after a glass or two of fizz.'

Sylvia had a wicked sense of humour and was a past master at showing people's characters in her shots.

'It'll be good to catch up with Sonia too,' she went on. 'She rarely comes to Suffolk. Too busy with work, and I dare say some time apart helps keep her and Lance's marriage fresh. She tells me he's so obsessed with his research that it's best to let him scuttle off and get on with it.'

It was Sylvia who'd put Eve and Viv up for the catering job.

'It was intriguing to see him again after so many years,' Eve said. 'And it'll be weird to see his children all grown up.' Once again, she thought of the family members who'd be missing. 'I'm looking forward to meeting Sonia as well; his first wife was still alive when I was with them.'

Sylvia nodded, her eyes serious. 'I never met her, but I've known Sonia a good while.'

'What do you think of her?'

'She's a hoot. Tough. Clever.'

Not vulnerable then. Eve was even more disturbed to know Lance and Lucy were keeping secrets from her. 'What does she make of Lucy Garton?' She couldn't resist asking. 'Lucy and Lance seem thick as thieves.'

Sylvia raised an eyebrow. 'She treats her as a fact of life. I gather she's been a live-in all-round help – housekeeper, childminder, PA, you name it – ever since Lance's first wife died. Everywhere Lance goes, she goes too. You probably know more about it than I do. Were Lucy and the first wife friends?'

Eve nodded. 'They were at Cambridge together, along with Lance. Then later on, Lucy was in a passionate relationship with Lance's brother. And then Lance's first wife was killed. Horrific.' She closed her eyes for a moment, unable to get the graphic images out of her head. 'You probably read the news reports.' It was how Eve had got her information.

Viv frowned. 'I don't remember anything about it. How long ago was this?'

Eve did a quick mental calculation. Lance's eldest had been

twelve at the time and he was thirty-four now. 'Twenty-two years ago.'

'I'd have been knee-deep in nappies.' Viv had three adult boys. 'Either that or up to my eyeballs at the teashop.'

'I know bits,' Sylvia said. 'Just what Sonia's told me, and snippets of gossip, but I never got the full story. Come on, Eve. Out with it.'

For a moment, Eve hesitated. She wasn't superstitious but it was the tale of a marriage brought to an abrupt end under the most terrible circumstances. She was due to wed Robin in just over three weeks' time and focusing on something so nightmarish made her anxious. She hadn't told Robin the story for the same reason.

She turned to him now. 'Do you already know what happened?'

He shook his head. 'I was still down in London at the time.' He'd been a detective there until informing on corrupt colleagues had forced him to go underground, changing his name, location and profession. The entire network was behind bars now, thank goodness, so he could be open about his past.

'I was down there when it happened too.' Eve had only moved to Saxford five years before – around the time that Lance and Sonia had married, in fact. 'But it made the national news, and of course it hit home for me, because of my link with the family. It's the same with the latest tragedy.'

They all nodded. They'd discussed the details of Lance's daughter's death, given the party was billed in part as a tribute to her.

Eve put down her glass of wine and turned to the others. 'Most of what I've got is second-hand tittle-tattle, laid over my background knowledge. I liked Lance's first wife, Jacqueline. She worked long hours as a human-rights lawyer, but whenever she was around, she was engaged and sparky. Bright of course, but also empathetic and energetic. It was hard to take it in when

I heard she was dead.' And it had been horrible to think of the three children Eve had cared for being left without their mother.

'Yes, yes,' said Viv. 'But what happened?'

'Lance was in the UK – it was before he got his first senior ambassadorial position. He'd come to Lockley Grange for a holiday, with Jacqueline and the kids in tow, as well as his brother, Bruno, and Lucy. They were infatuated with each other at the time.'

'I hear Bruno was the black sheep of the family,' Sylvia put in, 'but Lance brought him back into the fold. That decision led to Bruno and Lucy's relationship, according to Sonia. She didn't know any of them back then of course, but I gather Lance is unguarded when he's drunk and talks in his sleep too. I expect her insights are accurate.' She took up her tumbler and it caught the light from the fire.

'What else did she say?' Eve only had the public version of the story.

'That Lance still tries to justify himself when he's had too much to drink. He says his dad treated Bruno unfairly which made Lance more protective and that Bruno pulled the wool over Lance's eyes. And although he gave Bruno house room, he was never happy about his relationship with Lucy. He tried to get her to break it off with him.' Sylvia gave an ironic smile. 'Hypocritical, you might say – if he thought Bruno was an unsuitable match for his friend, why allow him to visit at all? But apparently, Lance's crowd flocked around when Bruno visited. He livened up parties and made Lance seem cool, so he didn't discourage him.'

It fitted with what Eve knew. 'I remember reading that Bruno had been expelled from every school he'd attended. The media said he'd been touring Europe with a band, getting into scrapes while Lance was at university. Then Lucy met Bruno at one of Lance's parties and was smitten.'

Eve thought of the quiet, organised woman she'd seen at Lockley Grange. In her experience, it was sometimes the most controlled types who went spectacularly off the rails and fell for the wrong people.

'What happened next?' Viv said.

'Jacqueline was worried by Bruno, from what the papers said.' Eve sipped her wine. 'She had her children to consider and the influence he might have on them. In the end, there was a massive row.'

Sylvia nodded. 'Sonia thinks Bruno had left drugs lying around the house, and that he was high half the time too.'

Having some of the gaps filled made the scene even more vivid. 'Jacqueline told Lance it was her or Bruno.'

She looked at Sylvia who nodded her agreement and took over the story again.

'When Bruno heard, he was livid with Jacqueline, and off his head on some drug or other. He'd already heard Lance trying to persuade Lucy to give him up. Sonia thinks the combination made him turn on them.'

It all fitted. 'The news reports say he got into his car, with Lucy in the passenger seat, all set to leave Lockley Grange for good, or so everyone thought, including Lucy. But she quickly realised he'd never intended to go without taking his revenge. He knew where Jacqueline was – out in the grounds, checking a fence that had just been mended. Lucy told the court she was terrified at how fast he was driving. She wanted to get out, but she couldn't. He'd locked the doors, and they were going at breakneck speed. In the end, she was sitting there helpless in the passenger seat when Bruno mowed Jacqueline down. He drove over her and through the fence and kept on going. He was caught, of course. In court, he said he was taking revenge on her and Lance – robbing Lance of his wife, just as Lance had tried to rob Bruno of Lucy.'

Sylvia closed her eyes for a moment and took a deep breath. 'He's out of prison again now.'

Daphne winced, her gaze on the table, hands clasped together.

Viv's eyes were huge. 'Poor Lance.'

'Poor Jacqueline!' Sylvia said. 'If he'd kept Bruno at bay, she'd still be alive, and Lucy's life would have panned out very differently.' She sipped her whisky.

As ever, the image of Jacquline filled Eve's head. Her lively brown eyes and long, dark hair pulled back off her face. Her quickness and her spirit. And then Eve thought of the three children she'd cuddled when they were tiny, and how they must have felt when they heard their mum was dead. To say nothing of the trauma Lucy had suffered. 'Lucy was already rising up the ladder in academia when it happened. She'd shone at university too – Lance was top in his year, but she was second. Everyone agreed she was destined for great things, but that all went out of the window.'

Sylvia drained her whisky. 'Sonia said Lucy could never go back to Cambridge. She wouldn't even leave the house for months afterwards. Lance came to see her at Lockley Grange each weekend and when she finally ventured further afield it was back to London, and in his company. I think Lance must have felt responsible. I gather he did everything for her back then. Though it benefited him too, of course. She became his right-hand woman, helping to run the household and look after the children. The youngest was only nine when Jacquline was killed, isn't that right, Eve?'

Eve nodded.

'Sonia thinks Lucy gained strength from focusing on them and Lance. They became her project. She lived in, travelled with them when required, looked after them when Lance worked and was his intellectual equal, sharing his problems. Sonia suspects he discussed all kinds of private work stuff with her, whether he was meant to or not. She says he has complete confidence in her, and vice versa.'

Eve looked at Robin. 'That fits with what we saw today. I can see how it happened, but I'd feel cut out if I was Sonia. She must have known the situation when she agreed to marry Lance, but I imagine the reality is claustrophobic.'

Sylvia nodded. 'I agree. I suspect it's no bad thing that Sonia's away modelling so much.'

Viv leaned forward. 'And now Lance's middle child is dead too.' She had three of her own, and Eve bet she was putting herself in Lance's shoes.

The latest death sat there like an uncomfortable lump in Eve's chest. Lance's elder daughter had fallen from a cliff in Cornwall around three months earlier and died. The 7 September. Eve could almost feel the warm little three-year-old sitting on her lap, but that child had been long gone. She'd been thirty-three when she died, and the deputy editor of a national newspaper. The weather had been terrible, the night of the accident – stormy, with high winds and poor visibility. The police assumed she'd missed her footing.

'It's brave of Sir Lance to carry on with the party,' Daphne said, 'and to present the whole thing as a celebration.'

'But a life *should* be celebrated.' Sylvia gave a wry smile. 'And Lance is a show-must-go-on sort, wouldn't you say, Eve?'

Eve nodded. 'Definitely.' Continuing would be a demonstration of strength.

'And the event was planned before the death, with people flying in from overseas, though the venue changed,' Sylvia went on. 'But I agree with you, Daphne. If you'd died recently, I wouldn't hold a shindig.'

'There you are,' Viv said to Daphne. 'Romance isn't dead.'

4

_____

When Eve and Viv arrived at Lockley Grange the following day, ready to offload their pastries, the entrance had been transformed.

Lance was first to greet them and seemed to read Eve's mind. 'It does look better, doesn't it? Sonia's idea. She's a model; she knows all about staging.'

'It works beautifully.'

The bank of lights and the gleam from the huge photo of the bronze palm tree were what caught her eye. The dark hallway beyond was all but invisible.

Lance walked with them towards the kitchen, but Eve and Viv assured him they could find their own way.

'You must have a lot to do,' Eve said.

He nodded, beaming. He didn't look a bit nervous despite the number of guests he was expecting and the press who'd been invited. Eve enjoyed meeting people, but public speaking wasn't her thing.

She and Viv went to and fro, carrying the pastries to the kitchen, stacking them ready for the hired staff to serve. By the time they'd finished they'd covered every surface, including a hatchway to an adjoining room.

'There's no room to transfer our food to the serving dishes,' Viv said. 'It's asking for trouble. What's the betting half the pastries land on the floor?' She seemed disinclined to leave.

'I'm sure the staff will find a way.' Eve steered her out of the door. 'We need to get back home, change and pick up the others.' Robin and Daphne were attending the party as well as Sylvia and her trusty camera.

Viv glanced at her watch. 'We're not in *that* much of a hurry.'

Eve took a deep breath and tried to relax. She was always ahead of time. 'Even so, we should leave the staff to it.' She hated people peering over her shoulder as she worked, and they probably would too. 'It's out of our hands now.'

But Viv turned right out of the kitchen instead of back towards the entrance hall. 'I'll just see if I can find them to have a very quick word.'

Eve would have to follow; she might need to smooth ruffled feathers.

'Oh my word,' Viv said, pausing by an open doorway. 'Look at this!'

They'd gone further away from the rooms Lance must use on his Suffolk visits. Here, the place felt abandoned. The room Viv had spotted made it clear life had been interrupted. The space looked frozen in time. Eve wandered in for a closer look; she couldn't help herself. Copies of *The Economist* and *Vogue* dating back twenty-two years lay on a coffee table, coated in dust. Desiccated insects decorated the mantelpiece and a paperback, still open, had been abandoned on the arm of a sofa. There was even a dried-out coffee cup.

Eve had wondered how Lance had coped with coming back. It seemed this was the answer: he'd holed up in a small part of the house and refused to look at the rest. Too many memories, she guessed.

'Let's go.' Viv's face was pale. 'It's creepy.'

They were just about to turn back when Eve heard a raised voice.

'This is just like you, Maynard.' Eve recognised Lance's rich tones.

Viv raised an eyebrow. 'Maynard is Lance's son?' For once she managed to whisper.

Eve nodded, picturing a scruffy four-year-old with tufty hair and loose shoelaces.

'I don't suppose you'd care to tell me *why* you need so much money?' Lance's voice reverberated with anger.

'It's an investment opportunity. Something only a fool would turn down and it's now or never. It's not as though you're short. I can pay you back with interest if you'll just trust me.'

'Trust you?' Lance's voice dripped with disdain. 'You're clever, Maynard, but not as much as you think.'

'Not as clever as you, you mean?'

Lance didn't reply.

'This is so typical. You can't bear to be challenged.'

'Far from it. What I can't bear is you expecting me to believe your ridiculous lies. Wait! Is someone blackmailing you?' He sounded panicked now, then muttered something under his breath. The only word Eve caught was 'conserve', which figured. They both had reputations to protect. A moment later he was clearly audible again: 'Has word finally got out?'

'Not as far as I know. I'm hardly likely to say anything, am I?' Maynard matched his father's tone. 'But you might have.'

'Don't be ridiculous. Of course I haven't.'

'Not even to Sonia?'

Lance huffed. 'Certainly not! Why would I? It happened years before I met her.'

'If you haven't talked then it must be Lucy!'

'So you are being blackmailed then!'

'I didn't say that!'

'It won't have been Lucy.' Lance's voice was quieter again. 'She's a hundred per cent loyal to you and me.'

'I don't think it's possible to be both these days. You and I are at each other's throats half the time. And if Lucy had to choose, she'd choose you.'

'It's not in my interest to have your grubby secret come out either. Lucy wouldn't tell.'

'Then it has to be you. Everyone knows you have no filter when you're drunk.'

'How dare you!'

A door down the corridor was yanked open.

Eve and Viv moved as one into the room with the abandoned magazines. Eve's heart was thudding hard, her chest tight as the pair of them waited.

From the shadows they saw Maynard storm past. Sturdily built, and well turned out in a dark suit. Jaw heavy, eyes mean. She tried to see the little boy she'd known in his features, but he was barely recognisable.

She was already familiar with the modern-day Maynard, though. He'd been a member of parliament for two years. She'd scanned the press coverage after he was elected and seen his photo again in the reports on his sister's death.

Thank goodness he didn't realise he'd been overheard. Eve wondered what the heck he'd done. It sounded serious enough to put anyone who knew about it in danger.

5

Later that evening, Eve stood in the reception hall with Robin, Viv and Daphne, feeling their way into the party. Eve was in her fitted green velvet dress, a glass of champagne in hand.

'You don't need to worry,' Robin said as her gaze ranged over the room. 'You look gorgeous whatever you wear.'

'Flatterer.' She gave him a smile. 'I'm not sure I like you being able to read my mind so easily. I have to say, you scrub up quite well yourself.'

He grinned. 'It took me hours to get the dirt from under my nails.'

A perennial gardening hazard. He looked a million dollars in evening dress. She couldn't believe they'd be married so soon. The thought still sent a thrill of excitement through her. After her disastrous ex had walked out, she'd never thought she'd feel so joyous again.

'Here's Sonia!' Sylvia had appeared in front of them with a beautiful blonde woman who was probably somewhere in her forties. She had wide blue eyes, high cheekbones and elegant bone structure. Eve could see why she was sought after as a model. Tonight, she wore a black figure-hugging dress with lace sleeves and a sweetheart neckline.

Eve shook hands. 'Pleased to meet you. I gather you're responsible for the party décor. It all looks amazing.'

Sonia gave her a wry smile. 'Thanks, but most of the Grange is stuck in the past, I'm afraid. I was surprised when Lance decided to host the party here, but he said he knew I'd make it work.' She laughed and rolled her eyes.

Maynard had joined them. It was three hours after his row with Lance but he still looked disgruntled. He turned to Sonia. 'You might not be the sharpest knife in the drawer, but you're very good at menu planning and making things look better than they really are.'

Ouch. Eve and Viv shared a grimace. The party guests nearby had gone quiet, just in time to hear Maynard's insult. Eve had been about to introduce herself and remind him of old times but now she held back.

'In a bad mood?' Sonia asked him. Perhaps she knew about the argument.

'Don't tease her, Maynard.' A tall man with sandy hair appeared beside them. 'Everyone's got their own talents.' He must have been listening to Lance. 'It's easy to see Sonia's.' He leered and Eve saw Robin frown. She was frowning too. The man must be drunk or an idiot. Or probably both.

If she'd been Sonia, she'd have felt like slapping him, but Sonia just smiled. 'Yes, it's a great shame I'm so dense, but I'm delighted that you appreciate my body. It's easy to see where *your* brain is located.' She stared pointedly at his trousers.

The man blinked, a flush creeping up his neck. Other people were laughing at him now, and he turned away, muttering something unsavoury.

'Sorry about that,' Sonia said, as Maynard went off to find himself a drink. 'I've been a fish out of water ever since I married into the Hale family. After five years I've got used to sticking up for myself. For a load of supposed intellectuals, some of the views they air are incredibly—'

She was interrupted by the chinking of a fork against a champagne bottle and Eve looked up to see that Lance had mounted a temporarily erected platform, complete with lectern. He looked down over his guests. 'My dear friends,' he said, 'thank you for coming to Suffolk for this special gathering. I'm both proud and humbled to have you here and I'll be round to talk to each of you presently. My formal speech can wait, as I'm sure you'll all agree.' There was gentle laughter and someone called out, 'Hear, hear.' 'For now, I want to focus on my wonderful, darling daughter, Jenna.'

Silence fell instantly.

'When I planned this event, I thought she would be here by my side, along with dear Maynard and Naomi. The fact that she's no longer with us breaks my heart.' He paused to take a juddery breath. 'She was known far and wide, but allow me to talk a little about her achievements.' He spoke of her upbringing in the Hale household, her triumphs at school and at Oxford, her glittering career in journalism, and the stories she'd broken. At last, he paused and took a deep breath. 'Please raise your glasses to her now. Darling Jenna.'

Everyone repeated the toast. Several people were crying, and when Eve turned to look at Lance, moments after he'd left the stage, she saw he was no exception. He'd held it together bravely for his speech, but no more. Maynard's eyes glistened too, and Lance was hugging a young woman with chin-length chestnut hair who looked very distressed.

Naomi. Eve recognised the hair colour, the dimpled chin and large eyes. Lance and Jacqueline's youngest, to whom Eve had sung lullabies and read baby books.

'The news of Jenna's death was an awful shock to all of us,' Sonia said, though she wasn't crying herself. 'We weren't close,' she went on. 'She didn't feel I was right for Lance and she never got past that. Years had passed, but I suppose it still felt as though I was replacing her mum.'

When Lance and his remaining children looked as though they'd recovered themselves, Sonia took Eve to be reintroduced. 'Maynard will behave himself when he realises who you are,' she said, with the same wry smile as before, 'especially with Lance listening in.'

As they approached, Lance pulled Sonia towards him. He was clumsy about it and Eve sensed he'd had too much to drink, just like the sandy-haired man.

'My darling,' he said to her. 'You look ravishing. And the décor and the refreshments are a triumph. You're in your element.'

'The food is down to Eve and her colleague,' Sonia said, which was just as well – Eve would have let it pass, but Viv would be bursting to remind him of the fact if she'd overheard.

'Of course' – Lance nodded at Eve, a twinkle in his eye – 'but you chose who to hire and you did it beautifully. Now, Eve, let me remember you to my children.'

But of course, they wouldn't remember. Not even Maynard. It was so long ago. They shook hands though, and Naomi said it was nice to see her again.

'Maynard's an MP now, as I'm sure you're aware,' Lance said. He sounded proud, despite the row earlier. 'And Naomi is an economist working for a charity focused on eradicating poverty.' He ruffled her hair as though she was still a child. 'An idealist like her mother. Naomi fights against the tide, just as Jacqueline did. People are animals unfortunately; they want to rise to the top at the expense of others and there's no way of stopping it.'

'Dad.' Naomi sounded tired, as though he'd said the same thing many times before.

'It's not the way I want it, it's just the way it is.'

She stood up straighter, so he could no longer pull her close.

'That's your view but it's not mine. I wish you hadn't given that interview pulling my report to pieces.'

Lance waved a hand. 'I thought we'd been through all this yesterday.'

'We didn't finish the conversation. You walked out of the room.' Naomi's face was pale, her knuckles clenched white.

'Why bother wasting my breath when I could see I'd never convince you?' Eve guessed the idea that he might be wrong hadn't crossed his mind. 'As for the interview, I had to say what I thought.'

'Very publicly.' Naomi was only just controlling her voice.

Rubbishing his own daughter's work was extreme, especially when he was wading into her area of expertise. Lance wasn't an economist.

Naomi began to walk away – an act of strength in Eve's eyes.

'I suspect she's in a bad mood because her partner couldn't make it tonight,' Lance said. 'That's theatrical folk for you. Apparently directing a play's more important than this event, even if you're months into a run. You'd think everything would run like clockwork by that stage.'

Naomi swung round. 'Don't be so selfish, Dad. The play's important!' She turned to Eve. 'It's been such a success that it's just transferred from a tiny venue in Edinburgh to one of the city's best theatres. The sort where critics from the national dailies turn up. I was the one who said it should take precedence.'

Eve nodded. Good for Naomi. She suspected it was Lance who felt slighted. He was welcoming and generous but she'd realised early on that he liked to be top dog.

'That's put me in my place,' he said, laughing, as Naomi strode away. 'Still, something's got her goat. We're close normally.'

How could he be so obtuse?

'She's already told you what it was,' Maynard drawled. 'You pulled three years of her research apart. She's not as good as she thinks she is, and you've forced her to face up to the fact.'

No wonder she was fed up. As for Maynard, he really was infuriating. Memories of him as a child filtered back into her mind. The way he and Jenna, aged just four and three, used to fight over who was best. Lance had encouraged them. He'd already started teaching them to read and played them off against each other, setting challenges, both mental and physical. Jacqueline had been worried that Jenna would come off worse, being a year younger than her brother, but rather than putting a stop to Lance's games, she'd egged Jenna on not to be beaten. Naomi, aged one, had been too young to get involved. She'd seemed like an oasis of calm in comparison.

Lance was shaking his head at his son. 'Nonsense. Naomi's a big girl with an excellent brain. She can fight her own battles.' He watched his daughter weave through the crowds until she was out of sight.

Maynard looked furious.

6

It was another half hour before Eve saw Naomi again. She was standing chatting with a small group including Maynard when Eve accidentally caught her eye.

'I'm sorry about earlier,' Naomi said, moving closer. 'It's Dad's night. I shouldn't have let my temper get the better of me. I hope I was less grumpy as a baby.'

'You were sweet.' It was funny to think of her on Eve's lap, eating a rusk. 'It can't have been easy when Lance gave that interview.' Eve had looked it up on her phone during a visit to the ladies'. Within days of Naomi producing her report he'd cast doubt on her conclusions. He was a man with plenty of contacts and his pronouncements had caused a stir because he was her dad.

'I was hurt, but I shouldn't have been surprised. I know his views are different to mine and he's never been backward in coming forward.' She paused, then took a deep breath and shook her head. 'All the same, he was a good dad to me growing up – it can't have been easy after Mum died. It's just that it's a crucial time for the charity. I'd got some interest in parliament and an appointment to go and speak to a group of MPs.'

Maynard rolled his eyes but she carried on. 'I think we could really make a difference, if only Dad doesn't put them off. Some of them seem to be backtracking now. You could put in a good word, Maynard.'

Maynard groaned. 'I can't tell them what to do. I've said I'll try.'

Eve wouldn't trust him to try for a minute. More memories came back of how he'd treated his younger sisters, hiding their toys and pulling faces. She remembered him ripping the head off a velvet rabbit of Jenna's, and putting the cat into Naomi's cot as she was sleeping.

Once again, she wondered what he'd done that was worthy of blackmail, and what he might do to resolve the situation. As an MP, he had an awful lot to lose.

In that quiet moment, she became conscious of Lance's rich laugh. He was surrounded by women now. Eve had already registered that he was good-looking, but the way they pressed in close made his magnetism even more obvious.

'He's got them eating out of his hand, hasn't he?' It was the drunk, sandy-haired man again, watching proceedings.

'It's always been that way.' Maynard's dismissive tone sounded almost genuine. Underneath it, Eve decided he was jealous.

'Plays away, does he?' The sandy-haired man grinned.

Maynard's look turned unfriendly. 'That's an unpleasant question to ask, even for you.'

'What do you say, Naomi?' The man turned to her. 'I notice Maynard's not denying it.'

Naomi's lips narrowed and Mr Sandy Hair looked at her speculatively.

The bad atmosphere was making Eve increasingly uncomfortable. She had a sense of foreboding, as though all the rivalry and resentment among the Hales was coming to a head. She was glad of the interruption when Lance stood up to give his second speech. It was fascinating to watch him. He managed to talk as though he was in a one-to-one conversation with each person in the room. Eve could imagine how successful he'd been as a diplomat. Not that there was anything diplomatic about the way he'd rubbished Naomi's research; she guessed he applied different rules in his personal life. Perhaps he felt threatened by his children, the young pretenders ready to replace him. That could be why his marriage to Sonia worked, assuming it did. They operated in entirely different spheres. No one would compare them, unlike him and Jacqueline, who had different careers but used similar skills. Eve knew their marriage had been passionate, but tempestuous too. She'd heard the rows.

Eve turned her attention back to Lance. He'd stopped suddenly mid-speech, his eyes on the lectern where he stood, his hand gripping its angled top. For a moment, Eve wondered if he was ill but then he snapped out of it, gave a quick snort, and carried on. There'd been some problem with his notes, perhaps. He sounded just as engaged and warm as before, but he shot the occasional livid glance at a woman of around Naomi's age with long dark hair. She twisted her hands nervously, face pale, eyes hollow; she looked exhausted.

When Lance finished, he met the young woman's eye and gave the faintest nod towards a corner of the room.

It was agonising. Eve felt sure he was going to tell her off. Doing it in the same room as the guests was unforgiveable, but there was an intensity in Lance's eyes and a fresh drink in his hand.

A moment later, he and the young woman had reached the 'quiet' space to one side of the partygoers. It wasn't at all private.

Eve heard bits of the dressing down, and what she didn't hear was echoed in shocked whispers by those standing closer by. The woman was Lance's research assistant and Lance was accusing her of mucking up his speech notes. Of deliberately leaving out an entire page to throw him off. And then he was telling her it hadn't worked because he was a professional and couldn't be 'destroyed' in such a basic way.

The word seemed way over the top. Even if the speech had gone disastrously, it wouldn't have finished his career. The woman was in tears, swearing she hadn't muddled his notes, deliberately or otherwise. That she'd checked them ten minutes before he started talking. Eve felt for her. Even guests who were too polite to stare couldn't help witnessing her humiliation. And she looked so worn out – after preparing for this very event, perhaps. Eve remembered being that tired once, and how impossible it was to keep your feelings in check. If the woman *had* messed up, it was probably because she was overworked.

Eve heard Lance's final words: 'It's not just about the speech and you know it. I've already warned you – you knew this was coming. You've betrayed me! You can wave goodbye to a career in international relations. No one will want to work with you by the time I've finished.'

Eve could believe it. He'd never done anything by halves. It was the other side of his passionate, intense coin. Already, he'd muddied her name in front of a large group of academics working in her field. He seemed intent on shutting the woman down.

She was left stranded on the opposite side of the room from the huge double doors, the best means of escape.

It was Naomi who went to her, taking her hand and putting an arm around her shoulder to shepherd her through the crowds. Lance watched them from a distance, his eyes angry. Most people had turned away. The show was over. But Eve was spellbound. Full of pity with no way of expressing it. It meant she saw the research assistant's look of despair before she and Naomi turned their backs on the crowd and huddled together, as if they were exchanging secrets.

When Eve could see Naomi's expression again, it was one

of total confusion. Then her hand was back on the research assistant's arm as she leaned in, speaking urgently. Eve didn't catch the words, but the research assistant's reply rang out, sharp with surprise. 'No. Of course not. No way.'

Then Naomi stood back, leaning against the wall as though to stop herself falling. She was fiddling with the zip on her navy velvet bag but her eyes were wide and unfocused. Whatever Lance's assistant had told her, it had clearly knocked her for six.

Eve glanced away and realised Lance was still watching Naomi too, his brow furrowed.

Lance's research assistant disappeared and Sonia came to check on her stepdaughter. They talked quietly and Sonia hugged Naomi; it was nice to see signs of their close relationship. Naomi had clearly accepted her stepmum in a way that Maynard and Jenna hadn't. Eve was glad her twins got on with Robin and that they were old enough to see things in the round. Naomi looked grateful for Sonia's support, but Eve still fancied she was holding something back. There was none of the urgent chat she'd exchanged with the research assistant. Eve couldn't imagine what that had been about.

The moment Sonia left, Naomi made for Lance. For the first time since Eve had met him, he looked scared. Uncertain. Naomi nodded towards the double doors and Lance went out of them ahead of her without so much as a murmur. Something in her eye must have told him she wasn't mucking around. Eve's sense of unease increased. If the Hale family was on the brink, hearing Naomi and Lance's conversation might tell her why. Once again, she thought of Naomi as a baby and her protective feelings came rushing back. It was no excuse, but she followed her anyway, muttering something to Robin about needing the loo.

But it was no good. There were too many people milling around for her to listen in as she had with Lance and Maynard.

It was another row though, Eve could hear that much, and several bystanders raised their eyebrows.

At the moment, the worst of the Hales' blow-ups were happening behind closed doors. The event was keeping a lid on things, but that meant there was nowhere for the pressure to go. In her experience, it was a recipe for disaster. The talk of betrayal, of careers destroyed, of years of work going to waste, and above all of blackmail, made Eve's mouth go dry.

She and the gang stayed until the party's bitter end, thanks to Sylvia's role as official photographer. Lance seemed to have sobered up a bit and was sweetness and light again, but Eve couldn't forget the events earlier in the evening.

She was walking hand in hand with Robin, ready to get her coat, when she noticed someone had dropped a handkerchief on the floor. She wasn't wild about picking it up – the last thing she wanted was to catch a bug before her wedding – but if she didn't do it, someone else would have to. She'd wash her hands immediately afterwards.

Eve held the hanky gingerly. Heck, what was that smell?

Robin frowned. He must have got it too.

'I'm glad I rescued this now.' She put the hanky in her pocket and strode towards the door, the hairs on the back of her neck lifting.

'I wasn't expecting you to get sentimentally attached to it.'

'Ha ha.' She gave him a look. 'Wait until we get outside.'

They'd come back in her car rather than Viv's clanking van and Eve went to find it on the sweeping forecourt. The rest of the gang were hard on her heels.

'What is it?' Viv demanded as she squeezed into the back seat with Sylvia and Daphne. It was on the cosy side. 'Have you spotted something fishy?'

'No. Chilli-ish.'

'What?'

Eve passed the handkerchief to Robin then released the clutch and drove off.

Viv must have been watching from the back. 'Ugh. Who uses cotton hankies these days? So unhygienic.'

'Don't worry.' Eve watched Lockley Grange recede in the rear-view mirror. 'I don't think anyone was using it because they had a cold.'

'No.' Sylvia coughed as Robin handed her the hanky. 'Mopping up chilli oil, more like.'

'Except we provided the food,' Eve said, 'and there was no chilli oil involved. Nor any in the kitchen that I saw. And who wipes up oil with a cotton hanky when there are paper napkins all over the place?'

'What do you think then?' Daphne asked.

Eve's eyes were still watering from the chilli fumes. She didn't like the way her thoughts were turning, but only one conclusion sprang to mind. 'There was a lot of emotion this evening when Lance paid tribute to Jenna. I'm just wondering if someone was crying crocodile tears.'

7

For the first time in many days, Eve thought about something other than her wedding as she tried to sleep that night. The handkerchief was topmost in her mind. Gut instinct told her the chilli oil was significant, and going to such lengths to appear emotional was odd. Eve wouldn't have thought badly of anyone who didn't cry. Grief took people in different ways, and the news of poor Jenna's death wasn't so very fresh. But it looked as though someone felt they must be seen to break down and that suggested a guilty conscience.

Eve kept pushing the thought away, but however hard she tried, it worked its way to the surface again. What if Jenna hadn't fallen from that cliff? What if she'd been pushed?

If it hadn't been for the turmoil she'd witnessed that evening, from the passionate arguments and deeply hurtful comments, to Maynard's blackmail-worthy secret, her mind might never have turned to violence. As it was, the thought took hold.

It would only wake her up further, but Eve felt compelled to leave her cosy bed to google Jenna from the spare room. She could have done it then and there, using her phone, but she didn't want the light to disturb Robin and her laptop would be less fiddly. She pushed the bedcovers back carefully, then pulled on her dressing gown before creeping across the landing.

A moment later, she was hunched over the computer, accessing the information she wanted. Much of it repeated what Lance had said in his speech. Jenna had been the deputy editor of the *Daily Reporter* and tipped for promotion before she was thirty-five. What a family; they were all at the top of their game. The press had reported various run-ins between Jenna and her dad, echoing the tensions between Lance and Naomi. He'd made barbed comments about her in interviews with rival papers, but Eve couldn't see him killing his own daughter because he was jealous of her success. She wasn't working in his field, so they weren't direct rivals, and if he felt threatened, Maynard was the most famous of his children.

After she'd investigated Jenna, she googled Lance too and found photos of his research group, including his beleaguered assistant, Erica Paxton.

Eve's feet were frozen and outside it was sleeting again. She went to fill a hot water bottle and crept back under the duvet next to Robin, wooden beams stretching over their heads.

After that, her mind circled round everything else she'd seen in the last two days. The fact that Lance had relocated his grand party to Suffolk to avoid Sonia coming into contact with an unknown guest. The knowledge that he and Lucy were keeping something from Sonia, supposedly out of concern. They were treating her like a child and that felt unhealthy.

And it wasn't only they who didn't take Sonia seriously. Maynard had made insulting comments about her intellect, and he hadn't been the only one. It made Eve angry. Sonia was clearly an intelligent woman. She'd developed her own way of dealing with the barbed remarks but she shouldn't have to. On top of all that, both Maynard and Naomi seemed to think Lance was sleeping around. Perhaps Sonia didn't know what was going on, though Eve suspected she was too worldly not to have a good idea, and too shrewd not to sense there were secrets being kept.

Her mind turned to Lance's row with Maynard. The four-year-old she'd once played with was a stranger now. A stranger demanding money, and a lot of it. It sounded as though Lance was right, and he was being blackmailed. He'd said Maynard's secret dated back years and it was clear Lucy also knew the truth. What on earth could it be, and who had talked?

Beyond all that was the appalling way Lance had treated Erica, his research assistant. She was only twenty-eight according to the university website Eve had found. Even if she'd made a mistake, it was abhorrent to bully and humiliate her in front of an audience. Lance had two sides to him: by turns warm and generous, then defensive and easily angered. And he'd accused Erica of betrayal. Either he was paranoid or there was more to their row than met the eye.

That had been followed by the intense exchange between Erica and Naomi. Eve could only conclude that Erica had confided something about Lance which had thrown Naomi into turmoil. She'd looked poleaxed, then demanded a word in private with her dad which had escalated into a furious row.

It was so late now that it almost didn't seem worth sleeping and Eve knew she'd dream if she did. There were too many disturbing thoughts playing on her mind.

But at last, she did drop off, and sure enough, the nightmare came. She lurched awake a little after five, heart thudding.

Robin reached out and held her hand. 'You had the dream again?'

She nodded. She'd finally confessed to him how often she'd imagined footfalls in the lane. And he knew the old tale: that hearing them signified danger. Half the villagers believed it. Eve's official explanation was that she conjured up the dream when she was upset. She hadn't yet told Robin it only ever came just before a death.

Downstairs, Gus, Eve's dachshund, whined. Deep down, she was frightened that it wasn't just her imagination, but what else could it be? Any other explanation would be ridiculous.

'Tell me,' Robin said, squeezing the hand he still held.

So at last she told him the bits she'd left out previously.

'There are more things in heaven and earth, Eve,' he said afterwards. 'You're no credulous fool, that I do know.'

8

As Eve set off to fetch Monty's trays from Lockley Grange the following morning, she felt better. The sleet had stopped and although the day was dark and overcast, the watery daylight was enough to dispel her night terrors. She drove inland, away from Saxford's coast, past bare trees, stark against the grey sky. At last, she reached the turning to the Grange, travelling back up the drive, the pool building to her left, the woods round to the right of the house. There were still signs of last night's party. As Eve pulled up, she spotted fellow villager Molly Walker and her team of cleaners through a window, busy with bin bags collecting rubbish and recycling. Molly lifted a champagne bottle and dropped it into a sack.

A woman in a dark dress and white apron let Eve in and invited her to go straight to the kitchen. Even the entrance hall was a mess. Someone had left a half-drunk glass of wine on a shelf, an extinguished cigarette floating in it. Eww. Poor Molly. There was something horrible about the smell of stale alcohol and tobacco in the cold light of day.

Eve was crossing the hall towards the kitchen passageway when Sonia descended the stairs.

'Morning!' She squinted at her. 'You look a lot more put together than I feel. We had people staying overnight and they simply wouldn't go to bed. Horrendous.' She laughed. 'You haven't seen Lance, have you?'

Eve shook her head. 'I've only just arrived.'

Sonia frowned. 'I'm not sure where he laid his head last night. I lost track of him.' Then she put a hand over her mouth. 'Sorry, that sounds bad. I don't think he's slipped into one of the guest bedrooms or anything, but he was celebrating rather wildly all day yesterday. One of the guests arrived early so the festivities had begun by midday. I suspect he nodded off somewhere and will be waking up around now with a crick in his neck.'

Maynard appeared in the doorway.

'You haven't stumbled across a sleeping father, have you?' Sonia asked him.

Maynard's look of distaste said it all. 'No, I'm glad to say. I wouldn't want the cleaners seeing him passed out.'

'I'm surprised about that,' Sonia said. 'You're not normally keen to guard his reputation.' She turned back to Eve. 'Most of the Hales have a marked competitive streak.'

Maynard sneered, turned on his heel and stalked back into the reception room.

Sonia followed Eve to the kitchen. 'Coffee, I think. Will you join me?'

Eve was about to politely decline when she saw that her and Viv's trays hadn't been washed up yet. Someone had propped them between the wall and a dresser where they'd been forgotten.

'Oh no!' Sonia said. 'That's a poor way to repay you for your hard work. Here, let me help.'

But it was a one-person job and Eve secretly liked to retain control. 'Please don't trouble. It won't take a moment. Though perhaps I'll take you up on that coffee.'

'Of course.'

They each got to work.

'It all seemed to go off very well last night.' Eve was partly making conversation, but she was curious to see if Sonia would comment on any of the tensions. She hadn't held back with Maynard just now in the hall.

'In the main, yes. I felt sorry for Erica.'

'It was hard to get such a telling off in front of everyone.'

Sonia pulled a face. 'Lance shouldn't have done that. He can't bear anything that makes him look foolish. When I challenged him on it once he blamed his parents. I gather they pitted him and his brother against each other.'

And Lance had repeated their behaviour with his own kids – or the elder two at least. You'd think he'd have realised it was a bad idea, but Eve had seen it happen before. People often complained about the behaviour of their parents, then mirrored it.

'Intellectual achievements were everything in Lance's family,' Sonia went on. 'Whenever he or Bruno failed, they were shown up in front of friends and relations. It was almost always Bruno who came in for a drubbing, but even if Lance "beat" him, his parents still pulled him up if he didn't get top marks. They certainly ensured the pair of them ended up as rivals. I often wonder if it was nature or nurture that made Bruno a killer. What's cleverness without love and understanding?'

Eve couldn't help thinking of the way Sonia had been slighted the night before. Objectified and patronised for what she did well. She wondered how Sonia felt after five years of marriage.

'Naomi seems to buck the Hale trend,' Eve said. It was she who'd first gone to check that Lance's research assistant was okay.

'I put it down to her being the youngest. I imagine she watched Maynard and Jenna tearing lumps out of each other and realised it was a mug's game. I've never heard her lay into either of them, though they've picked on her. All the same, she's driven – no pushover – and I love her for it.' Sonia laughed. 'Then again, I'm biased. She was the only one who accepted me marrying Lance. Maynard and Jenna couldn't bear that I was "so brainless" compared with their mother. They thought Lance was letting himself down.' She turned to Eve. 'Don't worry, I know I'm not brainless.'

'Thank goodness for that. It's perfectly obvious to me, but the way they treated you sounds horrendous.' Eve rubbed all the harder at a stubborn bit of cheese as she thought of the distress they must have caused.

'Thank you, but it doesn't bother me.'

Eve found that hard to accept. She was getting an adrenaline rush just thinking about it.

When the pair of them had finished their coffees and Eve had scrubbed the rest of the platters into submission, Sonia helped her carry her cargo back to her car.

Molly and her crew were outside now. It had been bitterly cold and damp last night, but empty bottles and glasses had still made their way into the grounds. People going outside to smoke perhaps, or for illicit liaisons.

Eve balanced Monty's platters on her hip and unlocked her car boot. Once she'd dumped them and taken the rest from Sonia, she gave Molly a wave. Molly waved back, looking game despite the debris she needed to clear. Eve felt grumpy on her behalf; it wouldn't have hurt anyone to bring their stuff back indoors.

Molly and a couple of her team were pottering towards the swimming-pool annexe as Eve thanked Sonia, got into her car and set off down the drive.

It was only as she glanced in her rear-view mirror from near the Grange's front gate that she realised something was wrong. Molly had been standing close to the annexe's window but now she staggered back, gesturing to someone from the team not to come closer.

Her body language told Eve something awful happened. Molly was leaning forward, hands on her thighs, as though to get her breath.

What the heck? Last night's dream was back in Eve's mind as she turned her car around and pulled up close to the annexe.

'Molly, are you okay?' She could tell it was a silly question.

Molly looked at her but didn't answer, just pointed over her shoulder towards the pool, her face pale, eyes wide with shock.

Eve took that as permission to look. And there, through the picture window, she saw the body of Lance Hale, slumped by the side of the pool.

9

Eve's first thought was of having to tell Sonia that her husband was dead. She'd been so light-hearted when she'd speculated about where he might be – snoozing in a corner somewhere, sleeping off last night's excesses. The truth would be devastating, even if the initial passion in their marriage was gone. As it would be for the rest of the family, despite the obvious tensions.

A crunch on gravel behind her made Eve jump. She and Molly wouldn't have to go to the house to break the news after all. Maynard had arrived.

'Oh hell.' He was looking through the pool window. He'd used the same sort of tone he might have chosen if he'd realised it was raining when he'd planned to play tennis. He turned away from the window as Sonia approached, her face immobile, her eyes on his.

'Lance?' She mouthed the word.

She'd been looking for him, of course. It wasn't unnatural to assume he'd been found.

Maynard nodded and shrugged. 'I always knew the booze and fags would catch up with him in the end.'

Molly rounded on Maynard as Eve bit back a selection of choice words. How could he be so callous?

Sonia stood, fixed to the spot.

'I suppose I'd better call that quack Acland,' Maynard said, as Sonia walked slowly towards the annexe and put her face to the glass.

A moment later she turned and shivered. 'Maynard's right. Lance had heart problems. We knew it could happen, but you never think it really will. He was on medication but he didn't take the diet Terence gave him seriously.'

'Terence?'

Sonia blinked. 'Our family doctor, Terence Acland. He's an old friend of Lance's so he came for the party. Tacked it onto a mini-break in Suffolk.'

Other household members were gathering now. Naomi looked most agitated of all. Sonia tried to hold her back, but she pulled away and went to stare through the window. Her expression made Eve curious. There were tears streaming down her cheeks, but she was frowning too and it looked like concentration – almost as though she was making some kind of mental calculation.

There were at least ten guests Eve couldn't identify crowded round. Three were shivering in dressing gowns, their faces creased, eyes adjusting to the light. Eve scanned their expressions; they all looked shocked. And over to one side stood Erica Paxton, Lance's research assistant. She was hovering further back than the rest and looking at the ground, her long hair falling forward so that it hid her eyes. In Erica's position, Eve would have adopted just that stance if she'd wanted to hide her reaction.

And then at last, Lucy Garton worked her way through the gathered group. Lucy, who'd worked for Lance ever since his brother Bruno had involved her in a murder. Lance had been her mainstay, according to Sylvia. When her world had collapsed he'd offered her a haven. They'd been intellectual equals, and thick as thieves, steering the Hale family ship together.

Lucy moved forward as though dragged against her will, her mouth hanging open, her eyes wide with horror. Like Sonia and Naomi she stared through the glass, then lifted her hands to her face and howled like an animal.

Not much later, uniformed police arrived, called because Lance had died suddenly, and Eve offered to stay in case they needed to talk to her. Everyone congregated in the reception hall where the party had taken place and the officers took down their contact details. In the end though, Dr Acland, a well-turned-out man with smooth dark hair and brown eyes, pronounced the death as natural causes. Lance's medical history combined with an examination raised no questions.

Several people looked tense, from Erica Paxton to Naomi and Sonia Hale. But who wouldn't, under the circumstances?

At last, a private ambulance arrived to remove Lance's body and Eve was free to go. The police left and the group in the reception hall were stirring when Lucy Garton glanced around the gathering.

'Did none of you see Lance in the pool last night?'

Everyone shook their heads and Maynard gave her a withering look. 'Someone would have mentioned it if they had.'

Lucy's eyes met his. 'Terence said the time of death was between one and three. I couldn't sleep and I saw two people near the pool at quarter past two.'

A murmur rose.

'What?' Sonia was sitting up straight now. 'What did they look like?'

Lucy shook her head. 'It was too dark to see, and too far away. I thought it was a man and a woman but I can't be sure.'

She looked at them each in turn, her brown eyes steady but her hands twisted, clutched tightly together in her lap.

'It could have been anyone heading to their digs after the party,' Maynard said. 'The drive goes that way.'

'But all the cars were parked further up, close to the house,' Sonia said, 'and this place is too remote for anyone to have walked here.'

'Oh, well, whatever!' Maynard sounded impatient. 'Perhaps it was a couple off for a quiet walk without their other halves. Either way, I'm sure they'd have called for help if they'd seen Dad. We're none of us monsters.'

Lucy glanced at him sharply, and Maynard looked away. Eve wondered if each of them was thinking of Maynard's secret. If Lance had been telling the truth, Lucy was the only person left alive who knew it.

10

Eve relayed everything that had happened to Robin when she got home, sustained by his firm hug and the attention of Gus, who seemed to sense her upset.

Later she told the tale again, this time to Viv during her afternoon shift at Monty's teashop. It was good to be able to pause, safe in the knowledge that their staff could look after the customers. They'd finally conditioned their new waitress, Emily, into waiting until people had finished chewing before offering more cakes or snatching their plates away. They'd been less successful with her friend Tilly. Eve had danced a jig when she'd handed in her notice. They'd been about to let her go after finding her absentmindedly digging into a customer's plateful of brownies as she stood by their table, chatting.

'It's a relief that Lance's death is natural causes,' Viv said. 'I could easily imagine Maynard bumping him off.'

Eve wanted to feel reassured too, but the tensions of the night before still filled her head. 'I agree, but what Lucy saw makes me wonder. Perhaps the people she spotted knew Lance was in trouble and didn't try to save him. Maynard and a girl-friend maybe? He was desperate for Lance to lend him money last night. Assuming he inherits a share of the Hale fortune he'll be sorted once probate goes through. He didn't deny it when Lance asked if he was being blackmailed. I wonder what he's hiding.'

It left Eve feeling jittery. All families had secrets, of course, but knowing Maynard's was serious made her feel complicit for saying nothing. Yet there was no investigation, no case to answer. And if she did tell the police, it would be her word against his unless Lucy filled in the blanks. Eve couldn't see her doing that; she was renowned for her loyalty to the family.

But doing nothing still made Eve twitch. Of course, getting involved would be crazy right now. It was three weeks until her wedding... That was all she should be thinking about.

Yet as Eve waited tables, she continued to worry over it. If she pitched to write Lance's obituary, she might find out more. The timing was terrible, but if she didn't get involved, she'd never know what Lance, Maynard and Lucy were hiding and if she should be acting on it. It was a can of worms, but her conscience nagged at her.

Could she walk down the aisle feeling happy if she'd turned her back on something that might affect Naomi badly? Eve's fondness for her had come rushing back. And what about Sonia, who was also in the thick of the Hale maelstrom, and a good friend of Sylvia's?

Worst of all, what if there'd already been a murder and it went undetected?

She spent half her spare moments that afternoon texting Jim the vicar about wedding readings and the other noting her thoughts on Jenna and Lance's deaths.

It was only when Jim replied: *Do we need to talk?* that Eve realised she'd included: *Need to consider practicalities of luring Jenna to the cliff to push her over.* in her latest text instead of adding it to her notes.

She sent a blushing-face emoji in response. It was lucky that

Jim knew about her hobby, but it showed that murder and weddings didn't mix. She should let this go.

'What on earth's the matter?' Viv said. 'You've just walked straight past a customer with a plate that needs clearing. It's almost like you're human.'

'Very witty.' Eve explained her quandary.

'Write an anonymous note to the police and let them worry about it.'

'They'll never follow it up. You know what Palmer's like.' Eve had dealt with the local detective inspector before, to pass on information she'd gathered while writing the obituaries of several murder victims. He shunned inconvenient clues. Digging for dirt on a powerful MP might affect his career.

Viv shrugged. 'It's not every day you get married. Don't put it all on the line now. Investigating blackmail sounds like a dangerous business, especially with Maynard involved. I could see him killing to protect himself.'

Ironically, that made up Eve's mind. What if Naomi or Sonia got in his way and he did just that?

By the end of her shift, she'd messaged her contact at *Icon* magazine to suggest Lance would make a good subject.

The situation at the Grange preyed on her mind for the rest of the day, but the following morning, *Icon* accepted her pitch and the die was cast. Eve called Sonia Welton-Hale to repeat her condolences and sound her out about some interviews.

'*Sylvia wondered if you might be in touch.*' Sonia sounded reasonably collected. '*She rang to find out how I was.*'

'It always feels wrong to contact relatives so soon after a bereavement, but I know Lance had a fascinating life and I feel closer to him than most, after I lived with the family.' It was a long time ago, but the memories had stayed with her. 'He was so welcoming to me. I'd love to tell his story.' And discover what he'd kept hidden. Had two people really stood by and watched him die? Or might it be even worse than that? Acland would be predisposed to decide the death had been natural, given Lance's medical history. She couldn't live with herself if she didn't dig deeper.

'*Come and get started whenever you like,*' Sonia said at last. '*I'm already at loggerheads with Maynard over the funeral and our guests have finally left. Someone to dilute us can only be a good thing. Sylvia said you've got a dachshund. Feel free to bring him too. He might help Naomi. She's in bits.*'

Poor Gus. He wasn't immune to other people's distress. All the same, Robin would be out and it would be better than leaving him alone.

Eve felt tense as she returned to Lockley Grange. The weather had turned even colder, darker and damper. If it froze, the drive home would be treacherous. She looked up at the empty windows as she got out of the car, and thought again of Viv's mention of ghosts. Jacqueline had been killed in these very grounds, and now Jenna and Lance were dead too. But it was the living that worried Eve. The Grange seemed full of a tumultuous mix of feelings, fierce and quite possibly destructive.

'C'mon, Gus!' Eve released him from his harness and he scrambled out of the car. 'We need to talk to Sonia first.' Maynard was the shiftiest member of the family on the face of it, but it was Sonia who'd invited her in. Besides, Eve wanted to know how she and Lance had met and how she really felt about the marriage. She'd have to have loved him a lot to get past Maynard and Jenna's behaviour, to say nothing of his drinking and rumoured womanising.

There was the matter of the conversation she and Viv had overheard the night before the party too. Who was the guest Lance and Lucy were trying to make sure Sonia didn't meet by switching venues to Suffolk, and what might Sonia have discovered if they'd attended the party?

It was Maynard who opened the door. 'I couldn't believe it when Sonia said you were coming back. There was I, imagining you were a harmless nanny-turned-baker, and it turns out you're a journalist, come to pick over Dad's bones. I hope it won't take long.'

It would feel like ages if he carried on like that. Eve glanced down and caught Gus giving Maynard a nasty look. He was an excellent judge of character.

She met Maynard's eyes. 'I won't bother you more than I have to, but your father was a well-respected and famous man. I'm sure you want to pay tribute to him.' She guessed her words would be as a red rag to a bull, but she couldn't resist trying to rile him.

He glared. 'He'd risen high, but he was on his way down again and he knew it. He'd started to treat me as a rival, yet he chose a lesser target to attack: Naomi and her little research project. I suppose he realised I'd play dirty if he came after me. Still, you're right; I'll certainly want to contribute to your article.'

Naomi's 'little research project'? Seriously? 'Good, but I must talk to Sonia first. As his wife, her input will be the most important.'

'But that's ridiculous. I—'

Eve was starting to enjoy herself but before he could say more, Sonia appeared. 'Please come through to Lance's study. We can talk there.'

It was good to turn her back on Maynard and walk away, though she'd relish quizzing him later. As well as discovering his secret, she wanted to know what made him so incredibly arrogant.

11

Sonia led Eve down a corridor near the front of the house and Gus pottered alongside them, sniffing at the skirting boards. 'Lance sorted out a few rooms for his use when he was down here working,' she said. 'He made his study and Erica's office comfortable, as well as Lucy's suite and the odd bedroom – but he avoided the rest of the house. Too many difficult memories.'

'Lucy's suite?' It sounded well established.

'She stayed here for a while after Jacquline died – she shut down, effectively. Lance gave her his mother's old set of rooms. I think it felt more secure than rattling round in the wider house.

'He had that blessed swimming pool built of course, to try to keep fit. He didn't seem to realise that he needed to get in there and actually exercise. He never cut down on the food, drink and cigarettes...' She gave Eve a smile which was irritated rather than indulgent. 'It wasn't unusual for him to head to the pool late at night, but only to lounge around and look over the park. I never saw him swim a width, far less a length.'

They entered a largeish room with a huge desk in the middle, chairs on either side. Beyond the desk was a view of the Grange's forecourt and lawns, with the pool annexe beyond.

'I'm so sorry.' Eve felt the need to express her sympathy, though in reality, Sonia didn't seem that sad. 'I guess diets often begin tomorrow.'

Sonia nodded and motioned Eve to a seat, bending to make a fuss of Gus before sitting down herself. 'So, what would you like to know?'

Gus shuffled off to investigate a corner as Eve replied, 'I wondered how the pair of you met.'

'He was a visiting dignitary when I was in Milan for fashion week, seven years ago.' Her eyes were fond suddenly as though she was back in the moment. 'My word, he was magnetic. That laugh and those intense blue eyes. I'm afraid I was hooked by the end of that first evening.'

Her choice of words was interesting. '*I'm afraid*' implied it had been a weakness, and possibly that she'd thought better of it since.

'I loved his excesses and his confidence,' Sonia went on.

He hadn't been without self-doubt though. His rivalry with Maynard, Jenna and Naomi showed that. 'So you and Lance were an item from that very first night?' Eve said. It sounded romantic.

Sonia nodded. 'He told me I was nothing like his first wife and he rejoiced in us operating on totally different levels. He said it meant there was nothing to argue about.'

His language felt significant too. He could have said they worked in different spheres, but 'levels' implied something else. 'Didn't you find that insulting?' The words slipped out before Eve could stop them.

'I'd realised by that stage that he was a bit of a bighead.' Sonia rolled her eyes and gave a tight, ironic smile.

Eve guessed she was angrier than she was letting on. She had spirit, you only had to look at the way she put down her detractors to see that. Eve could understand Lance bowling her over at first. She'd felt his charisma too. But as the years wore on, Eve suspected his attitude had started to rankle.

'I thought you might like to base yourself here in his study while you work,' Sonia said. 'You're welcome to look through his papers. Don't pay any attention if Maynard objects.'

Eve guessed Sonia would have checked the room's contents before offering her free rein.

Sonia's mobile buzzed.

'Please do take that if you need to.'

But she glanced at the screen and shook her head. 'It'll wait. Where was I? Oh yes, you must make free with the library too. It's just as it was in the old days, but I know Lucy put the books Lance wrote in there, as well as masses of reference material. There'll be goodness knows what else, I imagine. The family spent a lot of time down here when Jacqueline was alive, and I'm told Maynard used to live in the library. He was determined to be the cleverest of them all.'

She was being exceptionally helpful, which struck Eve as slightly odd. It wasn't that she'd expected her to be obstructive, but relatives were often too upset to think of the details Sonia was covering.

'What about family photos? It would be great to include some in the article if that's okay.'

'Of course.' Sonia nodded. 'You'll find plenty of them in the library too – both in frames and albums.' She shuddered suddenly. 'I had a look once, but it made me uneasy – like going back in time.'

Talk of the past provided the excuse Eve needed to ask about Jacqueline. It sounded as though her memory must have hung over Sonia. And Lucy would be a constant reminder of that painful history. 'You never knew Lance's first wife?' Sylvia said she hadn't, but Eve wanted to check.

Sonia shook her head. 'No, but I feel as though I did.' She

gave a wry smile. 'She's often mentioned. A first from Cambridge, then a career as a human-rights lawyer.' She grimaced. 'I suppose things would have got tricky logistically when Lance got his roles abroad, but she was dead by that time. Everyone says how wonderful she was and that Lance was devastated when she died. It was one of the reasons he wanted to go abroad – to try to forget. Be that as it may, Lance told me they fought like cats. You might know, I suppose.' There was a speculative look in her eyes.

Eve felt awkward and smiled while staying silent. It wasn't her place to say, but she remembered their spats all right. Hearing Lance at the party on Friday had reminded her of some of their flashpoints. Jacqueline had believed people could dedicate themselves passionately to the common good with the right systems in place. Lance thought she was a dreamer.

'It was Jenna I found hardest to cope with when Lance and I met,' Sonia went on. 'Maynard was rude and made his disapproval clear, but Jenna did everything she could think of to remove me from the scene.'

Eve raised an eyebrow.

'She wouldn't even admit defeat at our engagement party. She brought two alternative suitors for Lance. One last throw of the dice. Jenna said I'd show the family up at dinner parties.'

It was desperately disappointing to think that the little girl she'd played teddy bears' picnics with had grown up to be so supercilious. Eve took a deep breath and carried on. 'What were the suitors like?'

'Confident, with the obligatory first-class Oxbridge degrees. One was something senior in the civil service, the other a judge. I'm afraid I don't miss Jenna very much, though that's perhaps not a quote for your article.'

Her apparent accident had been horrific, but Eve couldn't blame Sonia. She hadn't seen her cry when Lance had paid tribute to Jenna on Friday night, so Eve doubted the chilli-oil hanky belonged to her. Anyone who knew her background with Jenna would understand her lukewarm response.

'Was Lucy welcoming?' It must have been a shock to the system for her to have another woman around the house after so many years.

'She took me in her stride.'

But of course, Eve knew Lance had consulted her when making his plans.

'I overheard her say once that I complemented Lance,' Sonia went on, 'whatever she meant by that.'

Once again, it made Sonia sound like an appendage.

'Right' – she got up – 'I'll leave you to it for a bit, so you can dig through Lance's papers and research. Then I'm sure you'll want to talk to the rest of the household.'

Eve thanked her. 'Sonia, before you go, could I possibly have a guest list for the party? And I wondered if there were any close contacts of Lance's who didn't attend. I should make sure I know who to speak to for his obituary.' She still wanted to know who Lance and Lucy had been trying to avoid. The person who might have told Sonia 'the truth'.

Sonia frowned. 'Lucy will have the list. I'll make sure you get it. Most people managed to attend, but an old university friend of Lance's had to cry off when the venue changed. He's shooting a film with a tight schedule, so he couldn't get out of London. Here. I'll write his details down for you.'

Felix Masters. That had to be him. Eve put the information in her bag for later. She couldn't wait to find out more.

12

Sonia left, but she was still in the corridor when Eve heard her make a call. 'Thanks for your concern, Terence, but I'm all right. You relax and enjoy your holiday!'

Her tone had turned sharp and impatient. She didn't want to be fussed over by the family doctor, clearly. Lance's death must have been a shock – unless she was responsible – but her attitude confirmed Eve's hunch that she was far from devastated by the loss.

Eve got to work on her laptop with Gus at her feet, under the desk. It was pleasingly immersive to sit in Lance's study. Everything gave her more insight into the man, from the novelty cigarette box decorated with a painted duck, to his exuberant fountain-penned writing which curled across page after page of paper. It appeared he hadn't taken life too seriously, except where his reputation was concerned.

There was personal correspondence in the desk as well as draft papers for publication, and it was fascinating. Once again, you could see his generosity: he'd repeatedly offered friends the keys to a place he owned in France for summer holidays and given freely to various charities. But when someone had written to challenge his views, Lance had clearly been incensed. He'd scribbled all over the letter in red pen, calling them a fool and worse.

Eve went looking for a draft response to the letter, grateful for Lance's old-fashioned habit of printing out emails and writing everything long-hand first. At last, she found it. He'd responded diplomatically, as you'd expect from his former profession, but there was a note across the bottom addressed to Erica, telling her to monitor the writer's output and run everything they published past him. Underneath he'd written, 'I intend to rip him to shreds.'

The more Eve looked, the more convinced she was that Sonia – or someone – had been through Lance's things before her. It was as expected; Eve would have done the same. As it was, a few of the files in his cabinet were out of order and the topmost papers on his desk were older than the ones lower down.

After an hour or so, Eve went to find the bathroom, telling Gus she'd be back in a minute. On her way along the echoey corridor, she heard a voice. Someone sobbing between their words.

She didn't mean to listen in – people ought to be able to grieve privately – but bar blocking her ears she couldn't help it.

'You know what it's like when you know something needs doing, even if it involves destroying someone you love?' It was Naomi. 'Before Friday I'd never have imagined I was even capable of it.'

Under the circumstances, her words were disturbing. Did she know something about her father's death? Perhaps she'd been involved. Lucy claimed she'd seen a man and a woman near the pool around the time he'd died.

As Eve reached the bathroom, a door to the corridor creaked open behind her. Snatching a glance, she saw Naomi appear, head down. She walked off in the opposite direction. Eve hesi-

tated a moment, but it felt too important to ignore. She wanted
to know who Naomi had been talking to. She stood outside the
room she'd occupied and knocked before walking straight in.
She could claim she was looking for Sonia.

But the room was empty. There was another door leading
off it, but when Eve checked, that room was deserted too.

Back in Lance's study, after she'd been to the bathroom, Eve
returned to her work. She was delving into another drawer
when she spotted the edge of a bit of paper she hadn't noticed
before, tucked under an Anglepoise lamp. It was black, just like
the lamp itself, which had helped to disguise it.

But when she pulled the paper out, she found that only its
edges were that colour – a thin black frame like Victorian
mourning stationery.

On the white centre of the paper, a message had been
typed:

> *You'll be on cloud nine at the party tonight, but I'm going to
> send you six feet under. You can't outrun your true self.*

Eve sat there, suddenly conscious of the cold room, the
draught whistling down the chimney and round the window
frame. The note could have been meant metaphorically. The
writer might have wanted Lance to know they intended to
destroy him. But Lance had literally died within twenty-four
hours – one heck of a coincidence, if it was one.

She wondered if the note had been posted or hand-deliv-
ered. The wording made it clear the writer was confident Lance
would read it on the day of the party. That implied precision
and made hand delivery more likely. It *could* have been slipped
under his door by one of the party guests who'd arrived early.
Sonia said the first one had turned up at midday. But it seemed
more probable that it had been a member of Lance's close circle,
who knew when he'd be in his study.

Eve wondered how he'd reacted when he'd read the note. She would have been on high alert, but she could imagine him shrugging it off. Thinking the writer planned to diss him in the press perhaps.

But wasn't it more likely that the note was from his killer? If so, then it was significant. They hadn't just wanted him gone, they'd wanted to terrorise him beforehand too, even if it meant leaving a clue.

Perhaps the note writer had come into the study to try to retrieve it – it could have been that which had caused the disordered papers. If so, she could see why they'd failed; it had been hiding in plain sight. Again, a search made a culprit from Lance's inner circle more likely. They'd have had time to conduct it.

She thought of Lance, giving his speech. Berating Erica. Maybe he'd thought the note had been from her. She remembered his words: *You've betrayed me!* He hadn't looked afraid, just furious, which would fit if he'd thought the note was about some wrangle over research and his reputation. But it could have been from anyone, and now Lance was dead. She couldn't ignore it.

She was just getting up to find Sonia when the study door opened and she walked in. Eve handed her the paper.

'I'm sorry. I found this under Lance's desk lamp.'

Sonia clutched it, breathing hard. 'I'll call the police.'

13

Eve was still at Lockley Grange when the police arrived. Inevitably it was Detective Inspector Nigel Palmer who came with his team to interview the family. As usual, Eve felt a surge of resentment at the sight of him. She always fed back anything she discovered when interviewing after a suspicious death and had found crucial evidence for him in the past. Palmer appeared to hate her for it.

'Ah, Ms Mallow. Why am I not surprised to find you here, poking your nose in where it's not wanted?'

Eve stood up and took a deep breath. 'I came to write a perfectly ordinary obituary and stumbled on the note Sonia Welton-Hale told you about. The moment I saw its significance I left Sir Lance's study.'

'And you expect me to congratulate you for that?'

'Far from it.' She'd long since given up expecting anything from Palmer, from politeness to an ounce of common sense. She had a lot of time for his sergeant Greg Boles though, who happened to be married to Robin's cousin.

Thankfully, Palmer handed her over to him once he'd warned her off getting involved. How much to say? In the end, she told Greg everything. He'd have to feed it all back to Palmer of course, who would think she'd had her ear to the door when she'd heard Naomi talk about destroying someone she loved. It couldn't be helped.

At last, Greg let her go home. It was a relief to go from a freezing-cold house, crawling with scientific support officers, to cosy Elizabeth's Cottage, where Gus planted himself firmly by the fire.

Robin must have read her expression. He put down the holly and ivy he was using to decorate and took her in his arms. 'What's wrong? What's happened?'

She looked at the cheerful red ribbon Robin had secured the greenery with and told him.

Eve had to wait after that – not something she found easy. She itched to get on with her interviews, especially now it looked as though Lance could have been killed. Questions filled her head and she googled like mad for background information, as well as leaving a message for the film director who hadn't been able to attend Lance's party. It was late the following day before Robin got news of the investigation via Greg. Palmer drove the entire team up the wall and Greg used Robin as a safety valve since he was a trusted friend. He knew some of his information went a little further – to Eve especially – but that flowed both ways. He saw the value in it.

'Gang meet-up?' Eve said, when Robin got off the phone. He nodded, so Eve used her WhatsApp group to invite Viv, Sylvia and Daphne round to share the news. They might have thoughts and insights, especially Sylvia, who'd known Sonia for years.

Normally, Viv's brother Simon would be in on proceedings too. He had fingers in lots of pies and was always useful, but he and his wife had gone off to catch some winter sun before Eve and Robin's wedding, their first holiday after a financial crisis the year before. They'd have to do without him.

At six o'clock that night they were sitting around bowls of cashews with glasses of mulled wine in their hands, warming themselves by the fire. Gus had already toured the visitors, receiving tickles and pats from each of them, and was now stretched out on the rug between the inglenook fireplace and the coffee table. He looked thoroughly relaxed and Eve envied him, but she was glad to see her friends. She wanted to develop a plan of action.

'What news from the police, Robin?' Sylvia's eyes were unusually serious. He hesitated for a moment and her intelligent gaze met his. 'I realise there's a conflict of interest because of my link with Sonia. I won't share what you tell me, but I can leave if you'd prefer... so long as I can take my mulled wine and nuts, naturally.'

Robin grinned. 'I wouldn't have dragged you across the road if I didn't trust you.' Sylvia and Daphne lived diagonally opposite them. 'But it's true. This has to remain absolutely confidential. We can't assume Sonia's innocent, however nice she might seem.'

Sylvia nodded. 'I believe most people would be capable of murder in the right circumstances.'

Daphne blinked. 'I don't think I would be.'

'Well, I'd kill for you if I had to,' Sylvia said. 'If you're not prepared to return the favour then I'll take it on the chin.'

'Can't you take anything seriously?' Daphne looked exasperated.

Sylvia reached for another nut. 'I'm deadly serious. Do the police know how Lance died, Robin?'

'The post-mortem showed an overdose of digoxin.'

'The heart medicine?' Eve had heard of it.

He nodded. 'Lance was taking it regularly. It's not the drug of choice these days – the dangers speak for themselves – but it's still given to people who can't cope with other options. Greg says Lance was allergic to the standard medication.

'There are signs that someone removed several doses from his supply. The likelihood is that they crushed the pills and put the powder into something that only Lance ingested. Unfortunately, all the dishes used on Friday night have been cleaned, but the most probable vehicle was cold coffee in a flask on a shelf in the kitchen. Lance always had a supply there on party nights, apparently. He tended to drink too much, so he'd go into the kitchen during the evening to down the coffee and sober up. Sonia would make it up for him but the whole household knew about the habit. On this occasion, she made the coffee early, because he started drinking at lunchtime. Unfortunately, the pathologist can't verify the time of death Acland gave – rigor mortis had worn off by the time he started work and it was no use relying on body temperature either.' He gave them a rueful look. 'They'd kept him cool at the funeral directors to preserve the body. But if Acland's assessment of between one and three a.m. was correct then Lance could have ingested the digoxin between one and six p.m. on Friday. He liked the coffee cold so he could swig it fast and reappear again.'

'And downing a strong-tasting drink quickly would be perfect from the killer's point of view,' Eve said. 'That and the fact that he was probably very drunk before he started on it. He'd be unlikely to notice a change in taste or any sediment.'

Robin nodded. 'It was cleverly done.'

Cleverness seemed to be a theme where the Hales were concerned and Eve included Sonia in that, whatever the others thought.

'On the upside,' Robin went on, 'it's doubtful people outside the household knew about Lance's coffee flask, and it looks as though the drink was doctored before most of the guests arrived.

Given that, our suspects are probably down to six: Sonia of course' – he glanced at Sylvia apologetically – 'then Lance's remaining children, Maynard and Naomi, as well as his research assistant Erica Paxton, and his employee and friend, Lucy Garton, who's been with him for decades.'

That made five. 'Who's the sixth?'

'The doctor, Terence Acland. He was a close friend of Lance's too. He was one of the few people who arrived early, and he knew Lance's habits and how easy it would be to pass the death off as natural. There's no clear motive for him yet, but Greg says Acland was sweating when he was interviewed.'

'In this weather, that's saying something,' Sylvia said dryly.

14

Robin rose to top up their mulled wines.

'I said it at the teashop, and I'll say it again,' Viv said, 'this feels like the wrong time to get involved, Eve. You're getting married, for heaven's sake. I know Palmer's a prize prune but just this once, I think you could leave him to—' She caught Eve's expression and stopped talking. 'Okay, I give up, but don't say I didn't warn you. What do you know about the suspects? I'll write down what you say.'

Eve looked anxiously at Viv's notebook, which was even more scrappy than the last time she'd seen it, full of loose pages with very little space left. She'd make her own notes once Viv had gone, just to be on the safe side.

'Just like you, Sylvia, I like Sonia,' Eve began cautiously.

'I sense a but coming.' Sylvia's smile was knowing.

'It sounds as though Lance had been patronising her for years and I think both Maynard and Naomi believe he was having affairs. I'm not certain she knew, or that she'd kill over it, but I find it hard to believe she'd take it lying down. In all honesty, she doesn't seem that sad that he's dead either. She hadn't walked out on him, so perhaps she stayed for a reason.

An anticipated inheritance maybe? He was a lot older than her and not in good health.'

Sylvia looked thoughtful, rather than cross, for which Eve was grateful. 'It's a fair point. She was besotted with Lance at first – he had terrific charisma – but I'm not sure how the land lay more recently.'

Eve remembered the way Sonia had talked about meeting him. *I'm afraid I was hooked by the end of that first evening.* 'I think reality might have set in. Does she inherit, Robin?'

'She gets a third of the cash. It's split three ways between her, Maynard and Naomi, and each of their shares increased when Jenna died. The properties are dealt with separately: Maynard gets Lockley Grange, the London house goes to Naomi and there's a place in France which will be sold, with the proceeds divided between the lot of them. There's plenty of money not tied up in bricks and mortar too. Sonia's inheritance will be substantial.'

'She definitely has a motive for Lance then.' Sylvia saved Eve from saying it. 'What about the chilli oil-soaked hanky, Eve? Do you still think it's significant and that Jenna could have been murdered?'

She nodded. 'I think it's very possible. But Sonia didn't cry on Friday night, so if someone was faking their grief it wasn't her. If Jenna *was* pushed, then surely Lance's death must be related. It would be a huge coincidence otherwise. Perhaps he pushed her, and someone poisoned him in revenge.'

But Robin shook his head. 'After what you said about the hanky, I asked Greg about Jenna's death. Lance was with Naomi in London at the time. Sonia was working on location on the Sussex coast, but she was at her accommodation by five. Lucy was in Surrey overnight at a B&B – she visited a friend nearby on the Sunday. That leaves Maynard, who says he was at home, though there was no one to vouch for him.'

'So unless Lance and Naomi are lying to cover up what

happened – which would be horrific – then they're out of it, but Maynard could be guilty. And Sonia and Lucy could have sneaked off and driven down to Cornwall too?'

Robin nodded. 'By the look of it, yes. *If* Jenna was murdered.'

Eve sighed. 'I still can't imagine anyone bothering to fake tears unless they had a guilty conscience.'

'We need to keep an open mind.' Robin sipped his drink. 'But gut instinct coupled with this latest death says you're right.'

'An unlucky family.' Sylvia's eyes were on Eve's. 'And if we're linking Jenna and Lance, what about Jacqueline, all those years ago?'

The same thought had crossed Eve's mind. 'It would be good to know if there's any possible question over the accepted version of events.' She glanced at Robin, who nodded.

'I'll ask Greg, but let's assume for now that that case was sound.'

'Okay.' Eve took another nut. 'So back to Jenna. If she *was* pushed off a cliff, and Lance didn't do it, then he can't have been killed in revenge for her death. We need to look at other motives. Perhaps someone wanted the pair of them out of the way, in which case, Maynard would be a strong candidate.' She reminded them of his and Lance's argument. 'He wanted money, and killing Jenna before Lance increased his inheritance.'

'Though he was clearly hoping Lance would just cough up,' Sylvia said.

'True.' Eve sipped her drink. 'But it's possible he'd already arranged the poison and asked in the hope of getting an advance on his inheritance.'

'Because probate takes ages, and blackmailers aren't known for their patience?' Sylvia's thoughtful eyes met hers. 'Yes, that's a point. Nasty.'

'Nasty does rather sum him up. But he might have other

motives for killing Jenna too. Either way, I think he's a suspect for both deaths if Jenna was pushed. It would be a horrific double murder, but I could see it. Of course, Lance refused his request for a loan, so he'll be short of cash until the admin's done. It means he'll need another way to raise funds to pay his blackmailer.

'Hushing up his secret provides another motive for killing Lance, of course. He was convinced he or Lucy had been gossiping about it, and that Lance was more likely because he's indiscreet when he drinks. Perhaps Jenna had found out too.'

'Do you think Lucy's in danger?' Daphne's eyes were anxious.

'It's possible. I told the police what I'd overheard, and Greg promised he'd warn her. I hope they'll find out what Maynard's hiding.'

'They've already tackled Lucy on the subject,' Robin said, 'but she claims she has no idea what secret Maynard was referring to.'

'Which is exactly what she would say as a faithful old retainer.' At least it would have put her on her guard. 'What did Maynard say? I presume the police asked him about it too?'

Robin nodded. 'He claims he had an affair with the wife of a fellow MP, and that it would be career-ending if it came out. He told Palmer he thought Lucy had picked up on it, but perhaps he was wrong. He says there's no question of blackmail. He wanted a loan from his dad to put into a business venture.' Robin pulled a face. 'Palmer lapped it all up, of course. Assured him he had no interest in the affair, so it won't get checked.'

It was just as Eve had feared. Palmer loved powerful people. 'Maynard's lying.' It didn't surprise her one bit. 'Whatever the secret is, it clearly happened ages ago, and Maynard's only been an MP for two years.' Eve thought it through. 'I think Maynard will arrange to pay off the blackmailer very soon and so he'll probably have to borrow money on the strength of his incoming inheritance. I assume he'll do each transaction in person, rather than leave an electronic trail, so I need to be ready to follow him if he makes a move.' If she could work out who he was paying, she might discover his secret and how much he had to lose.

'Maynard sounds like a strong candidate for the killer,' Daphne said.

'He seems like an odious man,' Sylvia agreed.

Viv drew a line under a section Eve assumed must relate to Lance's son. Eve couldn't help noticing that it also contained the words 'peas', 'salmon' and 'stain remover'. But she mustn't interfere.

'So, what about Naomi?' Viv said, looking up.

Eve sighed. 'Well, we know she has an alibi for Jenna, albeit one provided by her dad. She strikes me as a sympathetic character.' It was good to know one of the three children had turned out well. 'But she's still in the running. Perhaps she suddenly saw Lance for what he was: he couldn't take competition and she was starting to impress some very important people. I looked up the report she wrote for the charity she works for. It got an excellent response when it first came out. People in parliament were sitting up and taking notice. But after Lance's interview, rubbishing her ideas, those same politicians started to ask questions and some even made fun of her suggestions. Her appearance in front of the relevant committee has been postponed, and you can see from interviews how much she cares about her work. Perhaps she decided that the lives she could change were worth more than the life of her father. It's not out of the question. Did the police ask her who she was referring to when I heard her talking about destroying someone?'

Robin nodded. 'She says she made up her mind on Friday to hit back at Lance in the press. The gloves were coming off. She told Greg she feels terribly guilty for having such disloyal thoughts now that Lance is dead and that she was talking to a friend on the phone. The call was certainly made, and the friend backs her up.'

It explained why Eve hadn't found anyone in the room after Naomi had left. 'It could be true, but did she really believe she could destroy Lance that way? The reaction to his interview showed how powerful he still was. I wonder if she made up the story on the spur of the moment and managed to contact the friend to prepare the ground before the police got to them.'

Robin frowned. 'It's possible. I see she has a motive.'

'It makes me think of the note I found. *You'll be on cloud nine at the party tonight, but I'm going to send you six feet under. You can't outrun your true self.* It could be metaphorical, and fit with Naomi's plan to fight back. But if the killer wrote it, their hatred for Lance must have been all-consuming. The police would never have conducted a post-mortem if they hadn't left that clue, yet they went ahead anyway. I suspect someone tried to retrieve the note after Lance died, but it was still a big risk.'

Robin nodded.

Eve's thoughts turned to next steps. 'I need to interview Naomi and gauge how strong her feelings were. She was certainly livid with Lance when they argued after his speech on Friday night.'

'You'd think she'd be more cautious if she'd already put poison in his drink.' Sylvia was frowning.

'Yes, but I think she feels things deeply and she'd probably been bottling them up. Lance had walked out on her mid-argument, the day before the party, which must have made her furious. I could imagine her losing control, despite the risks. Plus, she thought she was letting rip in private. I guess she forgot how many people might be listening outside the door to his study.'

Robin put down his drink. 'Fair point.'

'How did she explain the row with Lance to the police?' They must have asked; Eve had told them about it.

'She said she was angry at the way he'd treated Erica.'

'No doubt, but I'd swear there was more to it than that.' It was frustrating. If she was the killer, she'd decided to act well before the row, but it might still relate to whatever had driven her. 'Did they ask what she and Erica talked about after Erica's dressing down?'

Robin nodded. 'Naomi said she was commiserating.'

Like heck.

'Speaking of Erica,' Viv said, 'what about her as a suspect?'

'She's in a similar boat to Naomi. She looked exhausted on Friday and if Lance's behaviour at the party was anything to go by, he could already have pushed her to the brink. All that talk of betrayal tells me their public row was just the culmination of something going on in private – I need to know what. I could see her sending the note and putting the poison in his drink. She must know his habits. They've probably been to conferences together and I'll bet she's seen him use his coffee flask. I need to talk to her too.

'And then there's Lucy. She'd also be aware of Lance's routine, of course. I imagine she knows him better than anyone. She could have invented the man and woman near the pool to muddy the waters. But if she's guilty, why draw extra attention to the death by mentioning them before anyone knew it was murder?'

'That would certainly be odd behaviour,' Sylvia said. 'She must have genuinely wanted to know the answer.'

'I agree. And she only raised it after the uniformed police who came first had left, presumably to protect the household. I hope it doesn't put her in danger, though she said she couldn't identify the people she saw.'

'The police have asked her about it now,' Robin said, 'but there's nothing further to report.'

'Did Lance leave her anything?' Eve would have thought

she'd be entitled to her share. 'She'd worked for him long enough, and it was his brother who ruined her life.'

But Robin shook his head. 'The will was redrawn after Jenna's death and his lawyer says Lance fretted over Lucy. Apparently, she'd told him very firmly that she didn't want anything. She was worried it might cause trouble with the family. She was well paid over the years, and I suppose she must have saved, living rent free since Lance's first wife died. All things being equal, she should be comfortable, but she doesn't benefit from his death. Lance left her a very pretty vase she'd always liked, but the lawyer confirms it's only worth a couple of hundred pounds.'

Lucy's attitude was interesting, but perhaps understandable if she already had what she needed. Eve wouldn't want to get embroiled in a family feud over inheritance either. She couldn't see Sonia or Naomi kicking up a fuss, but Maynard was another matter.

Eve rallied her thoughts. 'Lastly, there's Dr Acland. Terence. He's an unknown quantity, but I suppose I can see why Palmer's interested.' Even a stopped clock told the right time twice a day.

'He's supposed to be an old friend of Lance's,' Sylvia said, 'but old friends fall out and it can be devastating when they do.'

Eve nodded. 'And he was in an excellent position to cover up the death by claiming it was natural causes. He could have got his own digoxin, presumably, but if none of Lance's pills were missing, the police would immediately look for someone with easy access to the drug. Perhaps he took Lance's to avoid putting himself in the spotlight.'

She got ready to sum up her thoughts. 'Leaving Jenna aside for the moment, I'd say Maynard's top of the suspect list, but Erica's on my mind too.

'I'll watch Maynard like a hawk and hopefully follow him if he tries to pay off his blackmailer. I'll interview him as a priority as well. I also want to find out more about Erica, her working relationship with Lance, and what he meant when he said she'd betrayed him. It sounds as though their quarrel was acrimonious and ongoing. I need to know if she'd have killed over it.

'The others feel less urgent, but I'd like to know how important Sonia's inheritance might be to her and why Naomi and her dad argued so badly after she spoke to Erica. It might relate to any motive she had.

'Lucy's high priority for an interview too. She doesn't feel like a strong suspect, but she must have known Lance inside out. I must get to know Dr Acland as well, and lastly, I want to talk to someone who knew Jenna. If she was pushed, something must have triggered it. Hearing about her life just beforehand might give us a clue. Sonia got Lucy to email me a guest list for the party and I've spotted a colleague of hers who might fit the bill. She's still in Saxford – staying at the Cross Keys. Hopefully she'll talk to me.'

'How can we help?' Daphne asked.

'Sylvia's photographs might come in handy.'

Sylvia nodded. 'I've already reviewed them to try to identify the owner of the hanky. No joy, I'm afraid, but I'll go through them again.'

Eve leaned forward. 'Thanks. Any tiny detail might be relevant.' The police had copies too, of course. 'And we all need to be each other's eyes and ears. If any of the key players does anything, however insignificant, we can share it on the WhatsApp group and where possible, follow to see what they're up to.'

'The police have told the suspects to stay in Suffolk,' Robin said, 'so that'll help. Acland's in a rental cottage here in the village.'

'I can chat to Sonia if you like,' Sylvia said, placidly.

'I couldn't ask you to. It wouldn't be fair.'

'My conscience won't trouble me. I'll just be trying to confirm she's innocent.' She smiled.

After the gang had left, Robin took Eve in his arms. 'I know I can't ask you not to look into this,' he said, 'but I was cheering Viv on when she tried to put you off.' He held up his hands. 'It's all right – I know. You bonded with Naomi when she was little, you're a journalist and you're already involved. You wouldn't be the woman I love if you weren't determined to go for it. But I wish it hadn't happened now. The wedding's so close...'

Eve felt a stab of guilt. 'I know. Just as well I always organise things months ahead of time.'

He put his head on one side. 'You know that's not what I meant. Though there is your cousin Peter to contend with.'

Eve groaned. Peter had changed his mind about where to stay and when to turn up so many times that she could cheerfully bop him if he was within reach.

'Seriously, though.' Robin stood back, his eyes on hers.

'I know. I'll take care, I promise. But you're right about Naomi – she was so dependent on me as a baby and when I saw her again it all came rushing back.' In truth, she wouldn't feel happy getting married until she knew what had happened. How could she revel in the joy of the occasion if she'd left Naomi high and dry? 'Besides, I overheard things at the party that might be relevant.'

'Like when you sneaked off and claimed you needed the loo.' Robin's smile was wry and resigned.

'Exactly like that.' She might have known he'd sussed her.

15

Before Eve went to bed that night, she made her own record of that evening's discussion as planned in a beautifully pristine notebook. The whole process eased the tension induced by Viv's notes. Not that she wasn't grateful, obviously. At last, she had her summing up:

> <u>Key players/suspects</u>
> *Sir Lance Hale – diplomat turned academic*
> *Sonia Welton-Hale – Lance's wife, model*
> *Maynard Hale – Lance's son, member of parliament*
> *Naomi Hale – Lance's daughter, economist for anti-*
> *poverty charity*
> *Lucy Garton – Lance's live-in right-hand woman*
> *Erica Paxton – Lance's research assistant*
> *Terence Acland – Lance's friend and his and Sonia's*
> *family doctor*
>
> <u>Deaths, with means, motives and opportunities</u>
>
> <u>Jacqueline Hale</u>

Died 22 years ago – mowed down by Bruno Hale,
Lance's brother. Lucy was a passenger but no indication
that anyone but Bruno influenced what happened.
Case solved, Bruno guilty. For the time being, we assume
that Jacqueline's death is irrelevant, except for the effect
it must have had on the household.

Jenna Hale
Died 7 September after falling from a cliff in Cornwall
late at night.

Motives: Tenuous. Revenge on Sonia's part for the
terrible way Jenna treated her? But why now? And for
Maynard, Naomi and Sonia, the promise of an increased
share of Lance's fortune after his death.

BUT: If she wasn't killed, then why was someone so
keen to make sure they looked devastated at the party?

Means and opportunity: Not much strength required
and Lance, Maynard, Naomi or Lucy could probably
have talked her into walking the clifftops late at night.
Harder for looser connections like Erica and Dr Acland,
and also for Sonia. Lance and Naomi alibi each other for
the death, the others weren't checked or don't have
anyone to vouch for them.

Top suspects: Maynard (most desperate for money) and
Sonia (most antagonistic relationship)

Lance Hale
Died in the early hours of Saturday 30 November
between one and three (according to Acland – delayed
post-mortem means that can't be verified) of heart failure

*induced by an overdose of digoxin, probably adminis-
tered to his coffee between 1 and 6 p.m. on Friday 29
November.*

*<u>Motives</u>: Maynard, Sonia, Naomi and Erica all have at
least one: <u>Maynard</u>: to stop his secret spreading any
further and to inherit a fortune; <u>Sonia</u>: also for money
(but why now), and/or possibly because Lance was
having an affair; <u>Naomi</u>: to save her research project and
the children it might help (and/or for money); <u>Erica</u>: to
stop Lance destroying her career (as Lance implied this
was a live threat before their row at the party). No known
motives for Lucy and Dr Terence Acland.*

*<u>Means and opportunity</u>: All of the suspects probably
knew about Lance's habit of drinking cold coffee, and
each of them could have sneaked into Lance's rooms to
find his medicine. Acland would probably have found it
hardest since he wasn't staying at Lockley Grange. No
one has an alibi.*

*<u>Top suspect: Maynard (due to multiple motives and
level of desperation). But more info needed. Lance
accused Erica of betrayal – a strong word.</u>*

<u>To note</u>:

- *Lucy claims she saw two people – possibly a man
  and a woman – near the pool at a quarter past two –
  within the window when Lance died.*
- *Lucy told the police she has no idea what Maynard's
  secret is, but Maynard believes she knows.*
- *Maynard claims he had an affair with a fellow MP's
  wife, but he's only been in the Commons for two*

> *years and Lance implied his secret dates back far*
> *longer than that.*
> • *Maynard will need to access money soon if he's*
>   *being blackmailed.*

Once she was happy with her summing up, she texted the Hale family friend who'd worked with Jenna, asking if they could meet. Lucy's list of party attendees and contact numbers was a godsend.

Eve had hoped getting some details ironed out would help her sleep better, but in fact she dreamed of troublesome cousin Peter, crumbling digoxin into her wedding champagne.

On Tuesday morning, Sonia let Eve and Gus into Lockley Grange. Eve had called ahead to check it was okay, but it was hardly the best time to turn up. Sonia was clutching several newspapers and grimaced as she showed Eve the headlines:

Murder! Scandal hits troubled Hale family

Lance Hale killed, two decades after first wife

Third Hale tragedy – Sir Lance poisoned at drink-fuelled party in rural Suffolk

Some of Eve's colleagues really did scrape the barrel. Eve couldn't help feeling responsible for them. 'I'm so sorry.'

Sonia sighed. 'It was inevitable that they'd go to town. We'll just have to grin and bear it until someone's arrested and things calm down.'

Eve felt for her. The sooner that happened, the better. 'Thanks so much for arranging some interviews for me.' They'd discussed it during their phone call and Sonia had texted to confirm. Eve was down to see Maynard first, then Lucy and Erica later. She wouldn't normally relish dealing with a man like Lance's son, but as top suspect for his dad's murder, and possibly for Jenna's, she was itching to get on with it.

'I'll fetch you a coffee,' Sonia said, dumping the papers on a side table. 'Maynard's in the drawing room – cross the main hall, take the door in the far corner and then the door at the end of the corridor.'

Eve thanked her. It was the sort of place where visitors might need a map. As for the coffee, the Grange was cold, bordering on freezing. It would help to have something warm to clutch.

As she and Gus entered the main hall where Sir Lance had made his speech on Friday, Eve caught sudden movement. It was Naomi, crouched down, close to the floor, seemingly searching for something. She turned towards Eve, her eyes anxious, and stood up slowly, though Gus picked up where she'd left off, exploring the corner where she'd been, pushing his nose under a bookcase.

'Sorry,' Eve said. 'I didn't mean to startle you.'

She shook her head. 'I'm just jittery after what happened to Dad. I still can't believe it.' Tears filled her eyes. No chilli oil needed.

Eve rushed over. 'I'm so sorry. This is such a terrible time for you all.'

Naomi nodded.

'You've lost something?' Eve indicated the bookcase where Gus was still busily snuffling.

'Just some paperwork. It doesn't matter.' She walked away from where she'd been looking.

Eve's mind flashed to the missing page from Lance's speech. Could Naomi have removed it on Friday night as part of her plan to 'destroy' him? A guilty conscience would fit with the way she'd hurried to Erica afterwards when she'd got the blame. And possibly also with the black-bordered note, if it had been meant metaphorically.

Eve explained she was off to meet Maynard. She ought to be focusing on him, but she needed to know why Naomi had argued so violently with Lance on Friday night too.

'I'd love to interview you as well, if I may? Would tomorrow work? Say ten o'clock in the drawing room?'

Naomi nodded, though she flinched as Eve asked. She was afraid of something.

Eve left her and went to find Maynard. Someone had given the room he was in going over. It wasn't covered in dust and insects like the one Eve and Viv had found but it still felt strangely still, as though it hadn't seen the hustle and bustle of life for a long time.

Maynard didn't bother standing to greet her, which was no surprise. Worse still, he ignored Gus, despite Gus rolling over to have his tummy tickled. Ridiculous dog, but Eve still felt deeply affronted on his behalf. How could anyone not oblige?

'You said you'd like to contribute to your dad's obituary,' she said, taking a seat on a sofa. 'It would certainly help me to hear about your relationship. I can tell you weren't his number one fan, but I guess you loved him when you were little.' Eve felt sad again. 'He used to race you round the garden.'

'That was a long time ago. Everyone accepts their parents at that age.' He sat forward, his shoulders hunched. 'I've heard you work with the police. I wonder if it was you who listened in to my private conversation with Dad. You must have followed us.'

Eve said nothing.

'I can tell you that Dad had started to irritate me, but people don't commit murder out of annoyance. He was a threat to Naomi, of course, and to Erica. I see that. They're weaker than he was. But I'm not, so I had no reason to risk killing him.'

The man was poisonous. 'I never thought otherwise.' Eve smiled. It was possible Maynard was foolish enough to believe her. 'As for my links with the police, they're exaggerated. I've occasionally given them information I've stumbled across.

Nothing more than that.' She let that sink in. 'So, what was Lance like when you were growing up? I only got a snapshot of a few months when you were small.'

'But you know he was self-obsessed,' Maynard said. 'His work and his goals meant more to him than anything.' He shrugged. 'When the mood took him, he'd play "dad" in short bursts, and always with something wild and showy. Taking us out in a speedboat, or up in a balloon. A memorable outing he could tell his friends about, and then it was over until the next time.'

'He seemed like an interesting mix. I remember him as generous. He lent me and a friend his car once. My friend thought he was charming.' Eve wanted to push Maynard's buttons. It would make him share more and she needed to get to the bottom of Lance's character.

Maynard laughed. She could see the scorn in his eyes. 'Dad had an image of himself which was just as you describe: fun, charismatic, generous and passionate. And he could be all of those things so long as it didn't cost him anything. He had more than one car, and if you'd wrecked the one you borrowed he had the money to buy another. By taking him up on his offer, you made him believe in that version of himself. And I expect he enjoyed your adoration.'

That was a strong word, but in truth, Eve knew what he meant.

'It's that old thing about the ego versus the id,' Maynard went on. 'The id – the primitive, impulsive part of Dad's psyche – was revealed in all its ugly truth whenever someone poked him in a tender spot. Especially if his reputation was threatened. His dark side could come raging to the fore in an instant.'

Eve thought of the letter she'd seen from another academic, challenging his ideas, and Lance's response: the desire to tear his rival to shreds. She disliked Maynard intensely, but that didn't mean he was wrong about his father. A moment later, her mind turned to the black-bordered note she'd found in Lance's study. *You can't outrun your true self.* That sentence fitted so neatly with what Maynard was saying; she could easily imagine him typing it. She shivered, and Maynard spotted it.

'Cold as the grave in this wretched place. I can't believe the police won't let us leave.'

Thank goodness he'd misread her. She didn't want him to think she suspected him. Whatever the truth, she was sure he had the capacity to be dangerous.

'It wasn't just me that Dad infuriated,' Maynard went on. 'He drove Mum wild. She'd be working on a case, trying to focus, and he'd burst into her study and tell her she was ignoring him. We didn't see a lot of her either, of course, but at least she was predictable. She planned time with us, and not just when it suited her.'

It tied in with what Eve remembered. Lance had been effervescent and fun, but it was true, he could be selfish. 'I remember Lance's behaviour causing tensions with Jacqueline.'

Maynard nodded. 'They fought like cats. When Mum got fed up with Dad's brother Bruno staying with us, she gave Dad an ultimatum. Either Bruno went or she did. You read about it in the papers?'

Eve nodded.

'What you might not know is that Dad said he'd rather Mum went. He said Bruno was more fun than her.'

And then Bruno had taken Lucy in his car, as though to leave the Grange, and mowed Jacqueline down. How guilty must Lance have felt? No wonder he couldn't face sorting out the rooms which were so full of Jacqueline's presence. 'People say a lot in the heat of the moment. I suppose Bruno realised he wasn't in earnest. If he thought he'd won, perhaps he'd never have done what he did.'

Eve hoped she was doing the right thing, exploring the situation. It was so horrific it almost felt as though it should be off-limits.

'I think Bruno thought he was doing Dad's bidding.'

But Eve couldn't believe it. The idea that Bruno would be happy to serve life to please Lance was hard to swallow. They'd been rivals after all, and if Lance was bored with Jacqueline, he could have divorced her like any normal person.

'I'm sorry you've had to endure so much tragedy.' She really was, despite not liking Maynard, and what must Bruno's actions have done to Lucy? 'Jacqueline's death must have been unbearable for you.'

'I was tough enough to cope.' Maynard certainly wanted her to think so.

'What about your dad? He must have been in bits.'

'He was, at first. But I'd swear he started to think practicalities before the day was out. How could he limit the damage Bruno might do to his reputation, and who would look after us children? The papers ended up fawning over Dad – pouring out their sympathy and admiration for him coping as a single father. But he made damn sure that was temporary. I watched him eyeing Lucy, seeing how vulnerable she was. Coaxing her gradually into coming to stay with us. Not just for her sake, I'm sure. She became our live-in nanny, allowing him to go abroad.'

It must be exhausting, being that full of vitriol. Eve took a deep breath. 'Who do you think killed him?'

He shrugged as though she'd asked who'd cancelled the milk. 'I wonder about Terence Acland, our family doctor.'

'I know he got the cause of death wrong, but I suppose your father had had heart problems for a while. Perhaps it was an innocent mistake.'

Maynard raised an eyebrow. 'I might be more inclined to believe it if he hadn't kept popping up recently. I caught sight of him in London twice when I was out with Dad. Both times he scurried away after making a big show of being terribly surprised to bump into us. I thought he might be following *me*, though I'd no idea why. But since Dad's death I've made a few enquiries. Two of Dad's friends mentioned seeing Acland in similar circumstances, when they were with him. I don't know what he was playing at, but it can't be coincidence.'

As Eve and Gus left the room, Eve wondered. Was it possible Acland had suspected Lance of something and been monitoring his movements? And if he'd caught Lance at it, whatever it was, could he have killed him over it? He'd been in a prime position to sweep the death under the carpet.

16

Eve wanted to go back to Lance's study to write up her notes on the interview with Maynard, but she decided to nip to the kitchen and replenish her coffee first. It really was too cold to work without a warm drink.

As she approached the room, she saw Sonia through the open doorway, stuffing one of the many bouquets of flowers which sat on the worktop into the bin with a curse. She jumped when Eve cleared her throat. The house was full of twitchy occupants, not that it was surprising.

Sonia recovered herself, smiled at Eve and then groaned. 'Flowers from a series of males offering shoulders to cry on in the wake of Lance's death, if you can believe it.' She grabbed the next two from the pile and stuffed them into the bin as well, carrying on until the worktop was clear and the bin full.

Eve thought of all the admiring glances Sonia had had during the party and felt angry on her behalf. With a bit of imagination these creeps might realise she wouldn't be receptive. Even if her love for Lance had faded, she wouldn't instantly sign up for more of the same. 'I'm sorry. That's awful.' Eve explained her coffee mission.

'Please, go ahead!' Sonia bent to make a fuss of Gus who'd been standing patiently by her ankles, looking up, as though to catch her eye. 'Believe it or not, the heating is on, but it hardly makes a difference, the windows fit so badly. Would you like a heater? I'm sure I can find you one.'

'Please don't trouble. I'm well wrapped up.' Eve was wearing her warmest woollens.

Back at Lance's desk, she tried to focus on writing her notes, but the memory of Sonia in the kitchen kept coming back to her. The hurried way she'd explained her irritation and binning every bouquet the moment she realised Eve was watching. Something didn't feel right.

Eve was tense as she got up; she knew she couldn't leave it. Nonetheless, being caught rifling through the bin would be dreadful. Gus rose as well, name tag chinking, and looked at her appealingly.

'All right, you can come too.'

Before she left the study, she needed a plan. In the end, she took her coffee mug and a spare notebook with her. In the kitchen, feeling a sense of waste and shame, she deliberately spilled coffee over the notebook, leaving Gus looking perplexed. After that, she made for the bin, which she knew to be full. She took the bin bag out as she would have done if she'd honestly needed to throw something away and lacked the space. If anyone challenged her, she could say she was just trying to be helpful.

She put a new liner in the bin, dumped her notebook, then took the full liner outside to where the wheelie bins lived, screened from the house by a yew hedge. It would be a lot easier to go through the contents there.

After that, she removed the bouquets one by one. Gus was terribly interested and kept leaping up as though she was holding a slab of steak.

The first bouquet was from someone called Frank and said,

My darling, you know where I am. And how I've always felt about you. Call me any time.

Eve shuddered. No wonder Sonia felt tetchy. It was horrible to offer support with strings attached.

But the next three bouquets brought Eve up short.

Our sincerest condolences, Peggy and John Havers.

Please know we are all thinking of you and the family, the Wilson-Smiths.

And

So very sorry for your loss, Jemima Rosebury.

Why had those bouquets suffered the same fate as the one from Frank?

The next two were from single men, but there was no flirting or suggestion that they wanted to fill Lance's shoes.

And then Eve came to the last bouquet, the one Sonia had been holding when Eve entered the kitchen. And that was the most interesting of all. Someone – presumably Sonia – had removed the card that went with it.

Eve put the bouquets back in the bin bag, knotted it and put it in the general waste bin. Molly Walker was coming in to clean each day while the family were in residence. They'd hopefully assume she'd done it.

She walked back towards the house with Gus at her heels, her mind full of the missing greeting card. Had Sonia been having an affair? Maybe her lover had sent her flowers with something revealing on the card. If Sonia had been seeing someone behind Lance's back, that changed things. She'd probably have come off worse in any divorce settlement if he could show she'd been unfaithful. Whereas killing him would mean walking away with her third of the cash, straight into the arms of her lover. Eve needed to know how much difference the money would make to Sonia. She had a contact in the modelling world, the improbably named Heaven Jones. She could ask her how much Sonia might earn and pick up any gossip.

Eve was so preoccupied that movement to her right made her start. Erica Paxton, Lance's research assistant. Now *she* was acting oddly. Given where she was, she must have slipped out of the house via a side door, not the main entrance. She was skirting the building, flicking her gaze left and right and passing each window with caution.

Heck. Eve didn't want to leave Lockley Grange without explaining, but instinct told her it was important to follow. She watched as Erica sidled away from the house and through some bushes before turning towards the far end of the forecourt. She got into a dark-green VW.

Eve needed to act fast if she wanted to see where she went. Her eyes met Gus's and she put her finger to her lips before following Erica via a circuitous route. She had to keep hidden from both her and anyone watching from the Grange. It involved bending double behind a series of smart cars, from an Audi to a Range Rover. By the time she reached her Clubman, Erica was well down the driveway. Eve visualised the point where the drive met the road as she got Gus into his harness. It ran straight for a hundred yards or so in both directions. She could afford to wait until Erica turned before setting off. It was better than being spotted. As she lingered, she sent Sonia a quick text, claiming she needed a notebook from home, and promising to be back soon. Then she set off, holding her breath.

She let the breath out again at the head of the drive. She'd been right. Erica's car was still in sight. She was driving towards Saxford and Eve followed suit. It was grey again and the wind whistled across the flat landscape, coming in from the coast, thrashing the bare trees. As she and Erica got closer to the village it was clear that Erica wasn't heading for the centre. She overshot the turning towards the green and skirted the west side of the settlement instead, turning towards the sea to approach Saxford from the south. Eve slowed up. They were entering little-travelled roads. If Erica spotted her, she'd never believe Eve was there by chance.

Eve watched from a distance as Erica pulled up in the lane near a pretty red-brick cottage with vanilla-ice-cream coloured paintwork. Erica disappeared up a garden path, and Eve parked round the corner where she wouldn't be seen.

She twisted round to give Gus a reassuring pat, told him she'd be back in a minute and got out, turning her phone to silent and hugging herself against the cold. She wished she'd had time to fetch her coat.

Eve peered around a viburnum bush at the foot of the garden path Erica had taken, a car next to it in the driveway, and watched as Erica took an envelope from her pocket and eased it through the letterbox.

She was walking back up the path already, and Eve was wrong-footed. Until she'd seen the letter, she'd stupidly assumed Erica would go inside. Now, there was nowhere to run to. She glanced at the cottage next door. No car in the drive and no lights on inside, despite the dismal day. Taking a deep breath, she ducked into their front garden, then hid herself as best she could.

She waited, frozen in more ways than one. But before Erica could reappear on the pavement, a voice called her name. The tone was harsh and anxious, not friendly.

As tiny flecks of snow began to fall from the solidly grey sky, Eve pushed herself further into the hedge between the two houses.

Eve had a partial view through the laurel and she recognised the man who'd stopped Erica in her tracks. It was Terence Acland, Lance Hale's doctor, standing on the cottage's garden path, the front door open behind him.

'Don't run away.' His hand was on Erica's arm. 'Your plan won't work. We need to talk. Come in out of the cold.' His tone had gone from forceful to ingratiating.

But Erica was pulling back. 'Not here.'

'All right then.' He was testy again. 'What about the Black Cat Café in Blyworth?' It was the nearest market town. 'You know it?'

She shook her head. 'But I'll find it.'

'Today?'

She glanced at her watch. 'I can't. I've said I'll speak to Lance's obituary writer.' Eve was glad she wouldn't be stood up. 'The university have given me some urgent work to do too. I can meet you tomorrow. Mid-afternoon.'

Acland nodded at last. 'Very well. I'll see you there at three.' Erica turned to go but he still had hold of her coat sleeve. 'Erica? Hold your nerve until then. Anything else would be senseless.'

17

Eve could hardly flex her fingers by the time she let herself back into her car. She'd waited for five minutes after Erica had left in case Acland was keeping watch from his house. As she slipped into the driver's seat, she hoped fervently that the neighbour whose garden she'd occupied didn't have a doorbell camera.

She turned to pat Gus, then drove back to Lockley Grange, her mind full of what she'd heard. Erica and Acland were clearly mixed up in something together, but how did that relate to Lance?

Acland had been following Lance recently, if Maynard was to be believed. Meanwhile, Lance had accused Erica of betrayal. Had the pair of them been working together against Lance? Perhaps their plans hadn't come off and they'd taken the next step. If they'd wanted to bring him down, then killing him was the ultimate way of doing it. But why would his doctor and his research assistant form an alliance? Eve needed to know what they said at the Black Cat Café the following day, but she'd be recognised if she went herself. She hated the thought of sending a stand-in, but there was nothing for it. Back at the Grange, still stiff with cold, she returned to Lance's study and pinged off a message to Robin, asking if he could oblige. He messaged back moments later to agree. In his work-day clothes, neither Acland nor Erica was likely to give him a second glance. He hadn't dealt with any of the Hale household direct, except Lucy Garton, who'd booked him to tidy the garden before the party.

Eve had time to spare before she interviewed Lucy, then Erica. After what she'd just seen, the second interview was a priority, so she settled down at her laptop to do some background research. The process was frustrating. The Grange's broadband dropped out every fifteen minutes or so. How did Lance put up with it when he worked here? Maybe he spent more time thinking than googling. In the end, Eve linked her laptop to her phone to get data on the larger screen.

Erica's LinkedIn page told Eve which school she'd attended in London. Eve looked it up and found most people left with low grades and very few went on to higher education. Erica had defied the odds.

When Eve dug deeper, she found a JustGiving page where Erica had raised money for Cancer Research after her mother had died from the disease. It was clear from the messages that her father was no longer around either. She'd certainly had it hard, poor thing. Eve looked for any hint of siblings but found none. She had friends – you could see that from her Facebook profile – but family wise, she was alone in the world. Her job could have given her a feeling of belonging as well as an income and prospects. It seemed as though the Hales had treated her almost like family. Sonia and Naomi had both been concerned after Lance told her off on Friday. It meant his threat to cut her out didn't stop at her work. She'd lose her place in his household too. Eve guessed the hurt would have gone deep. But was it believable that she'd team up with Acland to kill him? Eve could see how they might egg each other on until they crossed that terrible line. And Erica and Acland could have been the man and woman Lucy Garton saw. But she couldn't guess at Acland's motive, and what would Erica hope to achieve by killing Lance, other than emotional satisfaction? If she wanted to keep her job then apologising was the obvious answer. Not that he'd deserved it.

Eve went back to her research again, looking for more up-to-date information on Erica. She'd published an impressive number of papers, usually with Lance as first-named author. Whether he'd done the lion's share of the work was another matter. She found other academics who'd complimented Erica and quoted findings they attributed to her, even if they appeared in papers published by Lance. She bet that hadn't gone down well. Lance had clearly hated competition.

And then Eve found something even more curious: a couple of positive stories mentioning Erica and *Maynard* in the same breath. That was odd. It wasn't as though they worked in the same area. The journalist involved was Monica Sutton, an old colleague of Eve's. That could prove handy.

Monica had linked Erica and Maynard because of their mutual connection to Lance. She could have spotted each of them doing well and used the fact to inspire one story, but to do it twice was weird. Lance would have hated it; he barely featured. Eve wondered if Monica had talked to Maynard and Erica together. She tried to imagine them being romantically involved but it was hard to see it. Still, Maynard might treat Erica differently to the way he'd treated Eve. It was something to consider. She made a note:

Lance accused Erica of betrayal. With Acland? What are the pair of them up to? Or with Maynard? Why the joint mentions in the press?

Eve messaged Monica, asking if she could buy her a coffee as soon as possible. It was no use calling her. Monica liked big stories and Eve was certain there was more to the articles than met the eye. Face-to-face wheedling would be required if she wanted to find out what.

After that, she checked there was no one in the rooms nearby, then called the model Heaven Jones. As soon as she explained what she was working on, she could hear the sad understanding in Heaven's deep melodious voice. It wasn't the first time Eve had picked her brains when working on the obituary of a murder victim.

'I know Sonia a little. She's still doing phenomenally well for herself.'

Eve couldn't ask her to dish the dirt on a friend. She'd have to tread carefully. 'She must be very well paid, I presume?'

'Oh, absolutely.' Heaven sounded a little envious. 'All those exclusive perfume advertisements. She'll be set for life.'

So unless she spent like crazy, she was unlikely to need Lance's money. It didn't mean she wouldn't be happy to have it, but it seemed less believable that she'd kill for it.

'I'm trying to get a handle on Lance and his connections. Did you know him at all?'

'Not well, but he was always charming, funny, clever. He paid attention to his guests.'

'Someone hinted he was having an affair. And actually, that Sonia might be too. But then people do gossip. I don't suppose there's anything in it.' Eve could feel herself blushing.

There was a pause. 'Anything's possible. Sonia's away a lot, but I've never seen her with anyone else. But Lance...' Her voice trailed off for a moment. 'I've heard the same gossip you have. And truth to tell, I spotted him buying an enormous box of chocolates once. It doesn't follow they were for a lover, but the box was pink, with hearts and flowers, and they won't have been for Sonia, that's for sure.'

It took Eve a moment. 'You mean because of her modelling work?'

'I'm afraid so. I know husbands can be scatty at times, but I'm sure Lance realised it was best to opt for flowers in Sonia's case. I don't think she had an easy time of it with the Hales.'

Eve remembered what Sonia had said about Jenna trying to fix Lance up with alternative women. 'No, I imagine not.'

'It was sad,' Heaven went on, 'but I didn't worry for her too much. She's her own person and I can't see her ever lacking work. She could have walked out any time she wanted.'

Yet she hadn't. Eve thanked Heaven and rang off.

As she stood, staring through the window at the dusky grounds of the Grange, a light dusting of snow lying on the grass, she saw Maynard walk past. He wasn't headed for his car and there was only one other reason she could think of for him to be out in such frigid weather: privacy. She needed to find out what he was up to.

Eve pulled on her coat and walked down the long corridor towards the back of the house, following the direction Maynard had taken. When she reached a back door, she could see him through the window, heading into a patch of trees around twenty-five yards from where she stood. Crossing the open patch of lawn between them felt like madness. She could well imagine Maynard poisoning his father. If he realised she'd followed him, she could be next. But his secretive behaviour compelled her to carry on. He might have arranged to talk to someone in person or be planning to make a call. Either way, it could make a huge difference if she heard what he said.

The light was fading fast now and the snow coming down more thickly. It was good news on both counts. Eve breathed a sigh of relief as new flakes filled in her footprints. Her dark coat would help her blend into the shadows too. Up ahead she could just see Maynard in his black woollen overcoat, but only because she knew he was there. He'd turned his collar up against the cold so she had to focus on his pale face to keep track of him.

At last, he came to a halt and pulled his phone from his pocket. Eve crept as close as she dared, aware of the very soft crunch her steps made in the new-fallen snow.

Maynard dialled. 'Well?' No pleasantries then. 'No, no. I know all that for Pete's sake.' He swore. 'I don't care what he's like, I need that money. Just give me his number.' He gave an exasperated sigh. 'At last. *Thank* you.' He rang off without saying goodbye.

A moment later he was redialling. 'Ah yes, the name's Jonathan Harris.' *Hmm.* 'I was given your number by a friend. I gather they've told you about me. No, no, I understand that. You'll get it back with the interest you specified to my friend. What? Yes, of course I realise the consequences if I can't pay, but that's not in question. I just need to come and get the cash. I can be with you tonight.'

Eve couldn't hear the words on the other end of the line, but the protesting tone was clear. Maynard must be after so much money that the person he was talking to couldn't get it in time.

'What?' Maynard sounded furious. 'You can't do this to me. I need it now!'

He stamped his foot. Eve was delighted that he wasn't getting his way. 'The weekend? Are you serious?'

From the long pause and the sound of shouting on the other end of the line, Eve gathered that the lender was in earnest.

'All right, all right. I'll come to you on Sunday night. Nine o'clock. Text me the address.' He jabbed at his phone, presumably to end the call, then started to type. A moment later, Eve heard a text going through. At a guess, he'd decided to message whoever was blackmailing him, rather than breaking the news on a call. He waited a couple of minutes after he'd sent the message. For the second time that day, Eve was chilled to the bone. Her hands hurt like crazy, despite her gloves.

At last, the sound of an incoming text came. Eve heard Maynard sigh with relief, then shake his head and say, 'Interesting that you'll wait. This really is all about the money then, not a desire to see my downfall.' He laughed. 'Thank God for that. It's a problem I can deal with.'

Eve guessed him babbling to himself was the result of nerves and relief. Something told her he had every intention of getting his money back again, whatever it took. She wondered if he knew the identity of his blackmailer. As for the lender, it was clearly a loan shark whom Maynard had never met before.

Eve stood stock still as he walked back towards the house then made herself wait ten minutes before she followed him inside.

18

With what little time she had left before her interview with Lucy, Eve did some background research on the woman. She'd been a high-flyer when she'd taken up with Bruno, just as Eve had heard. She and Lance had been contemporaries at Cambridge and evenly matched intellectually, though Lance had come top in his year, with her second. From what Maynard had said, maybe Lance wouldn't have befriended her if it had been the other way round. Lucy had got a 'starred first', whatever that was. Eve googled and discovered it required exceptionally high marks across a large number of papers. She must have worked extraordinarily hard. And then she'd done a PhD and more research after that, coupled with a lectureship. Perhaps that was why she'd fallen for wild, good-looking Bruno. A burst of rebelliousness at the end of a long stint of total focus. The horror of finding out what he was capable of must have been life-altering in the most dreadful way.

Eve had been told to meet Lucy in the suite Sonia had mentioned, up on the third floor of the house. She remembered it had once been Lance's mother's.

After knocking, she was admitted to a generously sized living room, complete with a neat sofa and two armchairs as well as a mahogany desk and an elegant wooden swivel chair, in keeping with the other period furniture.

Lance had certainly given Lucy a lovely home-from-home for when she was in Suffolk. It made Eve question her previous conclusion that the pair hadn't been lovers, but on second thoughts, she still couldn't believe it. Lance had been single for seventeen years after Bruno killed his first wife. He could have married Lucy, assuming she felt the same way. Instead, Lucy had given Lance her approval when he'd consulted her about Sonia, and Sonia said Lucy had accepted her. Perhaps Lance had simply rushed to give Lucy the suite out of guilt. She'd first occupied it in the aftermath of Jacqueline's death, after all, and it was his brother who'd left Lucy traumatised. In the back of her mind, Maynard's cynical words hovered too. If Lance had been hoping Lucy would look after his kids, presenting her with pleasant accommodation would have helped his cause, and once again, allowed Lance to see himself in a good light. All the same, her hunch was that he'd genuinely valued Lucy.

These days, of course, Lucy went where Lance did. She probably came down each time he visited Suffolk so the suite being well maintained made sense.

'Come in. Sit down.' Something about Lucy's clipped tone made Eve feel like a pupil being asked to enter the head-teacher's office.

'Thank you.'

Lucy motioned her to a seat. 'Tea?'

'Please. Milk, no sugar.' Eve sat on the sofa as directed and took the opportunity to size up Lucy's territory. There was a lovely carved statue on a mantelpiece, and the room glowed with lamps which reflected off a wall of glass-fronted cabinets facing the sofa and the door to the suite. Eve got a jolt as she saw herself in them and wished she'd tidied her hair after following Maynard. She ran her fingers through it the moment Lucy left the room, until she looked slightly less alarming. After that, she stood up to explore a little more thoroughly.

It looked as though Lucy was busy. Her desk was covered in many neatly ordered papers and from the way her chair sat – pushed back rather than tucked under – Eve had the impression she'd broken off from what she was doing to let Eve in. If she'd had to make time for her, it explained her brisk tone, though maybe she was restraining her emotions too.

Eve's attention was caught by the open web browser on Lucy's laptop. She'd been googling something to do with wills. That was interesting. Robin said she'd told Lance not to leave her anything, so what was she up to? Perhaps she suspected there was a problem with what Lance had left Sonia, Maynard or Naomi. They'd each gained a greater share in the Hale fortune after Jenna died; Eve wondered if it was something to do with that.

In the background, she spotted the tabs of various shopping sites. An antiques store, Hamleys toys, and a high-end furniture outlet. A combination of Christmas shopping and planning for the future, perhaps, if she would shortly set up on her own at last. Robin had implied she'd been well paid over the years and the tabs suggested she had money to spend.

Eve couldn't completely quell a stab of guilt for snooping, but after a murder she couldn't apply the usual rules.

She thought of Lucy in her own home after twenty years of running someone else's. All the hustle and bustle followed by quiet. It would feel strange.

When Lucy reappeared with their drinks, Eve was looking innocently out of the window. The suite faced the garden and the woods beyond. The view might not have changed for a hundred years and looked reassuringly traditional, in stark contrast to what was going on inside the Grange. 'It's a beautiful outlook.'

She caught Lucy bite her lip and wondered if she'd said the wrong thing. She'd probably miss it.

But as Eve sat down and Lucy handed her her tea, she sighed. 'Maynard's made it clear he'd like me to stay and it's this house he inherits. I'll have to make up my mind.'

It was interesting that Maynard wasn't pushing her out; he wasn't exactly full of the milk of human kindness, which might explain Lucy's reticence. She'd told the police she didn't know anything damning about him, but his desire to keep her under his nose might suggest otherwise. Treating her generously was sensible if she was a threat. The thought made Eve anxious. If he'd killed his dad to hush up past sins, he might end up doing the same to Lucy. She'd be a sitting duck if she stayed on. 'I guess it might be nice to have your own space after all these years.'

'Perhaps.' Tears sprang into Lucy's eyes and she wiped at them furiously with a tissue from her pocket, then met Eve's gaze. 'You have to understand that Lance saved me after Bruno killed his wife. You know how it happened? That I was in the car with him?'

Eve nodded. 'I'm so very sorry. I can't begin to imagine how you must have felt.'

Lucy looked down at her lap. 'I was consumed with guilt.' The words came out very quietly. 'I don't know how I could have been such a fool, but I'd fallen for Bruno to the point of obsession. Lance warned me – he did everything in his power to make me see sense – but I didn't listen.' Lucy seemed back in the moment. 'Instead, when Jacqueline said she wanted Bruno out, I was furious with her. When I got into the car with him, I was telling him how much I hated her. I'd dashed round my room, packing, and I set out on that journey knowing I'd follow him wherever he went. I felt powerless to opt out.' She closed her eyes for a moment. 'Hardly the feminist icon, am I?' Her head was in her hands but at last she looked at Eve again. 'Never in my worst nightmares did I imagine what he'd do, but I should have realised he wouldn't go quietly. Looking back on it now, I think I was as out of my mind as he was, despite not taking any drugs.'

'It must have been horrific when you understood what he was planning. Did he drive straight to where Jacqueline was?' Eve couldn't imagine the terror she must have felt as realisation set in.

Lucy nodded. 'He said, "Let's say goodbye to Jacquie before we go." Then before I knew it, he was driving across the lawn towards her with his foot to the floor. He was staring out of the windscreen, leaning forward in his seat. I couldn't get out. He'd locked the doors, and we were going so fast...' Her hands went to her face. 'It took me weeks to remember anything beyond that. Now, I think I recall Jacqueline looking up as we barrelled towards her, but it might be a false memory.'

False or not, the thought made Eve feel sick. How could you ever put something like that behind you?

'I always worry—'

But she was stopped by a noise in a nearby room and Eve fumed inwardly at the interruption. She heard Sonia's voice faintly. 'No, it'll all have to go, I suppose.' Then a pause as someone else said something.

Lucy got up, her eyes anxious. 'The soundproofing between the bedroom and the next-door suite's very poor.'

'Thank you, Molly,' that was Sonia again, 'but I must do it myself. You could vacuum in here though, that would be lovely.'

As the vacuum started up, Lucy closed her bedroom door to act as an extra barrier between them and the next room. Hopefully she'd feel able to confide now. Eve leaned forward. 'Sorry, Lucy, you were saying you always worry?' *Please* pick up where you left off.

She swallowed and nodded. 'I always worry that Jacqueline saw me alongside Bruno. She must have thought I wanted her dead too.' She looked at Eve with helpless eyes – a far cry from the organised slightly brusque woman Eve had met when she'd first come to the Grange. Perhaps she'd had to maintain that facade ever since the killing just to avoid crumpling in public.

Lucy took a juddering sigh. 'I'm sorry. That's such a selfish thing to worry about. It's hardly important compared with Jacqueline losing her life.'

'I can understand it playing on your mind – I'm sure it would on mine too – but if Bruno drove at such speed, I doubt she'd have even registered what was happening before it was over.'

'I really hope you're right.' She spoke very quietly, but with great intensity. After a long pause, she continued. 'Anyway, I couldn't function properly for a long time afterwards. There was no question of my going back to academia. I could never have stood up in front of a sea of faces to give a lecture. After worrying about my future if I followed Bruno, I resigned anyway, and hid myself away. It was horrific for the children, and Lance too, of course.'

Yet Lance had managed to carry on – thrive and fly in fact. But he hadn't been in the car that killed his wife.

'Lance made it clear from the start that I'd always have a home with him and the family,' Lucy went on. 'I was so grateful to him. I remember sitting there marvelling that he could look beyond me going off with Bruno – and what it had led to.' Her eyes were wide, as though she was lodged in the past again. 'People think it's odd that I never went back to my career, but Jacqueline's death was too great a burden. I kept blaming myself.'

Perhaps guilt was something she and Lance had had in common. Maynard said Lance had declared he'd rather lose Jacqueline than Bruno, because Bruno was more fun.

'I threw myself into helping Lance and the family,' Lucy went on. 'And Lance said he couldn't have coped without me. Three motherless children. Naomi was only nine at the time, Jenna eleven and Maynard twelve. They boarded when Lance went abroad, but I was there for them before that and during the holidays.'

'It must have been hard, trying to fill in for their mum.'

She nodded. 'Hardest with the older two. They were angry at everything: Jacqueline's death, their dad, each other. And Naomi for being less trouble and better liked than they were.' She looked down. 'It's horrible to confess, but it was far easier to bond with Naomi than the others. She had a calm about her – a separateness. She watched their fights but didn't join in. I praised her for it and tried to encourage the older two to cooperate, but lashing out and competing over everything was already ingrained. And I soon realised singling Naomi out as a good example made things worse for her. Maynard was especially jealous, though he never admitted he cared.'

It must have been a trial, and hard on the heels of a horrific and traumatising event. 'Did you ever go for counselling?'

She shook her head. 'I didn't feel I deserved it. I was actually quite glad when Maynard and Jenna played up. It felt like a just punishment.'

No wonder she wanted to talk now. Eve would be sensitive with the information she used.

'What about Lance? How did he cope after Jacqueline's death?'

'He put on a brave face, after the initial shock.'

But a brave face and a lack of true sorrow might look quite similar.

'He treated me as his mainstay. Took me as his companion to formal dinners, introduced me to his colleagues. We talked over his work, which gave me something to get my teeth into.' It sounded as though he'd made her feel special – something he excelled at. And like Maynard said, it hadn't cost Lance anything. Quite the reverse, in fact. It seemed she'd been so grateful for his support and forgiveness that she'd treated him like a demigod. He would have loved it.

'I spent the rest of my time organising Lance's life and running the two houses. It was always frantically busy. There was no time to think and that was what I needed. Having that one, strong, clear focus saved my life.' She looked at Eve intently. 'I ensured that everything ran smoothly, and that Lance was saved from further pain. You understand?'

Eve nodded. It sounded as though the mission had been a guiding star, dragging her on through a long, dark night. Hero-worshipping Lance had been an essential part of the process.

Eve went on to ask Lucy what Lance was like to work for. She said he was full of energy and drive, appreciative of her efforts, and willing to collaborate, with her at least. He was always 'determined to succeed, and for the children to do so too'.

'I heard he played them off against each other. Especially the older two. It explains the rivalry you mentioned.'

Lucy cocked her head. 'He thought it would boost their chances in the big, wide world. He used to worry that Naomi wouldn't be tough enough.'

But as far as Eve could see, he'd found it hard to accept when they fulfilled their promise. He couldn't resist keeping them in their place: somewhere below where he was.

When Eve got up to go, Lucy followed her towards the door. 'I've been reading up on the help you've given the police in the past.'

As before, Eve began to downplay it, but Lucy fixed her with her gaze. 'I'm glad you're working on Lance's obituary. Even I never knew him properly. He had hidden depths. You won't give up trying to work out what happened, will you?

You'll question everything, especially if you think the police have got it wrong?'

The words seemed loaded. 'Is something worrying you? Do you suspect someone or have information you haven't passed on?'

But Lucy just looked back at her. 'I want justice to be done, that's all. It doesn't always happen.'

19

Lucy's words about justice filled Eve's head as she left her suite. What had she meant about it not always being done? Had there been more to Jacqueline's death than met the eye or did she suspect that Jenna had been killed? She sent Robin a text, asking if Greg had come back with any update on the ins and outs of Jacqueline's murder. The news reports made it sound open and shut, but the journalists might not have known everything. After that, she walked quietly around the house. She wanted time to think, and she half hoped she might overhear something useful, but there was nothing. At last, she went back to Lance's study to carry on working until her interview with Erica.

She continued to go through Lance's papers and belongings. The police would have searched the room, of course, and removed anything they thought was significant, but she might find something that meant more to her than it did to them. In particular, she wondered about Lance's rumoured lover.

Eve scanned the study, looking for hiding places the police might not have found. She doubted they'd removed every book, for a start. It was a dry-looking collection of tomes and Eve ran her finger along them, feeling for any volume that might have something tucked inside. But then she thought of Lance's personality: the way he ran at life. She couldn't imagine him carefully placing love letters or other secrets into a book. He'd dash in and shove them somewhere, pausing only to rub his hands with glee before he sat down. She imagined him dashing in now. Where would he go first? To the hooks by the door to hang up his jacket? They were fixed to a free-standing Victorian dresser, meant for storing coats, hats, umbrellas and gloves.

Eve searched the dresser's drawers, knowing a scientific support officer would have got there before her. There was nothing of interest. Then she took the drawers out and looked underneath and behind them, still with no luck. And besides, it was as she'd thought before, she couldn't see Lance making a lot of effort when squirrelling something away.

At the top of the stand was a shelf, above eye level, even for a tall person, but reachable if you were Lance.

Eve moved a chair so she could climb on top and check it, but of course it was empty too. It was disappointing, and she stood there for a moment, looking down at the dresser, feeling fed up.

And it was then that she saw it. A gap between the back panel of the dresser and a glove drawer which sat just in front of it.

And in the gap, from this angle, Eve could see some papers. She got down from the chair carefully, as though anyone listening might guess at her momentous discovery if she made a noise.

A moment later, she was easing the papers out. For all her analysis of Lance's character and his probable behaviour, she hadn't truly expected a result. She caught her breath as excitement made her insides flutter.

The papers were a weird, eclectic mix, all secret, but for a variety of reasons. There were receipts showing how much he smoked and drank. Eve knew Lucy had put in a bulk order at Saxford's village store when they arrived but Lance must have kept some of his spending private. She imagined him slipping the evidence behind the glove drawer until he had time to dispose of it properly, then forgetting all about it. Some of the receipts dated back months. Much more interesting was a note in Lance's handwriting, easily recognisable now she'd trawled through his papers.

Darling, come and meet me tonight at the pool. I'll head down there once things have quietened down. Let's talk, I

The note broke off mid-sentence. It didn't follow that Lance had written it on the night of the party, but Eve thought it was likely. Perhaps he'd been interrupted by someone knocking on his door. He'd have been right by the stand when he went to open up, so the gap behind the glove drawer was a logical place to hide it. Maybe he'd been writing to the person who'd knocked, and he'd issued the invitation direct instead. Either way, the note hadn't been sent. If only she knew what had happened. Lucy thought someone had been hanging around the pool when Lance died, but they couldn't have gone there to kill him. The overdose had been administered much earlier. And Lucy had seen two people, not just Lance's 'darling', whoever that might be. Eve guessed at Sonia, Naomi or a lover. And having talked to Lucy she couldn't imagine that lover being her. Eve went through the rest of the papers after that. At last, she found a note which was not in Lance's handwriting.

Forgive me writing. I couldn't bring myself to ask you directly, but am I right? Are you feeling the same way I am? I spend all my time thinking about you but if I've misread the signs, please let me know – gently! – and I promise I'll banish these thoughts from my mind. It feels wrong to even ask given you're already attached. xxx

The writer might have been too cautious to sign the note, but Eve recognised this handwriting too, thanks to reading the communications that went between Lance and his assistant.

It was from Erica.

20

Eve stood there considering the note to Lance from Erica before photographing it, along with his note to someone asking them to meet him by the pool. After that, she put everything back where she'd found it. The question was, what had Lance felt when he'd read Erica's note? Had he returned her feelings and was she the lover his children had picked up on? If so, Eve doubted Naomi had known it was Erica. She'd been friendly towards her after Lance told her off, whereas Eve had a hunch she'd have been angry if she'd known. She and Sonia seemed close; Naomi would probably have taken Sonia's side.

But if Erica and Lance had been lovers, the doctor, Terence Acland, might have known the whole truth. He'd been following Lance around, so he could have seen for himself. How would that fit with the pair of them meeting up in secret?

Eve couldn't fathom it, but any relationship with Lance made Erica look even stronger as a suspect. Him wanting to end her career was enough, but if the relationship had also been smashed to smithereens it would only make it worse. And Eve could believe there'd been a relationship. Lance had accused Erica of betrayal. Perhaps he thought Erica had been seeing someone behind his back. The only person Eve had seen her meet secretly was Terence Acland. It was worth considering him as the other man, if there'd been one. Eve had so many theories, but they were all built on sand. For a second, she imagined Erica and Acland agreeing to finish Lance off together, then going to the pool to make sure he was dead. It might save Erica's career, but Acland would have to love her an awful lot to collaborate on such a terrible plot.

She was about to interview Erica. She wasn't sure how to talk to her without giving away her suspicions. Facing her with some intrusive questions could help determine how angry she'd been with Lance, though. If she'd already transferred her affections to Acland, she might not mind him ending any relationship, but his determination to torpedo her career would still be a powerful motivator. She'd worked so hard for it – and for him. Eve remembered how exhausted she'd looked on Friday night.

She repeated her earlier exercise of prowling quietly around the house in the spare time before talking to Erica. This time, she got lucky. Way down one of the back corridors, she heard Naomi's voice.

'I just want it done without anyone finding out.' There was a pause. 'No, that's okay. I expected it to be expensive. And you're willing to do as I asked? I know. I'm sorry, but you're the only one I trust.' Then her tone changed. She sounded wrung out. 'No, but you can see why not. It's all such a mess and the timing's terrible. I can't tell her. Not yet.'

Eve wandered back to Lance's study to pick up her notebook, Naomi's words playing in her head. The terrible timing must refer to the aftermath of Lance's death, so the 'her' was probably Sonia or possibly Lucy. But what secret was Naomi keeping from one of them? And who was she hiring, and why? It sounded ominous – as though she wanted to tidy up after a problem. But if so, it couldn't be at the Grange. She could do that herself. The thought took her to Jenna's death, but she still couldn't believe someone like Naomi would conspire with Lance to kill her sister. If Naomi committed murder at all, Eve's gut told her it would be a spur-of-the-moment act, resulting from a loss of control. She felt it was just possible she'd poisoned Lance, but only if he'd drunk the coffee before she could change her mind. Though of course, Eve might be wrong. Robin always told her to keep an open mind.

As if on cue, a message from her fiancé popped up, coming back with Greg's information on Jacqueline Hale's death. There were multiple witnesses to back up the official version of events. A group of friends who'd been visiting had seen Lucy and Bruno storm out.

The crew working on the fence close to where Jacqueline had been killed had seen Lucy screaming as the car hurtled towards Lance's first wife and confirmed that Bruno had been in the driving seat. They said Lucy was tugging on the door handle, trying to get out.

It was so horrific that Eve felt overwhelmed all over again, but it was a relief to have it clear. Whatever effect Jacqueline's death had had on her family, there was no secret to uncover.

She sent a message to the gang's WhatsApp group, suggesting supper at the Cross Keys. They needed to hash things out together.

After that she went to find Erica in her study, just along the corridor from Lance's.

Erica's deep-set eyes met hers steadily as she stood back to let her in and offered her tea. Eve accepted just as she had with Lucy. It would give her time to assess her before she put up too many defences. Erica worked carefully and in silence, using a kettle in the corner of the room. Eve knew she'd lost her immediate family and there was a photo on her desk of a man and woman holding a baby. She guessed that might be Erica and her parents; the timing looked right, judging from the fashions. Erica had ornaments too, including a wooden carving of a wren.

'I made it for my mum when I was at school,' Erica said, following Eve's gaze as she delivered her tea.

'It's beautiful.' It was so carefully worked. Eve guessed she'd loved her mum very deeply.

Erica sat down. 'I feel awkward talking to you about Lance. Everyone knows we were on bad terms the night he died.' She frowned. 'I checked his speech ten minutes before he stood up to give it. The pages were in the correct order and none of them were missing.'

It was clearly paramount from her point of view that Eve knew this, despite all the larger things going on. Her professionalism really mattered to her.

'Maybe someone knocked them to the floor and muddled them when they put them back.'

'Maybe.'

'You think someone mucked them up on purpose, and stole a page?'

There was a pause. 'I wondered if Lance might have done it himself.'

She certainly wasn't trying to hide the bad blood between them, but that could be a double bluff. 'Why would he do that?'

'There's been some positive coverage about me in the press lately.' Eve didn't admit that she'd noticed it too. Her old colleague Monica Sutton had agreed to meet Eve in London on Saturday. She should find out more then.

'You'd think he'd be pleased that one of his team was getting some recognition,' she said.

Erica gave a hollow laugh. 'That wasn't the way Lance's mind worked. If my stock went up, he automatically felt his was going down.'

It was the same attitude he'd had towards Naomi and her report. It can't have been conducive to an affair, but of course the love note Erica had written to Lance could be old. 'Was he always like that? Or was he a better boss at the beginning?'

Erica sighed. 'Much better at the start. He gave me my big chance and treated me as his protégé. I worked my fingers to the bone, all hours, day and night, because my career means so much to me. And when Lance made demands, even if they seemed unreasonable, I went with it. He could be very compelling.'

It was clearly a pattern. When Lance was in charge and his good will cost him nothing, he was sweetness and light. But when Erica had started to get noticed, the primitive, instinctive part of his personality had been unleashed and he'd moved swifty to clip her wings. 'What kind of unreasonable demands did he make, if you don't mind me asking?'

Erica paused a fraction longer than should have been necessary. 'After-hours work. Stuff that wasn't strictly to do with the research project.'

She seemed to read Eve's look. 'Maynard's got it into his head that his dad and I were having an affair, but he's wrong. It was nothing like that.'

It wouldn't be unnatural to deny it. 'Whatever it was, it still sounds hard to deal with.' There'd been an imbalance of power. 'Tell me he didn't get you picking up his dry cleaning and buying Sonia flowers.'

Erica gave a quick laugh. 'Nothing like that, but it was out of order. I should have said no, but he wielded a lot of power.'

And now that power was at an end.

21

That evening, Eve sat with Robin, Viv, Sylvia and Daphne at the Cross Keys. They'd managed to bag the table closest to the fire again. It crackled and popped as a light flurry of snow danced past the window, lit by the lamp just outside.

Eve had a heartening pie in front of her, crammed with rich gravy, chestnut mushrooms and shallots. She took a sip of her Malbec and glanced around the table. 'Lots to report and I need your input because my head's spinning.'

'Tell all, immediately!' Viv was diving into mushroom stroganoff.

Eve had updated her list, so she didn't forget anything. 'Let's go in order of most likely suspects. First, we have Maynard. He inherits a third of his dad's fortune, plus Lockley Grange, and he has a secret which Lance might have gossiped about. He could have wanted to stop him spreading it any further; it certainly sounds as though he's being blackmailed.' She relayed the conversation she'd heard in the grounds of the Grange, then finished a mouthful of pie.

'Next, there's Erica, and she's moved up the suspect list for Lance.' She explained about the note Erica had written to him and how she'd said he made 'unreasonable demands'. 'She admits Maynard thought they were in a relationship, though she denies it. She might have decided it would be better to present her version of events before I heard it from someone else. If they were lovers, then Lance accusing her of betrayal takes on a new significance. Perhaps she'd finally seen through him and hooked up with someone else.'

'Dr Acland?' Viv asked. Eve had updated the WhatsApp group after that adventure.

'Possibly. There are definitely tensions between them, which would fit if Erica had talked Acland into helping her kill Lance. And her motive's clear: Lance was intent on ending her career. He told her at the party that she knew it was coming, so she'd have had time to plan the murder. Acland would know exactly how much digoxin to use to bring on a heart attack and he was in the perfect position to present the death as natural causes. But there are caveats. If the black-bordered note came from the killer, it's hard to imagine Erica sending it. I can see she might want to frighten Lance to punish him, but I'd say she's far too controlled to give in to temptation like that and risk triggering an investigation.'

'It's still possible it was typed by another member of the household and meant metaphorically,' Robin said.

'True, but it feels like too much of a coincidence. And as well as that objection, I can't see Erica's motive for Jenna, if she was killed too.'

Sylvia steepled her fingers over her boeuf bourguignon and frowned. 'I can't help seeing your point. What do you conclude then?'

Eve closed her eyes, but no enlightenment rushed into her head. 'I'm not sure. I think we need to focus on what we know, dig further and wait for the mist to clear. The facts are that Erica and Acland have something to hide, and that Lance asked Erica to do something which made her uncomfortable, yet at the time she loved or respected him enough to agree. Whether she and Lance became lovers is an open question. Maybe he turned her down or she saw through him before they got that far. Or maybe they were still involved when he died, and he asked her to meet him at the pool that night.' She explained about the note Lance had written but never handed over.

'What about Acland?' Viv asked. 'Anything more?'

'Just that he and Erica seemed to disagree about how to deal with their secret, whatever it is. He said Erica's solution wouldn't work; he was desperate to talk to her before she did anything.'

'I'll make sure I'm in the Black Cat Café when they meet tomorrow,' Robin said.

'Thanks. And lastly for Acland, Maynard thinks he was following Lance before he died. Again, that makes me wonder if there was some kind of plot afoot.'

'Who's next on the list?' Daphne tucked her silver hair behind her ears.

'Sonia. And sticking with the topic of affairs, I wonder if she's been having one.' Eve explained how she'd gone through the flowers which Sonia had binned and found the bouquet without a label. 'She seemed irritated, infuriated even, when I discovered her disposing of that first bunch. Assuming she removed the label herself it suggests a guilty conscience and a revealing message. She could have killed Lance in preference to going through a messy divorce. She gets a third of his fortune after all. But from what my modelling-world contact tells me, Sonia's probably already wealthy. I find it hard to believe she'd kill out of greed.'

'And what about Naomi?' Sylvia asked. 'I liked her the one time I met her, but I don't know her well.'

'I like her too, but she's got secrets.' Eve relayed the latest phone call she'd overheard. 'She's prepared to pay a lot of money for someone to do a job for her and her sense of urgency set my radar off.'

'And you heard her talk about having decided to destroy someone on the day of the party.' Viv was bolt upright in her seat. 'It sounds pretty dodgy.'

Eve nodded. 'And at the end of the most recent call, she talked about the timing being terrible and said: "I can't tell her, not yet." I wonder if there's something she needs to break to Sonia or Lucy, but if so, I doubt it's anything to do with killing Lance. I can't imagine she'd confess her guilt, even though she and Sonia seem close.'

'And what about Lucy Garton?' Robin asked. She hadn't had time to fill him in before coming to the pub.

Eve relayed her conversation with Lance's right-hand woman. 'I can't see any motive for her. She doesn't inherit and you told me yourself she specifically asked Lance not to leave her anything. From what I can gather, she's comfortably off and if she wants, Maynard will keep her on. But I think she might be worried.' Eve explained how she was researching wills when she'd gone to interview her. 'She started off quite brusque, but I think that's a defence mechanism. I suspect she's suffered pent-up trauma ever since Jacqueline was killed and it's possible she's never let her feelings out. I found it worrying, the way she asked me to search for the truth because justice isn't always done.' She looked at Robin. 'But the information you sent me about Jacqueline's death leaves no room for doubt. Bruno was guilty and he was punished, so I don't think she's talking about that. It made me wonder about Jenna's death again. Lance and Naomi alibi each other but there was no one to vouch for Maynard. I suppose Lucy would go to the police if she could prove anything, but I wonder if she suspects. It's concerning, because she also knows Maynard's secret, though she's denied all knowledge to the police. I'm glad they asked her about it at least; it should make her aware of the danger.'

'Have you reported all the latest stuff to pea-brain Palmer?' Viv asked.

'Up to a point.' Eve's gaze slid to Robin, who raised an eyebrow. Eve normally passed on anything relevant the moment she heard it. 'I've emailed Greg saying I think he needs to ask Maynard if he's being blackmailed again, and that Sonia might have a lover. And I've suggested he might talk to Lucy about Jenna's death and to Erica about a possible relationship with Lance – she mentioned the rumour about it to me herself. But I haven't told him to go and look for a note from Erica behind Lance's glove drawer, for instance, or repeated word-for-word what I heard Maynard say.'

Robin put his head in his hands.

'The trouble is, it's so specific. The family will guess exactly where the police got their information and whoever killed Lance will find a way of ejecting me from the house. Long-term, the police will learn more if I'm allowed to stay than if I over-play my hand.'

Robin took a long swig of his stout.

'She does have a point,' Viv said, patting Robin on the shoulder.

Eve turned to him. 'That's why we need to be the ones who follow Maynard on Sunday evening, when he leaves to keep his nine o'clock appointment. If he succeeds in borrowing the money, he might go straight to the blackmailer to drop it off. I think he's had to ask for an extension, so I guess time will be of the essence. He was talking to himself after he got it – I think he was so relieved it made him unguarded. He's decided that the blackmailer's only motivated by money, not the desire to ruin his reputation, which clearly reassured him. He thinks he can "deal with them", which sounds ominous. It looks as though they're communicating by text.'

Robin took out his phone, looking resigned. 'Sunday at nine. I agree, *someone* has to be there. Dealing with the blackmailer might involve violence, and it's as you said before, if we find out who they are, we might discover the secret and possibly why Lance died.'

'There you are, you see,' Viv said. 'You and Eve will be on the case, so there's no need to worry about Palmer not knowing the finer details.'

Sylvia smiled. 'You can say you spotted Maynard acting suspiciously and decided to tail him on the spur of the moment. You knew the police wouldn't make it in time if you called them.'

'And the authorities do have the most crucial information, thanks to what Eve has passed on,' Daphne added hopefully.

They were all very loyal.

'All right,' Robin said. 'You win.'

'You're not allowed to go yet,' Viv said, as Eve started to gather up her stuff. 'I've got something urgent to discuss with you.'

'About the murders?'

'No, you noodlehead. About your wedding cake. Moira's given me a revolting bride-and-groom cake topper and it doesn't match my vision. I need your help to explain to her why we won't be using it.'

She produced a photo. It was very much not Eve's sort of thing either.

She was actually quite pleased to be presented with a different challenge. Moira from the village store, Eve could handle. 'Consider it done.'

22

Back at home, she mapped out plans for the case with Robin.

'Do you forgive me for not telling the police everything?'

He gave her a wry smile. 'Let's say I understand your motive, even if I don't officially approve. I just hope flouting the rules doesn't come back to bite us, that's all. So' – he got up to stoke the fire, causing Gus to stir in his basket – 'what's next?'

'Naomi's agreed to talk to me tomorrow. I want to ask her about the final row with Lance to see if I can work out the background. I'll explore more of the house too, and listen in to any conversations while I'm at it. Then later, I've got an appointment to talk to an old family friend of the Hales who ended up working with Jenna.' Her text in reply to Eve's had come in while they were at the pub. 'She came to Suffolk for the party and she's staying at the Cross Keys. I'm hoping she can tell me what was going on in Jenna's life just before she died. If she was killed, something major must have triggered it. And I can't wait for your updates on what Erica and Acland talk about at the Black Cat Café either. I'll need to arrange an interview with him when I can too.'

Robin nodded. 'I'll make sure I'm in Blyworth on time.'

'Thanks.' She had high hopes for the following day.

At ten o'clock the following morning, Eve sat opposite Naomi in the drawing room as arranged. Gus had pottered up to Eve's interviewee a little hesitantly, as though he could sense her tension and upset, but as Naomi stroked him, she began to look calmer.

Eve started with gentle questions to put her at her ease. Her relationship with her dad sounded as though it had been good as she'd grown up. She was less resentful than Maynard about the time Lance had spent working and she'd clearly felt encouraged in everything she did.

It was in marked contrast to the impression Maynard had given. Eve explained what she'd gleaned from her interview with Naomi's brother. 'I wonder why you came through your childhood with such different memories.'

Naomi looked sad. 'Looking back as an adult, I think I get it. Dad found it hard if we questioned his judgement, and by the time Mum died, Maynard had already started doing that, aged twelve. The same went for Jenna – she was eleven. But I hadn't made that switch into pre-teen mode. I think he felt I was on his side. Then after Mum's death, Dad went abroad, and we spent most of our time at school or with Lucy. It meant Dad and I never locked horns in the way he, Maynard and Jenna had. It's only recently that our relationship's become more challenging.'

'The interview he gave about your research must have been a blow.' Eve would have been devastated, but she wasn't used to a dad like Lance.

Naomi looked utterly exhausted. 'It came as a bolt from the blue, but I should have expected it. It was the first time I'd really put myself out there. He was determined to preserve his position as top dog and terrified of anyone laughing at him. His solution was to get them to laugh at me instead.' She gulped back a sob. There was no doubting her deep hurt. 'I'd seen him do it to Maynard and Jenna, so I knew what he was capable of.'

'I'm sorry.' Eve watched her eyes and ached for her inside, but her emotion made her wonder afresh about Naomi as a killer. 'It sounds painful. Someone mentioned you had a horrible run-in with him on Friday night too, after he'd shown Erica up.' The trouble was, if Naomi knew Eve had helped the police in the past, she'd see she was digging, however subtly she tried to put it.

Sure enough, Naomi's eyes were wary. 'I shouldn't have lost control like that. It was wrong to let other people overhear.'

'Erica told you something that shocked you?'

There was a long pause. Naomi was looking down again, stroking Gus. 'Dad used her in an unforgiveable way. It made me so angry that I tackled him about it immediately.'

Perhaps she could have poisoned Lance as well as writing the black-bordered note and losing control at the party. It would have been risky to show her feelings, but her hurt hung in the air. It was intense.

Eve let the silence ride, hoping Naomi would say more about the way her father had used his research assistant. When she didn't speak, Eve tried to prompt her. 'Erica said he'd made some unreasonable requests.'

But instead of encouraging Naomi to say more, she looked oddly thrown. How did that make sense?

'I can well imagine,' Naomi said at last.

Eve wished she could ask Naomi to explain what she knew outright, but push too far, and she'd probably get herself thrown out of Lockley Grange. The killer – either Acland or someone from the household – had every reason to want her gone. So instead, she expressed her sympathy again and left Naomi to it.

. . .

Back in Lance's study, Eve wrote up her notes from their talk and wondered what lay behind Naomi's words. She was increasingly frustrated at having to wait to get more information on Maynard too. When her shoulders got stiff, she prowled around the house to see if she could see what he was up to. She managed to find the room he'd chosen to work in, and at one point caught him on the phone, but he was only talking about his parliamentary duties.

In desperation, she went to the library Sonia had mentioned. She hadn't seen Maynard go in there, but he was supposed to have frequented it as a child and Lance's books and the family photos were there too. She wanted to see them.

The moment she entered the room, she was glad she'd come. It was atmospheric: decorated dark red and full of bookcases with gilt detailing. The centre of the room was bare, so that it felt spacious, but on two sides there were comfortably worn chairs next to leather-inlaid desks.

Eve found a dedicated section for Lance's books and picked out his memoirs of life as a diplomat, as well as the academic volumes he'd published. She'd borrow them to read at home if Sonia had no objection.

After that, she skirted the room to get the measure of the place. Sonia was right, it was an eclectic mix. There was everything from classic fiction to detective mysteries, to reference books and travelogues. Lots on international politics too, as you'd expect from Lance's career. Perhaps they had got Maynard interested in standing for parliament.

She found a section for children's books over on the north side of the room, including several on academic subjects, as well as novels and collections of poetry. She pulled out a volume catchily titled, *Multivariate Calculus and Mathematical Models*. A sign that Lance and Jaqueline had been hot-housing their kids?

But the inscription inside wasn't from them. Someone had written in black ink:

Bet you can't understand any of this, Jenna. I'll read it when you've given up. Mosh. 2005.

Mosh?

Maynard something, something Hale? Only child though Eve was, she still knew enough to guess it was the sort of dedication a certain kind of brother might write. She found Maynard on Wikipedia on her phone. Maynard Oscar Simon Hale. *Hmm.*

After that, Eve pulled out several similar books to prove to herself that Maynard was just as nasty as he seemed. She found one he'd given to Naomi on economics.

To Naomi, who's always asking questions. Dad might see it as a sign of cleverness, but if you're asking, you don't have the answers. They're all in this book if you can understand it. Mosh, 2004.

How old had Naomi been then? Eve thought back and did some mental maths. Heck, only eleven. So Maynard would have been fourteen. It would have been after their mother died, when Lucy had stepped into the breach to keep the family on an even keel.

Eve was no economics expert, but the book looked degree level to her. She checked and found Amazon agreed.

It was a similar case with the book he'd given to Jenna. They could have been child prodigies. It wasn't impossible when you looked at their careers. But from Maynard's inscriptions, Eve couldn't help thinking he'd wanted to crush their ambitions before they got going. What better way than giving them books they couldn't hope to understand?

It was a horrible, mean-minded thing to do, but it fitted. Lance had brought him up to be desperately competitive and Jacqueline, not wanting Jenna to lose out to her big brother, had only encouraged her to fight back all the harder. It seemed Lucy had tried to call order, but by that time it must have been ingrained. Maynard had been determined to hold his sisters back so he'd shine by comparison.

Eve's other takeaway was that if Naomi had been asking clever questions about economics when she was eleven, she must be exceptionally bright. Her charity job was less flashy than Jenna's or Maynard's, but she might be the most talented of them all.

For a moment, Eve considered Maynard killing Jenna to rid himself of a sibling rival. Was Naomi in danger too? Even if he'd murdered his father to get money and guard his secret, he'd effectively wiped out another family competitor there. But surely, he wouldn't go through them all? She suspected he'd be ruthless enough, but he couldn't hope to get away with it.

Except no one even suspected Jenna had been pushed off that cliff, and Lance's death had very nearly been written off as natural...

After she'd replaced the books, she went on to examine the rest of the room's contents.

She found the photograph albums Sonia had told her about and flicked through old family groups with a lump in her throat. There was one of Lance and Jacqueline looking impossibly glamorous on an exotic beach, their three children standing in front of them. Eve guessed Naomi had been around five at the time, Jenna seven, and Maynard eight. He looked sullen, it had to be said. Jenna had been striking, even at that age. Imperious looking with her head held high, her hair swept back. But it was Naomi's adoring expression, focused on Jacqueline, that got to Eve. Mother and youngest daughter looked so happy, and Lance's expression was proud. Thank goodness they hadn't known what lay ahead. Within five years, Jacqueline would be dead.

Eve was having one last look at the books when she spotted one that made her pause: an old volume on poisonous plants with a tattered green cloth cover. It couldn't relate to Lance's death, of course. His medication might be derived from foxgloves, but no one had given him the plants direct. All the same, she was moved to pull the book from its shelf and have a look.

It had fifty pence written on the inside cover in pencil. A jumble-sale find by the look of it. So who had wanted to research the topic? Perhaps Jacqueline had picked it up, anxious at the Grange's extensive grounds, where anything might be growing. Eve could imagine her scouring the flowerbeds for plants that might harm her young children.

As she turned the pages, she found the book fell open naturally on an entry about belladonna. Deadly nightshade. Close to the spine of the book, where the pages were sewn in, she saw there was a speck or two of something. A bit of dried plant? Eve shivered in the cold, high-ceilinged room. Whatever it was, it didn't look as though anyone had looked in this book for a long time and her theory about Jacqueline's protectiveness still held good. She could have rushed in from gardening to check a plant, wanting to reassure herself.

It had to be something like that, surely? The only historical unnatural death she knew of was Jacqueline's, and she hadn't been poisoned.

23

Eve drove Gus home from Lockley Grange that afternoon, ready to meet Robin, who'd been to eavesdrop on Acland and Erica at the Black Cat Café. After that, she was going to meet Jenna's friend and colleague Judith Tyler at the Cross Keys.

She was back at Elizabeth's Cottage having a cup of tea when Robin returned home. She reached the door as quickly as Gus and almost fell over him. Robin gave her an apologetic look as he shut out the cold, kissed her and made a fuss of the dachshund.

'A bit of a letdown, I'm afraid.'

'They didn't show?'

'They did' – he took off his coat and beanie – 'and I don't think they recognised me, but Lucy Garton did.'

'Lucy?' Eve was struggling to keep up. She poured Robin a mug of tea and handed it to him.

'Thanks.' He held the drink close to his chest, as if for warmth. 'Yes, she was there too, and I doubt she believed my presence was coincidental, any more than I think hers was.'

'I wonder if she suspects Erica and Acland. She told

everyone she couldn't identify the couple she saw by the pool, but she might have been trying to guess.'

Robin nodded. 'I thought perhaps she was after the truth, just like us, but if so, she was clumsy about it.'

Eve put her arm around Robin. 'I suppose she's not lucky enough to have someone she can send on her behalf. Maybe she doesn't know who to trust.'

'I can see she's in a tricky position but I'm still trying to forgive her for scuppering what could have been a very enlightening mission.'

'Erica and Acland left?'

'Uh-huh. They crept off but I'm sure Lucy saw them before they escaped. I followed them, of course. I thought Lucy might too, but I'm guessing that was a bridge too far. A waitress had just delivered her tea and cakes, so she'd have created a kerfuffle if she'd walked out.'

'It's odd. She's renowned for her cleverness; you'd think she'd have planned it better.' But Eve agreed: it was hard to believe her presence was a coincidence. There were plenty of cafés to choose from in Blyworth. 'Where did Erica and Acland go?'

'They sat in Acland's car, where there was no possible way I could hear them. I don't think Erica trusts him. She wasn't keen to get inside, any more than she wanted to enter his house when you saw her there. I stayed long enough to check she got out okay but I've no idea what was said, only that Acland looked more relaxed by the time they'd finished.'

'Thanks for being so dedicated. But darn it.'

'Eloquently put.'

'Do you think there's any chance that they're lovers?'

Robin looked thoughtful. 'I certainly wouldn't have said so. They didn't even act like people who knew each other well.'

'Bang goes another theory.'

He put down his mug and turned to give her a hug. 'I might be wrong. At least you've still got Jenna's friend to meet with.'

'True. I only hope she says something enlightening. Acland's agreed to talk to me tomorrow too, so I'll be entering his lair.'

'What time?'

She knew he'd offer to wait outside as backup, in case she ran into trouble. 'First thing. I have to confess, I checked your bookings to make sure you'd be free before I agreed.'

He kissed her. 'That's just what I wanted to hear.'

Eve met Judith Tyler in the snug at the Cross Keys, thankful for the warmth of the pub. It was only a short walk from Elizabeth's Cottage, but the weather was still bitter and it made her fingers hurt. She bought Judith a mulled cider, decided to have one herself, and settled down to ask her about the Hales. She'd start off with questions about Lance – it was what Judith would expect – then work her way round to Jenna and what life had been like for her just before she died.

'Thanks for agreeing to talk to me. It's great to find someone who knew Lance for so long. You were at school with Jenna?'

Judith nodded, her red hair falling forward, pale fingers gripping her warm drink. 'We met at primary school. After that, I spent almost as much time at their place as I did at home. Awful that both he and Jacqueline were murdered. I still can't quite believe it, but things were always intense with the Hales.'

Eve had her own experience of that, but Judith might know more. 'Intense? How do you mean?'

'Feelings ran high. No one did anything by halves and they didn't moderate their behaviour in front of me much. If there was a row brewing, I used to beg Jenna to take me up to her room, but she always wanted to join in.' She shook her head.

Eve had noted the same lack of moderation of course, and

recognised the desire to hide. 'I know Lance and Jacqueline used to quarrel. They hired me as a stand-in nanny one summer.'

Judith gave a quick smile. 'I'm glad I'm not giving anything away. Didn't it blow your mind that they could be at it for days?'

'Absolutely. And then the passionate reconciliations...'

Judith and Eve shared a grimace. 'So awkward!' They'd spoken at once.

Judith laughed now. 'Especially for an impressionable child like myself. But I thought Lance was fun. They both were. The thing that got to me was the competitiveness. Not just between them, but between Jenna and her brother too.'

It was the same old tale, but it was useful: the perfect chance to ask about Lance's dead daughter. 'I've chatted to Maynard and Naomi of course, but I hadn't seen Jenna since she was tiny. She liked to win then, just like her dad?'

'Poor Jenna, yes, she did. She and Maynard used to fight – I mean literally, fists and all – if there was a dispute about who'd done best at something. Lance used to set them puzzles and time them to see who'd finish first. I wished he'd stop. All hell would let loose.

'Don't quote me on this, but I did sometimes wonder if there was a bit of divide and rule going on. If ever Maynard or Jenna challenged him, he'd distract them with something like that, and they were so hot-headed that it worked a treat. Naomi was younger, of course. She didn't have the same "it's-not-enough-to-succeed-others-must-fail" approach.'

It backed up what Eve already knew. She nodded. 'Naomi must be reeling after the death of her sister and father in quick succession. And the news of Jenna falling must have been dreadful for you too of course – a massive shock.'

She waited to see if Judith contradicted her – if Jenna had been upset about anything, she might have wondered if she'd jumped.

'It was. The police talked to me afterwards. They wanted to know if she'd been depressed, but actually, I'd noticed a new energy about her. I was sure she was up to something, but when I asked, she just laughed and told me I'd see.'

That only made Eve more suspicious. 'I'm so sorry she never got to pursue it, whatever it was. Another promotion perhaps?'

Judith hesitated, and Eve decided she'd better justify herself. 'Sorry – it's weird. It's Lance I really want to know about – for the obituary – but having looked after Maynard, Jenna and Naomi as kids, I keep getting distracted. I felt very close to them at the time.'

Judith sighed at last. 'I can imagine. Truth to tell, I'm not sure Jenna's excitement related to her career.' Her brow creased. 'I saw her leave the office one lunchtime with an older man who looked faintly familiar. There was something about the way they went off together. They looked secretive. Jenna had the hood of her coat up, though it wasn't raining. After a couple of days, I managed to place him – Leonard Clarke, a friend of Lance's from back in the day. When I looked him up, I found he's Lance's chief rival in academia now; they worked at the same university. I couldn't help wondering what her business was with him. I had some idea she was planning to get her own back for all the snide comments Lance had made about her.'

24

Back at Elizabeth's Cottage, Eve and Robin cooked supper, then settled down to discuss the latest developments over pasta with chorizo, peppers and parmesan.

'Jenna sneaking off with Lance's arch-rival shortly before she died makes one wonder,' Robin said.

Eve nodded. 'If she was plotting something with this Leonard Clarke, then horrific though it would be, I could imagine Lance pushing her. From the way everyone talks about him, it's clear he couldn't cope with being challenged. But he's alibied by Naomi and her involvement's a lot harder to swallow.'

'You know she's keeping secrets. And you said yourself it sounded as though she was hiring someone to tidy up after her.'

Eve sighed and prepared another forkful of food. 'I know. But she seems principled compared with her dad and Maynard. She works for a charity trying to improve the lives of impoverished children. I could just about see her finishing Lance off if he put her work in jeopardy – her upset over the article he wrote is intense. But conspiring with Lance over Jenna's death's another matter.'

'All the same, fathers and daughters have been known to lie for each other. And perhaps you're a bit too close to Naomi.'

That might be true, but was she really the sort to cold-bloodedly plot the death of her own sister? Eve just couldn't accept it.

A fresh thought struck her. 'Of course, Lucy's made it her mission to protect Lance and she went down to Surrey the night Jenna died. I suppose it's not impossible she sneaked out and went all the way to Cornwall to kill Jenna to protect him. But she was actively encouraging me to root out secrets and ensure justice is done. It would be weird to do that if she's guilty.' It was a puzzle. 'Erica could have done it on Lance's behalf too, if she'd fallen in love with him, but I doubt it. It would demand a really warped sense of loyalty and she seems too level-headed. Erica said Lance had made "unreasonable requests", but that would hardly cover murder.

'I think Maynard still feels more likely for Lance and Jenna, though I don't see how Jenna meeting with Lance's rival might prompt him to kill her. It's not as though *he'd* do it for Lance's sake.' It made her case against him less convincing. 'Have the police pressed him on the blackmail yet?'

Robin nodded. 'Greg was vague about why he was asking him again. Said he was acting on an anonymous tip-off and didn't mention his phone call. Maynard denied it as strenuously as before, but Greg says he looked shocked and angry. I'm afraid he might still guess you're the source of the information. You need to take care.'

Eve nodded. 'What about Erica? Did Greg ask her again about her relationship with Lance?'

'She said the affair was a figment of Maynard's imagination.'

'I feel bad for not showing them the note she wrote now.'

Robin put his hand on hers. 'In reality, Greg's treating an affair between them as a definite possibility. And the note doesn't prove Lance returned Erica's feelings. He wouldn't be any more certain if he knew about it.'

Eve felt marginally less tense after the reassurance.

Robin sat back in his seat. 'So, what's the plan?'

'I'll email the work rival after supper and see if we can talk on Saturday when I go to London to meet my journalist friend. He's a natural interviewee for Lance's obituary, as they're in the same field. I want to know what he and Jenna were up to, though extracting the information could be tricky. But first things first, tomorrow, I'll tackle Terence Acland.'

Eve returned to Dr Acland's holiday rental the following morning. She took her car, so Robin had somewhere to sit. It was far too cold for him to hang around outside, whatever he said. She left him parked just out of sight of the cottage with an open call to her mobile. If she ran into trouble, he could be with her like a shot.

'I'm so sorry for your loss,' Eve said when Acland let her in. 'I gather you and Lance were old friends as well as doctor and patient.'

He sighed and led her down a pristine, narrow hallway to a pleasant holiday-cottage sitting room, complete with plenty of chintz. 'That's right. I still feel terrible about missing the digoxin overdose, but poor Lance ignored every bit of advice I gave him. I'd been worried his heart would give out for the last five years.'

That was probably true, even if Terence was guilty or knew he'd been killed by Erica.

'You got on well?'

He nodded. 'He could be infuriating of course. I knew he could improve his health if he tried. But his devil-may-care attitude went with a fun-loving personality.'

They talked about Acland's memories for a while, then Eve

decided to leap in and take him by surprise. 'I gather you know Erica Paxton well too. A friend said they saw you together in Blyworth.'

He twitched visibly and there was a long pause. 'We bumped into each other,' he said at last. 'We've met before because I often visit the Hales but it's no more than that. I offered to buy her a coffee because I knew she must be shaken up. She agreed, but then got upset and left before we started our drinks.' He spread out his hands in a gesture of help-lessness.

'So you never got to chat, to find out how she was doing?'

Acland looked her straight in the eye. 'That's right. I must try to get her to open up at some stage, or encourage her to share her feelings with someone else. She's not my patient, of course, but I'm concerned for the welfare of the entire household.'

It was satisfying to catch him out in a lie, but this wasn't getting her anywhere. She wondered whether to risk going further.

After a moment, she said, 'The friend who recognised you both thought you got into a car together, but I guess she was mistaken.' She let the sentence hang.

Acland sighed and looked at her with what felt like a studied bedside manner. 'Between ourselves, that's true. I wouldn't want this going any further, but in all honesty, I suspected she'd been having an affair with Lance. In fact, I'm damned sure she was.' But 'damned sure' wasn't the same as knowing. 'So you can see why I was so worried about her feelings.'

He *sounded* honest.

'When she rushed out of the café, I tried to talk to her again. It doesn't do people any good to bottle things up.'

'Ah, I see.' But Eve was sure that wasn't what they'd talked about. Erica had been nervous of Acland. She hadn't wanted to sit in his car or enter his house, but it looked as though he'd had the power to persuade her. The offer of listening therapy didn't fit.

'Lance was the sort of person to drag you along in his wake,' Acland said, 'but he had his vices, and not just food and drink. I don't think Sonia ever realised. Now, if you'll excuse me, I have an appointment.'

'Of course.' As Eve thanked him and left, she pondered what he'd said. He'd sounded intense as he'd talked about Erica's affair with Lance. She wondered if he'd fallen for her himself. If so, perhaps he'd hoped to reveal the truth to Sonia and get her to put a stop to it, leaving the way clear for him. He was way older than Erica, but then Lance had been too.

In that scenario, he could have killed Lance in a moment of desperation, to get Erica to himself. But that still didn't fit: whatever had happened, it looked as though Acland and Erica had been in it together.

25

Eve was back in her Mini Clubman with Robin, who was layered up with gloves, beanie and a thick grey scarf and jacket. The colour suited him.

He'd heard everything that went on thanks to the open call, and they discussed the basics.

A moment later, Eve reached into the glove compartment and pulled out her beanie and scarf too.

'You're getting well togged up for the drive home.'

She gave him a sidelong look. 'I hate to say it, but I was planning on hanging around a little longer. Out of sight, obviously.'

He grinned and rubbed his hands. 'I had a feeling that might be coming. You're wondering about the appointment he claims to have?'

She nodded. 'He might have made it up to get rid of me, but I'm curious. I imagine the only people he knows down here are linked to Lance. You don't mind waiting?'

'I'd have suggested it if you hadn't.'

'I'll tuck myself behind that bush near his house and keep watch.' With more time to plan, she wouldn't have to sneak into the neighbours' garden this time and she knew Robin would be okay sitting tight. He and Acland had barely crossed paths and he was so bundled up she doubted even his best friend would recognise him.

As Eve stood waiting in the spot she'd chosen, she felt her phone vibrate and snatched a quick look. Viv. A moment later the vibrating stopped, and a text appeared.

Urgent. Leaf or seashell stencil design for icing?!

Before Eve had managed to put her phone away a second message popped up.

Or lace, or something more whimsical?

The word whimsical rang alarm bells. She was about to send a one-word reply when she heard Acland's door open. She shoved her phone back in her pocket and hoped Viv would await further instructions. The wedding cake design wasn't *that* urgent.

So, Acland must be going out, not receiving visitors. That complicated matters. She'd have to see if she could follow him. It was possible she'd be able to hear what was said if he met someone in public.

She waited, but still Acland didn't appear at the end of his drive. Perhaps he was taking his car – heading outside the village. She craned round the bush and guessed she was right.

Acland was manhandling something around a metre long by half a metre wide, wrapped in a navy blanket. What on earth? He had his boot open and lowered the hidden object carefully inside. After that, he stood there a little longer – making sure the object was secure, perhaps – then closed the boot and slipped into the driver's seat.

She texted Robin, telling him to get ready to drive. They'd need to set off quickly, but she couldn't return to her car until

Acland was out of the way. Watching him head up the lane, past Robin and away from Saxford filled her with urgency. The moment he'd turned the corner she raced back to the car and was still closing the passenger door as Robin set off. She took a deep breath. It would be all right. He could only be heading for the main road that led towards the A12.

She told Robin what she'd seen. 'Whatever he's transporting, it's something he minds about.' Eve wondered if it was secret too, or if the blanket was simply to protect it.

It took her another five minutes to remember Viv's text, by which time she found her phone contained several more messages.

What about frogs dancing?

Where on earth had that come from?

Or dachshunds doing pirouettes?

A little bit more understandable.

Or a circus scene with you as a trapeze artist and Robin as a strong man? If too sexist, could reverse roles.

Hmm.
Are you goading me into replying? Eve texted back.
As if, came the reply.
Eve turned to Robin. 'How about seashell patterns on our wedding cake?'
Robin frowned. 'Unexpected topic switch. But yes, lovely.'
Eve texted back their choice. The sea meant a lot to her. She'd been brought up close to the ocean in Seattle, where her parents still lived. Nowadays there was nothing like walking

Gus along Saxford's beach, so bracing in winter and uplifting in the warmer months.

Robin drove carefully, taking care not to make them noticeable to Acland. As soon as the roads got busier, he made sure there was at least one car between them and Acland's BMW. At the A12, Acland turned towards the capital.

'I hope he's not going all the way home,' Eve said.

But in fact, he turned off at a pretty market town in Essex. They followed him cautiously through backstreets until he stopped on an olde-worlde shopping street full of half-timbered buildings. Robin overshot, as Eve watched what Acland did in the rear-view mirror.

'I couldn't see which store he went into, but we'll spot him if we walk back that way.'

Robin nodded as he pulled the keys from the ignition, got out and locked up.

'I'll keep my hat on and take a peek.' Eve was already walking up the pavement. 'If he's here to sell something I hope he'll be too busy to notice me.'

They walked past midweek shoppers pushing toddlers in buggies, and made their way to where Acland was parked.

The business he'd entered was called Fallowfield Antiques. *Interesting.* Robin pulled a chocolate bar for each of them from his jacket pocket and they stood chatting outside the next store along, as though they'd paused to take a break. Eve could just see past Robin into Fallowfield's, where Acland had placed his bundle on a large counter in front of a man in a dark suit.

Slowly – agonisingly so from Eve's point of view – Acland unfolded the navy blanket. Underneath was something red and gold. Painted wood, maybe? The man behind the counter looked delighted. He was nodding and smiling.

Acland, on the other hand, looked anxious. Eve saw the edge of his smile too, but he was shuffling from foot to foot and glancing over his shoulder.

A lot more nodding went on and Acland handed over some paperwork, then the dealer gave him something in return.

'I think he's about to come out again.' They'd finished their chocolate, so Eve led the way into the next-door business – an interiors store – where they pretended to look round as they watched Acland drive off. Their eyes met and as one, they muttered compliments about the merchandise then retreated.

'Heading next door?' Robin raised an eyebrow.

'I thought it might be an idea.'

Inside Fallowfield's, the proprietor had yet to take Acland's goods away, just as Eve had hoped. It was a very pretty cabinet, the background red, the foreground decorated with horses and cattle. Eve detested playacting, but in this case, it wasn't hard. If she'd had the money, she would have been delighted to take it home. For a moment, she cast her eyes over the antiques near the front of the store, just as Robin was doing, but then she 'caught sight of' the cabinet and tugged at his sleeve. 'Look!'

A second later she was rushing up to the counter, smiling at the proprietor. 'It's just come in? Goodness, it's beautiful.'

He nodded and smiled back. 'Tibetan. Nineteenth century. A wonderful find for us. So often people sell online these days. I'm delighted we haven't missed out.'

Eve sighed and looked down at the fine paintwork. 'I suppose it will be way out of my budget?'

'Ah.' The man's eyes were kind. 'Possibly. Out of most people's, I should think, though we'll advertise online ourselves and I know we'll find a buyer. We'll price it at nine thousand pounds.' Eve winced and he looked sympathetic. 'It's always worth enquiring. It could have gone for much less if it wasn't in such good condition, or lacked the right paperwork.'

'Do you mind if I take a photograph of it and one of your cards?' They were lying on the counter. 'I have a friend who might be interested.'

'Of course.' He stood back while she took the shot.

In the end, Eve left with some vintage playing cards. Viv always insisted she had a cast-iron will, but she had a weakness for old games.

Back in the car, Eve took her keys from Robin and returned to the driver's seat. 'Interesting.'

'Absolutely. What's your take?'

She started the ignition. 'It seems unlikely that he'd bring something he owns to a holiday cottage in Suffolk, only to drive halfway back to London to sell it.'

'Agreed. So he probably came by it in Suffolk, and as far as we're aware, the only people he knows there are the Hales.'

'Yes. It doesn't sound like he stole it from them, unless he managed to steal the paperwork that goes with it or had inside help.' Eve thought of Erica, only to dismiss the idea. 'Even then, it's unwieldy. It wouldn't be easy to smuggle it out of the Grange without someone seeing and although it's high value, it's not a fortune. I can't see someone who can afford a BMW taking that risk.'

'No. So that leaves someone giving it to him.'

It seemed most likely to Eve. 'But why? That's the question. There are plenty of good antiques stores near Saxford. He didn't have to drive all the way out here. The whole operation feels clandestine. What if one of the Hales was using the cabinet to pay Acland off, without telling the rest of the family? Lockley Grange is huge and half the rooms have been unused since Jacqueline died. It's likely no one would notice it disappearing.'

'If Acland's squeezing someone, he's playing a dangerous game.'

'You said it. Perhaps he's Maynard's blackmailer and he demanded something as a down payment. Or maybe he knows who killed Lance and is using that to extort money. Of course, that could be Maynard too.'

'If he's being blackmailed twice over, he'll be desperate by now.'

It was an unnerving thought. 'Or maybe Acland found evidence of the affair between Erica and Lance after all. In which case, Erica could be his target. If it went public, it might make it harder for her to get another role in academia. People would see her as a troublemaker.'

Whatever the truth, Acland could still be guilty of murder. With other secrets in the mix, discovering he was a blackmailer didn't prove anything.

26

Eve paused in Saxford to drop Robin off and walk a very overexcited Gus. She printed out a copy of her photo of the Tibetan cabinet too. She had plans for that.

After grabbing a bite to eat, she returned to Lockley Grange with Gus in tow. Naomi let them in and made a fuss of the dachshund, but her face was still pinched and worried. She never quite met Eve's eye.

In Lance's study, Gus pottered under the desk and sniffed at the edge of the rug as Eve got back to work, writing up notes from her interview with Acland and what she'd seen later. She'd been at it for half an hour when she got cramp in her wrist and decided to stop and walk around the room.

Everywhere was cluttered. It looked as though Lance was careless with anything not crucial to his work. His shelves were crammed with defunct invitations, postcards, paperweights, photographs, pens and pencils. He couldn't have appreciated any of them properly; it would have driven Eve up the walls, but she guessed Lance had been oblivious. He'd probably had no clue what was on the shelves – anything could be there.

The thought made her look more closely. And it was then

that she found it. She swallowed, her legs feeling wobbly. A very ordinary-looking pen, except when you examined its end, you could see it hid a webcam. Eve could understand the police missing it, everything was such a jumble, and unless you studied it closely, you'd never notice. For a moment, Eve wondered if someone was watching her now, but when she investigated, she found the pen contained an SD card. It must be gathering images for someone to view later.

What were they after? Perhaps it was to do with Lance's supposed affair with Erica and Sonia had put the camera there.

But if it had been her, then why hadn't she removed it after Lance was killed? The device was subtle, but she surely wouldn't risk the police finding it and asking questions; it would make her look guilty.

The same applied to the rest of the household, of course. The one person who'd find it harder to retrieve the hidden camera was Acland. She'd heard him asking to come round to check on Sonia, but Sonia had turned him down – got irritable in fact, at his pushiness. Perhaps he'd been hoping he could pick up the pen. It fitted. He'd been caught following Lance too.

At that moment, Eve's mobile rang. Sylvia.

'Hello, how's life?'

'*Interesting. Or possibly so, anyway.*' There was a pause. '*Are you up at the big house?*'

'Yes.'

'*Ah, well then, there's no need to comment on anything I say if it's awkward. I'll just give you the gist. I had coffee with Sonia this morning.*'

'Ah, thank you.'

'*It's a pleasure. I'm not sure if it's relevant but she got a text while we were together which clearly irritated her. She tutted, rolled her eyes and said, "How many more times?", before stuffing the phone back in her pocket. It rang a short while later and she excused herself, picked up and said: "Will you please stop?" I got up and left the room to give her some privacy. In reality, of course, I listened in.'*

'You're one in a million.'

'*I know.*' Sylvia laughed. '*Anyway, I'd say she's got an admirer and she's trying to keep them at bay.*'

Eve thought of the flowers which Sonia had stuffed into the bin. 'Because it'll look bad?'

'*I don't think so,*' Sylvia said. '*I think they're making a nuisance of themselves, and she's not interested. It sounded as though the would-be lover was trying every trick in the book to get her to change her mind. Needless to say, she dug her heels in.*'

Eve pondered the facts. 'Thanks, Sylvia.'

'*Any time.*'

After she'd rung off, Eve sat there feeling stupid. She bent to pat Gus and whispered to him under the table. 'I think I got it all wrong.' She'd been imagining Acland might be interested in Erica, and following Lance out of jealousy, though that had never quite made sense. But what if it was Sonia who Acland had fallen for? Perhaps it was he who'd sent her the flowers and badgered her on the phone. He could have followed Lance to try to catch him out in an affair and set up the webcam for the same reason. Perhaps he thought proof would finally get Sonia on his side, but she wasn't interested and probably never would be. What a creep.

A man who wouldn't take no for an answer might be capable of anything. If he hadn't managed to find evidence of an affair, maybe he'd decided that killing Lance was his next best option. Yet it was he who was blackmailing someone, if the beautiful cabinet was anything to go by. Eve wished she knew Maynard's secret. On Sunday, she'd follow him – see what he did next – but it felt like an awfully long wait.

She looked at where the pen had sat. If Acland had planted it, he wouldn't have got a recording of Lance slipping Erica's note behind his glove drawer. It would be out of shot. Even so, it looked as though he'd been obsessed with watching Lance, so it was interesting if he *hadn't* unearthed an affair with Erica. Eve remembered Acland's words. He'd said he was 'damned sure' they were sleeping together, not that he knew they were. It didn't sound as though he could prove it. It made Eve wonder if Lance had turned Erica down when she wrote to him. Maynard claimed the affair was real, but he could just be making mischief.

Thoughts were piling in and she tried to put them in order. Acland could have killed Lance out of jealousy if he was obsessed with Sonia. But it looked as though he was black-mailing someone too. Maynard, possibly.

And perhaps Erica and Lance *hadn't* been sleeping together, even if Erica had wished it. She could have decided to kill him after he'd rejected her and threatened to end her career. The latter motive felt more believable to Eve and had clearly been on the cards before last Friday. Eve remembered Lance's words at the party. 'I've already warned you – you knew this was coming.' Either way, it looked probable that Erica and Acland had had a shared interest in Lance's death.

Eve put the SD card into her laptop, handling it with a tissue. She hoped against hope that it would show her something useful, but there was nothing of interest. After she'd replaced it, she texted Greg Boles to explain what she'd found.

She was so distracted that she almost forgot her plan. She'd noticed that the household were in the habit of making tea, mid-afternoon, and it was almost that now. Time to make some waves and see what came of it. She printed out the photo she'd taken of the Tibetan cabinet, then left the study, telling Gus to wait, and went to the kitchen. There, she left the print-out next to the kettle.

After that, she hid in the room beyond. It was an old dining room, she guessed, and was linked to the kitchen by a hatchway. It made it the ideal place to wait as each member of the house-

hold came in for their tea. Eve peered through a chink in the
hatchway door, holding her breath.

Maynard was first to arrive. She watched as he picked the
photo up, frowned and peered at it closely. When Naomi
joined him, he asked her about it, his tone irritable.

'This anything to do with you?'

She peered at the paper too. 'No. How odd. It's very pretty.'

Maynard mimicked her. And to think he was in charge of a
constituency. If the voters could see him now.

Sonia came in next and said she had no idea what the photo
was doing there either. They all agreed they'd never seen the
cabinet before, as did Erica when she appeared. She seemed
keen to leave again as quickly as possible. She edged round
Maynard, as though she couldn't bear to be near him.

She'd gone by the time Lucy arrived. She looked at Eve's
photograph and her eyes opened wide.

'Well I never, I haven't seen that cabinet in a long time. I
assumed Lance had got rid of it. Are you thinking of selling it,
Sonia?'

'It's not up to her,' Maynard said. 'But I don't think it's here
anyway. I've never seen it.' If he'd given it to Acland, he'd want
to play down any notion that Lance hadn't sold it years ago.
'Perhaps it's got something to do with Eve Mallow,' he added.

'Why on earth would it have?' Naomi still sounded drained.

'Well, if none of you put the photograph here then who else
is there? We should go and ask her.'

Heck. Eve waited until they'd trooped off towards Lance's
study, then went to the loo, ready to reappear looking innocent.
Gus helped; he was distracting everyone except Maynard by
being adorable when she got back. Eve did her best to look casu-
ally confused when they asked about the photo, though battling
adrenaline made it a challenge.

Overall, her mission had failed. She'd hoped Maynard
would look shocked, not mystified, when he saw the picture. He

could have been acting, but why would he, unless he'd guessed she was watching? It was an unnerving thought. The upshot was, she was none the wiser about who had given the cabinet to Acland, and whoever it was would be even more careful than before.

27

Before Eve left the Grange for the day, she asked if she could speak to Sonia alone.

Sonia raised an eyebrow. 'That sounds ominous. But of course. Shall we talk in Lance's study?'

But Eve couldn't get the thought of the hidden camera out of her head. It might not be working but the whole room felt uncomfortable now. 'Do you mind if we have a change of scene?'

She looked at Eve curiously. 'Not at all. Come up to my room instead if you want privacy.'

It wasn't next door to Lucy's suite as Eve had expected, but down on the second floor. Yet Eve was sure Sonia and Molly had been talking about sorting through Lance's stuff when she'd heard them through Lucy's wall. Perhaps it was a storeroom or something.

But there was no evidence of a male presence inside Sonia's room. Even if she'd been clearing out, she didn't think Sonia could have removed all traces so quickly. She was starting to think Lance and Sonia had had separate rooms. It could mean that Lance had slept next door to Lucy, but try as Eve might, she still couldn't see them as lovers. She had the feeling that Lucy had given up on the idea of that sort of happiness a long time ago. There was something closed-off about her.

Once again, Eve thought of the way Lance had treated Sonia – like a favourite pet who was very good at putting on parties and making rooms look pretty but was beneath him intellectually. Why had she stayed? If Acland was to be believed, Lance could have died at any moment over the last five years. Perhaps she really had got one eye on his money. It didn't mean she'd killed him.

'Come and sit down.' Sonia motioned her to a sofa. 'So tell me, what is it?'

Eve took the seat she'd been offered. 'It was just something Dr Acland said when I interviewed him earlier. To be honest, I started to wonder if he was obsessed with you and given what's happened, I thought I should warn you about it. Though you might already be aware.' It was one way to get her to open up, and the warning seemed reasonable under the circumstances.

Sonia gave a hollow laugh. 'Thank you, but don't worry. I'm well aware. I suppose he told you Erica and Lance were having an affair too.'

Awkward.

Sonia sighed. 'You can take it from me that they weren't, though Maynard's got a bee in his bonnet about that too. He's been needling me about it. I could cheerfully throttle him.' She took a deep breath. 'Sorry. Not the thing to joke about right now.'

Eve wasn't sure she *was* joking, though she did sound genuinely convinced that Acland was wrong about Lance and Erica.

'Letting Terence down gently hasn't worked, so I'm telling it to him straight. I'm afraid he exaggerates our connection. We were left alone together once after a dinner party. I accepted his compliments graciously because I didn't know what else to do and I didn't want to hurt his feelings. Ever since then he's acted as though I'm promised to him.' She pressed her fists to her eyes. 'He sent me one of the bouquets you saw me bin just after Lance's death, complete with a disgustingly presumptuous note. It's really getting to me.'

Eve could well understand it. It sounded as though the situation had moved from annoying to unnerving. 'Have you told the police?'

Sonia looked at her lap. 'Not yet. I don't want any publicity. I'm worried he'll make it sound as though I led him on, and I can't have that.'

She must feel trapped. Eve guessed any hint of an affair might make Sonia look guilty, especially in the eyes of someone like DI Palmer.

Back at home, Eve prepared for another meet-up with the gang. Viv arrived in time to 'help', which meant the cashews were all but gone when Sylvia and Daphne arrived. Luckily, Eve had been prepared (as always) and brought out a spare bag.

'Where on earth were you hiding them?' Viv looked dumbstruck.

Eve just smiled, then turned to Sylvia. 'Thanks for talking to Sonia. I'm afraid you were right. It was Acland calling and he sounds obsessed with her.'

Daphne shuddered. 'How horrid.'

'You can say that again.'

'So where are we on suspects?' Viv was still going strong on the cashews.

'Maynard's still top for me. I can't forget how desperate he sounded for money or the way he suspected his dad of spreading his secret. Lance was far less discreet than Lucy from what I can see – inclined to get drunk and talk.'

'But Acland is up there with him. It seems pretty desperate

to spend so much time stalking Lance to prove to Sonia that he was having an affair. Sonia doesn't want to go to the police, but they need to know.' She and Robin had talked about it the moment she got home. 'In the end, I contacted Greg to tip him off. He's sworn he'll deal with it quietly – just keep an eye on what Acland is up to. I could see Acland killing Lance from jealousy. And it's just possible Erica helped him, probably to protect her career. But if so, then I don't get how Jenna's death ties in, assuming it was murder. Neither of them seems to have a motive.'

'What's Erica like?' Sylvia asked.

'I'd say quietly determined. She fought a lot of battles to get where she is.

'The others are further down the suspect list, but Naomi gets an honourable mention. She's keeping secrets – hiring someone to do something sensitive. I just don't know what yet.

'Switching to Jenna's death, I've got an appointment with Lance's arch-rival, Leonard Clarke, who met with her shortly before she went down to Cornwall. I wonder if they were plotting something that could have damaged Lance. He had an alibi, of course.' She glanced at Robin and held up a hand. 'And I know. It was provided by Naomi, so it's not as strong as it might be.' But her opinion hadn't changed. She couldn't see her conspiring to kill her big sister. 'I hope I'll find out more from Clarke.'

Sylvia patted her arm. 'Good luck.'

That night, Eve found it hard to sleep. Acland and what probably his hidden camera gave her the creeps and him and Erica meeting secretly made her worry. Eve thought of Erica sending Lance the love note, then realising she'd been barking up the wrong tree. Then later, Lance humiliating her in front of all his guests.

Then there was Sonia, who seemed vulnerable, Maynard, who was abhorrent, Lucy, who'd acted like Lance's watchdog and Naomi, who'd decided to destroy someone the day of the party. As she fell asleep confused thoughts mingled in her head.

She came to in the small hours in a cold sweat and realised Robin was awake by her side.

She could just see his eyes glint in the near darkness. 'I had the dream again.' The thudding feet, down in Haunted Lane. This was ridiculous. 'At least Gus isn't whining this time.'

Robin stopped stroking her arm.

'What?'

'I'm sorry, but he was whimpering, just before you came to. I think that's what woke me.'

The following morning, Eve was working a shift at Monty's when her mobile vibrated. *Robin*. She dashed into the kitchen to take it, Viv at her side, alert to her quick movement.

'*Greg's been on the phone,*' he said when she picked up. '*He went round for a chat with Acland on the back of what we told him.*'

Eve could tell from his tone that something was wrong. Her throat tightened. 'What happened?'

'*He found him collapsed on the floor. Dead. They'll need a post-mortem to find out more, but I'm betting it's not natural causes.*'

28

Eve was reeling from the news about Acland. She hadn't liked what she knew of the man but that didn't mean she'd wished him dead. Guiltily, thoughts of her wedding filled her head too. The case was getting more complicated, not less. She'd pushed herself into the Hales' inner circle because she'd felt she had to. She'd been full of determination to solve the case before her marriage. Now, she felt she'd been arrogant. And probably selfish too. Robin hadn't complained about her involvement after airing his misgivings, but he'd be much more relaxed if she left it to the police.

She needed to make sure this latest tragedy made a difference. Where did Acland's death lead her? Had he killed Lance and been killed in revenge? In which case Lucy might fit the bill. She'd seen a man and a woman close to the pool when Lance died, and she'd been in the Black Cat Café when Acland met Erica. Perhaps she'd been onto him, and she'd been devoted to Lance. Eve remembered the animal-like howl she'd given when she'd seen his body.

Eve couldn't think of anyone else who'd kill to avenge his death. He'd destroyed his closeness to Naomi when he'd written his damning article, and Sonia's marriage to Lance had lost its shine.

No, Lucy seemed most likely if that was the motive. But there were other possibilities, of course. If Acland and Erica had conspired to kill Lance, Erica could have killed Acland over what to do next. He and Erica could have fought over Acland's blackmailing – it was an extra risk.

Alternatively, Acland might have been innocent, but a threat to the killer, and finally, the killer could have needed him and Lance dead for different but related reasons. Eve looked at her watch. It would be hours before Greg contacted Robin with any news and the Hales would be tied up with the police. She'd better wait before she headed back to Lockley Grange.

In the end, Eve went to see Moira, the village storekeeper, to see if she'd heard anything. As a collector (and spreader) of news, she was second to none. Eve could tackle her over the bride-and-groom cake topper Viv had mentioned too. She held the conflicting conversational themes in her head and felt faintly hysterical.

'Ah, Eve dear!' Moira said brightly as the shop bell jangled and Eve hastily closed the door to keep out the cold. 'Another terrible tragedy I hear, and I suppose we must assume poor Dr Acland was killed as well. Have you been up to the Grange? I'm sure the Hales must be in a state of shock, so soon after dear Lance's death.'

Dear. Moira always behaved as though she knew the great and the good personally, even if she'd only met them to deliver food.

'I haven't been up today. I guessed they'd be busy with the police.'

Moira looked disappointed, but then brightened. 'But I'm sure you have an idea of who might be guilty. A second death must have narrowed down the suspects.'

Eve thought of her earlier musings. Lucy, Naomi or Sonia.

Or Maynard. Or Erica. *Hmm.* 'I'm not at all sure yet, but what have you heard, Moira? You're so well connected, and I know people confide in you.'

She hoped she wasn't laying it on too thick, but she needn't have worried; Moira was simpering.

'Well, Eve, I couldn't possibly claim that, of course, but it's very good of you to say so. I had Dr Acland in here only yesterday as a matter of fact, just before we closed. I must say he looked quite jolly then, poor man. When I commented on it, he said Lance's death had knocked him for six, but he'd just had a bit of good news, which had cheered him up a little. I was curious, but I didn't like to pry, of course.'

She wasn't even blushing. Eve stifled a giggle. 'Of course not. But it's only polite to make conversation.'

'Exactly, Eve!' Moira looked relieved. 'That's just what I thought. So I said how pleased I was to hear it and asked if it was business related. That gave him the option of a simple yes or no.'

Hmm.

'He agreed that it was, in a kind of a way, so I waited, because I didn't want to interrupt him if he was about to say more. After a moment, he said he thought the income from a scheme he was involved in had dried up, but it turned out there was more.'

The power of simply leaving an awkward gap in conversation. *Well done, Moira.* 'That's interesting. Thank you. At least he was upbeat at that point.'

She nodded. 'Just what I thought.'

'By the way, Moira, I wanted to thank you for the cake topper you gave Viv.'

Moira beamed. 'Well, something borrowed, you know. Paul and I had it on our cake!'

Her enthusiasm made Eve feel even more mean, but there were limits. 'I'd love to put it out on the day,' somewhere where it wouldn't be seen, perhaps, 'but I wasn't going to have a topper on the cake. Yours in particular is such a special piece, I think it would distract from Viv's icing. She might get more commissions if people focus on what she's done, not the decoration on top. I wouldn't want to ruin her moment.'

Eve apologised to Viv mentally for being patronising, but it would save hurt feelings.

Moira was smiling, so it was worth it. 'Well, Eve, if you think the topper will grab everyone's attention I quite understand. It was the best that money could buy, back in the day.'

As Eve walked home to find Gus and Robin, she wondered what Moira's interaction with Acland meant. When he'd mentioned an income-generating scheme that was doing better than hoped, had Acland been talking about his blackmail? Perhaps he'd doubted Maynard would come through with more money because of the delay. If he'd been proved wrong, it might be that Maynard had managed to get a loan sooner than anticipated and Eve had missed the chance to follow him. She really hoped not. Of course, Maynard could have been bluffing about getting the money. It might just have been an excuse to visit Acland and kill him.

29

Back at Elizabeth's Cottage, with Gus at her feet at the dining room table and a fire roaring in the grate, Eve rang Sonia to see if the police were still with them. She wanted to speak to Erica first, on her return to Lockley Grange. Her secret interactions with Acland made her top priority and there was a chance she could shock her into revealing more of what she knew.

'Eve!' Sonia sounded breathless as she picked up. 'I was about to ring you. Inspector Palmer's still working his way through interviews over here, but I'm done. Can we meet?'

'Of course.' Eve considered her options. 'Can I buy you tea and cake at Monty's?'

Half an hour later, Eve was sitting in the teashop. She'd already told Viv she'd solved the Moira cake-topper problem, and been hugged in response.

Sonia had arrived, and Eve was requesting Viv's winter warmer selection for her: cupcakes flavoured with sloe gin and spices, as well as a second variety with sticky ginger and cinnamon. A pot of assam completed the order.

Sonia looked harried, as though she hadn't slept, though the news of Acland's death hadn't broken until that morning. Perhaps guilt had kept her awake, but worry over who'd killed Lance was an alternative explanation.

Eve wondered how her interview with the police had gone, and if they'd asked about Acland pestering her. Greg had promised to treat the information sensitively, but the murder had probably thrown that out of the window.

'I'm sorry,' Eve said to her. 'You must be in a state of shock.'

Sonia nodded. 'It's horrific, and after what I said to you yesterday, I was worried you'd get the wrong idea. I'd had it up to here with Terence, but I'd never have done him any harm. I just wanted to keep my distance.'

'I would have too.'

Sonia nodded. 'Thanks. It was pointless me holding back about it to the police in the end. Someone must have cottoned on and reported it because Inspector Palmer asked about his pestering almost immediately.'

Eve felt guilty for not owning up, but she'd swear Sonia had no idea and keeping their relationship friendly was paramount if she wanted access to Lockley Grange.

They paused their conversation for a moment as Emily delivered their order.

When she'd retreated, Sonia carried on. 'The inspector seemed quite taken with the idea of me killing Terence to get him off my back, or possibly in revenge, if he'd killed Lance.' Sonia sighed. 'Or both, of course. I pointed out that there are umpteen people who treat me the same way Terence did.'

'That's appalling.'

She nodded. 'I can't decide which is worse, that, or the way people underestimate me. I discovered my agent was creaming money recently, as though I wouldn't notice. I enjoyed setting him straight, then sacking and reporting him.'

'I'll bet.' It was a satisfying thought, but the original slight made Eve furious.

'Once Inspector Palmer had given up saying I killed Terence out of fear or in revenge, he jumped on an alternative theory,' Sonia added. 'That Terence's fixation with me was invented and it was actually the other way about.'

Worse and worse.

'He suggested I'd killed Lance to be with Terence, only for Terence to reject me, whereupon I did the obvious thing and killed him too. What's one more murder, after all?' She gave a brittle laugh.

Eve was so indignant that she had to take a deep breath before she replied. 'He's clearly clutching at straws.'

Sonia gave a wry smile. 'I thought so too, but it doesn't mean he'll let them slip out of his grasp.'

'How do you think Dr Acland's death relates to Lance's? Assuming that it does, that is.' She didn't bother asking who she thought was guilty. That would involve naming one of her household and Eve was sure she'd never do that.

Her eyes met Eve's steadily. 'I don't know. There are various possibilities, of course.' She named the ones Eve had already thought of. 'What I can say is that Terence and Lance's friendship had been rocky recently. Once Terence decided he wanted me, it was as much as he could do to be polite to Lance. Lance noticed the change and I hoped he might switch doctors. But then suddenly, although Terence was still coming on to me, things changed. I came back to our London house one day to find them all-but slapping each other on the back. It struck me as a lot of false bonhomie, but they were both going along with it.'

Weird.

Viv appeared at Sonia's shoulder and asked if they'd like more tea, despite the large pot sitting there in front of them.

She'd be desperate to know what was being said, but Eve would love it if she developed a little more self-discipline.

'Thank you, but I'd better get back,' Sonia said, standing up. 'I'll call you as soon as we're clear of police, Eve.'

Viv looked nervous now, as well she might. She pulled an agonised face as Sonia left, the bell over the teashop door jangling. 'Did I ruin something?'

Eve raised an eyebrow. 'As luck would have it, no.'

Viv grinned. 'Phew, now, please don't be strict. Tell me what she said.'

Eve went to help Viv bake red velvet cupcakes, and filled her in.

'It sounds as though Acland and Lance were scheming over something,' Viv said.

Eve nodded. 'And whatever it was, it was more important to Lance than Acland's obsession with Sonia, which is saying something. What a horrible creep.'

'Do you think Lance would have paid Acland to kill Jenna?'

But that was a bridge too far in Eve's mind. 'It's hard enough to imagine Lance wanting his own daughter dead. The only definite motive we have for that is competitiveness between them. It looks as though Jenna was cooking something up with Lance's arch-rival, but even if that's true, killing her in a cold-blooded, carefully planned way seems far-fetched. And as for Acland, why would he risk his lucrative career and an already comfortable life to commit murder, even if Lance offered him a huge sum?'

'Hmm.' Viv began to whisk her cake mix. 'Perhaps you're right. But in that case what were they up to? It's pretty fishy that they're both dead now.'

She was right; it was.

30

Eve had just finished a lunch of parsnip soup and crusty bread when Sonia called to tell her the coast was clear at Lockley Grange. She was glad to know she wouldn't risk bumping into Palmer. She texted Erica next, asking to talk, and received a response, agreeing to a three o'clock appointment. Eve was glad to have it booked in, though she wished she could have seen Erica's face as she got the message. She wanted to know her state of mind. If Erica and Acland had had any involvement in Lance's death, she'd surely be terrified. Someone had come for the doctor, and she might be next. Eve would need to tell Greg what she discovered to protect her, whether she was guilty or not.

She drove over to Lockley Grange having primed Robin about her plans and coordinated times. She'd take Erica outside to talk and he'd be there too, hiding in the woods in case Eve ran into trouble. He was travelling separately to avoid being noticed.

When Eve found Erica at three and suggested a walk, she saw the alarm in her eyes. Eve could understand it. It was another bitterly cold, grey day and the light was fading. No one

would choose to hold a meeting outside unless there was something intensely private to say. It was unkind, but Eve was glad
Erica had picked up on her intent. Her nervousness should
make it harder for her to keep her feelings hidden.

Eve still couldn't fathom how Erica had been involved in
Lance's death, but she had hints and hunches. She would claim
to know more than she did and see how Erica reacted.

They paced across the hard, frosty lawn to the east of the
Grange in silence and the world was silent too. No birds sang
and the wind was still. As they reached a wooded area where
Scots pines shut out even more of the light, Eve turned to Erica.

'Let's carry on walking. It's too cold not to. But after Dr
Acland's death, I needed to talk to you in private.' She paused.
'I'm sorry, Erica, but I know you and Acland were at the pool
when Lance died.' She hoped she sounded convincing. It made
a lot of sense. Lucy had seen a couple and Eve had witnessed
the pair of them skulking around together. They'd both seemed
scared and panicky.

Erica opened her mouth, her eyes huge. 'How—' But then
she stopped herself. It was too late, though. If she wanted to
know how Eve knew, it meant Eve was right.

'Please, tell me what happened.'

Erica's mouth was working. At last, she spoke. 'It's too late.
There's nothing I can tell you.'

She'd know that Eve would report anything she said to the
police. She might guess that Eve was short on evidence too,
given she hadn't been to talk to them already. She was sharp, so
she'd see her best option was to keep quiet, but she wasn't
unmoved by what had happened. The emotion in her eyes was
almost overwhelming and tears were welling.

'Look, I'll tell you what I think happened. You don't have to
say anything.' Erica was an open book now. Eve was sure she'd
be able to tell if she struck gold. 'I think you worked your fingers
to the bone for Lance ever since he hired you, and that he saw

your dedication and took advantage. Got you to do tasks that weren't in your remit and treated you like a skivvy. I think he only got away with it for so long because he was kind and exciting to begin with and you fell for him.'

Erica shook her head vehemently, but Eve went on. 'He rejected you but what really mattered was his determination to ruin your career. You've given everything to get where you are. He accused you of betraying him – I don't know why – but whatever it was it made him so angry you panicked. It's no wonder you were desperate.'

Erica looked frightened now, but it didn't necessarily mean she'd killed Lance. She might just realise what a strong candidate she was.

'I think you and Acland talked and you found he hated Lance as much as you did, but with far less justification. He was jealous because Lance had Sonia. He told you the correct dose of digoxin to give Lance a heart attack and you slipped into the kitchen and put it in his coffee last Friday afternoon.'

'No!' Erica's hands were over her mouth, tears streaming.

'You and Acland went to the pool to make sure the overdose had done its stuff and were seen, though Lucy didn't recognise you.'

Erica was shaking her head. 'No, no, no.'

'What then? How was it?'

'I can't talk to you about it. If you report me to the police, they're bound to think I'm guilty. All I can tell you is that I'd never have done what you're suggesting. There are many good reasons why not, one in particular, but I...'

Eve waited.

'It doesn't matter. The chief reason is that I'd never ever kill anyone. And why would I risk going to check Lance was dead if I was responsible?'

But Eve could see the temptation from the killer's point of view. Their strength of feeling might drive them to it, and people who killed weren't necessarily rational. All the same, in her heart of hearts, she believed Erica. 'So what really happened then?' Eve had another scenario in mind that was just as believable. 'You went to the pool to try to reason with Lance? You wanted to convince him not to ruin your career?'

The passion shone from Erica's eyes. She gave a very slight nod of her head, but for the purposes of going to the police, there was no firm evidence Eve could give. Erica was thinking this through.

'It was unlucky timing,' Eve went on. 'Lance had his digoxin-induced heart attack while you were there. And Acland was there too. He was convinced you and Lance were having an affair; he probably followed you to get proof he could show Sonia.'

The look Erica gave in response was expressive enough.

'You didn't raise the alarm because Acland said there was nothing to be done and although you didn't know the death was murder, you didn't want anyone accusing you of bringing on the heart attack by arguing with Lance.'

Erica was crying again, huge great sobs. Eve was sure she'd got it right now.

'Acland wouldn't want to explain he'd been there either, of course. Admitting he'd been spying on a patient would hardly be ideal, but he could have been guilty of a lot more than that. He had a motive for Lance's murder.'

Once again, Erica shook her head strongly.

'You might have watched as he went through the motions of trying to revive Lance, but he was a doctor. He'd know how to make that look convincing.'

At last, Erica spoke. '*If* I'd been there, as you say, I'd never have left without raising the alarm unless I was completely confident Acland had done all he could to save him.'

That was interesting. Acland had been obsessed with Sonia. Even if he hadn't administered the digoxin, Lance's death would have taken him one step closer to his goal. Sonia didn't want him, of course, but it seemed he hadn't accepted that.

Perhaps whatever he and Lance had been cooking up together had been so appealing that he'd wanted Lance to live after all. Or maybe Erica was wrong, and Acland had simply put on a good act.

Eve thanked Erica for talking to her and apologised for the upset she'd caused. She had no proof but she was pretty much certain she was innocent, and that life had been tough for her, over and over again. She wished she hadn't had to grill her like that, but time felt doubly pressing with the latest death. And what if Acland wasn't the last? That thought, and the wedding countdown, were making her stomach churn. She needed answers.

They made their way silently back towards the house, Erica wiping her eyes and Eve feeling guilty. After they'd parted, Eve texted Robin to thank him for standing guard. She hoped he wasn't frozen solid. Then she pondered possibilities. Could Lance have told Acland Maynard's secret and agreed to share any proceeds from the resulting blackmail? Perhaps Lance wasn't as well off as he seemed. The Grange was falling apart, after all. If that was the arrangement, Acland had two reasons to want Lance dead: Sonia, and the prospect of a sole share of the profits. But it made no sense. Maynard didn't have the money to pay, and Robin had said Lance's fortune was sizeable.

What was it Eve wasn't getting? Surely something had to become clear soon.

31

It was completely dark now, but the sky had cleared. Looking out of Lance's study window, the shadows under the trees were blacker than ever. From somewhere nearby, Eve heard a mobile ring, but couldn't catch any of the conversation. It seemed to provoke a reaction though. Movement. Hurried footsteps going past the study door. It sounded as though the call had been a summons.

Eve waited a moment, then rose and opened the door stealthily. She was just in time to see Naomi disappearing round a corner, entering one of the corridors that went towards the back of the house.

Gus got up. She almost made him stay, but the excitement in his eye made her relent. Besides, his presence would make her look innocent. No one expected a spy to have a dachshund with them. She put her finger to her lips to let him know absolute silence was required, then turned towards the door again and exited the study.

By the time she reached the back corridor, Naomi had disappeared. Eve walked on cautiously. She could be in any of the rooms off the passage, or have left the house via the door at the end if the person who'd rung was outside. Eve decided that was more likely. A call implied something complicated to organise. You'd think anyone at the house would just message or drop by.

Sure enough, when Eve peered through the window at the end, next to the door which led outside, she could see Naomi hugging herself against the cold. She was talking to a man of around her age with floppy dark brown hair. He was carrying a crate, but Eve couldn't see what was in it. She badly wanted to hear their discussion and if she waited, she'd lose out. Without giving herself time to debate it, she eased open the window, praying it wouldn't creak.

'It's the last time I want to resort to burglary,' the young man said.

'I know, I know.' Naomi's voice was shaking, either from the cold or emotion. 'I'm sorry. Truly.'

'I think a neighbour saw me.'

'Hell.'

'Naomi, if the police get involved, I'll tell them the truth. I've got too much at stake not to.'

She hung her head. 'I know you have.'

He nodded.

Eve sensed they were good friends, but what she'd asked of him had strained that to the limit.

He handed her the crate.

'Thank you. Safe journey.' She sounded tired and sad, and it was clear she was about to come back inside.

Eve closed the window as Naomi watched her visitor retreat. She wished she knew what the man had given her. It was a risk, but she nipped back up the corridor and let herself and Gus into one of the large, bare rooms, which would allow her to peek as Naomi came back along the corridor. She'd be sunk if Naomi happened to choose the same hiding place to look at her delivery. Still, the odds were good. There were plenty of abandoned rooms to choose from.

Eve held her breath as she heard Naomi re-enter the corridor, then stood behind the open door to the room she occupied, peering through the narrow vertical gap between the door and its jamb.

As Naomi approached, she could just see the top of the crate. The contents looked like paperwork: notebooks and files perhaps? Whose were they, and what did she want with them? That was the question. Whatever the source, they were stolen.

Eve was lying low, determined to wait a good few minutes before risking the return journey to the study, when she heard Maynard's voice.

'What's all this, then?'

Naomi gasped and Maynard laughed. Eve visualised him waiting at the end of the corridor, blocking her route.

Naomi swore. 'Grow up, Mosh! You nearly gave me a heart attack.'

'Just like dear old Dad,' Maynard said. Then added, 'Oh come on. Let's not pretend we'll miss him. Whoever bumped him off did us all a favour. What I'm interested in is who's been to visit and what you've got there.'

'Go away!'

It was no good. Eve would have to reveal herself. She wasn't sure Maynard was guilty, but she feared for Naomi. Her heart was going like the clappers. She moved into the corridor, motioning for Gus to stay, and approached the pair at speed.

'Oh look, it's the spy,' Maynard said nastily. At least his attention was off Naomi, and Sonia appeared at that moment too.

She looked at them each in turn. 'I came to see what all the fuss was about.'

'Naomi's had a mysterious delivery,' Maynard said. 'I dread

to think what she's keeping from us, and Eve's been eavesdropping, true to her name.'

Eve was glad the corridor was shadowy. She hoped it would disguise her flush. 'That sounds a good deal more exciting than the truth,' she said, not bothering to keep the edge from her voice.

'That being?' Maynard sounded highly sceptical.

'I was looking for Gus. I'm afraid I left the study door ajar and he went walkabout. Sorry, Sonia.' She turned to the woman. 'It was kind of you to invite me to bring him. I should have thought he might cause chaos.' She apologised mentally to her dachshund for taking his name in vain. 'He gets very excited when there are new places to explore.'

'And did you find him?' Maynard's voice dripped with disdain.

'Yes, I did. Gus!' Eve called down the corridor and the stoical hound appeared on cue, scampering up to meet them, tail wagging.

Sonia bent to fuss him, and Eve enjoyed Maynard's obvious irritation.

Naomi had taken advantage of the distraction to disappear, taking the crate with her. Eve would have done the same in her shoes. She wondered what she was hiding. Just because Maynard made her skin crawl, didn't mean she should ignore what his sister was up to.

'Can I just say, Maynard,' Sonia was saying, 'that I take a dim view of you insulting someone who's here at my invitation. I'm sorry, Eve. Maynard, I need to talk to you about some legal stuff, if you please.'

Back in Lance's study, Eve bent to stroke Gus. 'You're a dog in a million. You do realise that, don't you?'

But her gratitude to him was mixed with anger towards

Maynard. He was a piece of work. She thought of the books he'd given to Jenna and Naomi with their nasty, belittling inscriptions, then sat down at the desk and put 'Mosh' into Google. If Naomi still used the nickname, perhaps Maynard did too, as a handle on social media, for instance. He'd have formal accounts for his work, of course, but there might be something personal out there. It would be interesting to lift the lid on any unguarded posts.

She found nothing on any of the larger social media sites. Where Maynard had a presence, it was all tied into his identity as a member of parliament. But she did get one result, on a creative writing site. It was called *Tales of the Unexpected*, presumably after the Roald Dahl stories. She could see from the content that the genre was similar: dark tales with elements of crime and horror.

Frustratingly, though, Mosh – or Maynard if it was he – had removed all their content years ago.

Removed by the author Dec 2006.

He'd been sixteen back then. Too early for him to have taken it down in case the newspapers dredged it up after he'd entered parliament. Perhaps he'd just found it embarrassing by that age. Eve wondered how old he'd been when he'd uploaded the stories, assuming it was him at all, but that information wasn't given.

It probably wasn't relevant, but Eve thought back to him ripping the head off Jenna's velvet rabbit. She could imagine the sort of cruel stories he might come up with.

Whatever he'd done or not done to Lance, he was a deeply unpleasant man.

32

The gang met that night in the Cross Keys, huddled in the cosy snug.

Toby had brought them their food and Eve had wild venison steak in a port sauce. It tasted like heaven and was warming her through nicely. She sipped her Pinot Noir and turned to Robin.

'So, what does Greg say?'

Robin referred to his notebook. 'It's looking like the method for Acland matches the one for Lance Hale. Digoxin. They've rushed through tests on a mug which had traces of sediment in it and the toxicology reports on Acland's body will probably confirm it.'

'So the police don't think Acland killed Lance?' Viv said.

'Probably not.'

'To be fair, the idea of him following Erica to try to prove she and Lance were having an affair fits just as well as him going there to check the poison had worked.' Eve relayed the two scenarios she'd put to Erica to those in the gang who hadn't yet heard about it. 'I think he believed evidence of the affair would bring Sonia to his side, though he was deluded. She wasn't interested.

'I can see why Acland and Erica kept quiet about their presence, and why they were on edge with each other. If they both assumed it was natural causes, it must have been a heck of a shock to learn he'd been poisoned.'

'I should say so,' Daphne said.

'So why was Acland killed, do we think?' Sylvia attacked the game pie in front of her. 'It's interesting that he was on the spot when Lance died, but if the poisoning took place earlier, inside the house, it's not as though he's likely to have witnessed anything.'

The same thoughts had been occupying Eve's mind, but there was more than one possible answer. 'Acland appeared to be blackmailing someone, don't forget. Maynard, most probably, so it could be he who killed him. If it *was* Maynard, we might get circumstantial evidence to support it on Sunday night. He was meant to be visiting that loan shark to get the money he needs, but if the funds were for Acland, perhaps he'll cancel.' She sipped her wine.

'You and Robin are going to wait in the van near Lockley Grange and follow him if he leaves the house?' Viv had her notebook out again and was writing sideways in a margin. Eve could hardly bear it.

'That's right. Of course, he might still want cash to tide him over, but I hope we'll be able to see what he does with any money he picks up. If he brings it back home, it'll suggest his blackmailer is no more.'

Viv nodded. 'Makes sense.'

'Who else is high up your suspect list, Eve, in the light of Dr Acland's death?' Daphne cut up a beautifully golden roast potato.

Eve swallowed more of the delicious venison. 'I think we have to consider Lucy Garton. She could have done a copycat killing to confuse the police. She'd worked for Lance for years and I could hear the pain in her voice when his body was found.' Such anguish. 'She might have killed Acland in revenge, if she thought he was guilty, whether he was or not. And he still could have been. Erica seems convinced his attempts to resuscitate Lance were genuine, but she's not a medic, and Acland was fixated on Sonia. I can't get it out of my head.' Eve turned to Sylvia. 'As for Sonia herself, I imagine she's relieved Acland's gone and I don't think her and Lance's marriage was in good shape, but that doesn't mean she'd kill the pair of them. She didn't feel she could report Acland, though. She was worried he'd imply she'd encouraged him, which probably says a lot about the sort of man he was.'

Sylvia was frowning. 'I'm surprised she didn't go ahead anyway. She's tough as nails, as I'm sure you've seen by now. And if, as you say, her marriage was in its death throes, then why worry over Lance being jealous? I can see it might affect her divorce settlement, but it sounds as though she's well off anyway. I doubt she'd care.'

It was true, and not speaking up in case it made Sonia look guilty didn't make sense either. Acland's pestering had clearly been going on since well before the murders. She could have reported him to the Medical Council weeks ago. Eve would never judge her for not doing so, but it did feel out of character. 'I think her not leaving Lance is odd too,' Eve said. 'None of it adds up to a convincing motive for either victim, but I'd feel happier if I could explain it.'

'So Maynard's still top of our list,' Robin said, 'followed by Lucy, for Acland?'

Eve nodded. 'I think so. Gut instinct says Erica is innocent. She looked so upset when I talked to her, but I didn't get any hint of guilt. And going to the pool to reason with Lance fits.

'But again, there are still questions to answer: what tasks did

Lance give her that were unreasonable? She won't say and I'm not sure how to find out.'

'And Naomi?' Viv asked.

Eve told them about her secret visitor that evening. 'She's got an accomplice breaking the law on her behalf. It's not impossible he broke into the Hales' London home to steal papers of Lance's. Or he could have stolen something from Acland's place. If I knew the answer, it might change everything, but as things stand, she doesn't strike me as a likely killer.'

'She's too nice?' Robin said.

Eve gave him a look. 'I know. Nice people can do terrible things.'

33

Eve and the gang covered next steps before they left the pub. Eve's trip to London was the following day. She wanted to find out what had made her media contact, Monica Sutton, decide to write complimentary articles about Maynard and Erica. After that, she planned to confirm that it was the film director, Felix Masters, whom Lance and Lucy had excluded from Lance's party. She needed to know why it had been so important to keep him and Sonia apart. And lastly, she'd talk to Lance's arch-rival, Leonard Clarke, with the aim of finding out why he'd been meeting Jenna in secret, just before she died. Lance couldn't have pushed his daughter unless Naomi had lied, but in the back of her mind, thoughts of Lucy still floated. Would she have killed for him? Without even asking him perhaps, if she thought Jenna was set to ruin his life?

By eleven o'clock the following morning, Eve was sitting in Monica Sutton's office in a tall glass building, overlooking a canal far below. She'd spent the train journey to London digesting the news headlines.

LATEST DEATH IN HALE SHOCKER

HALE FAMILY DOCTOR LATEST VICTIM – WHAT MADE HIM A
TARGET?
DEATH IN RURAL SUFFOLK – WHEN WILL VILLAGERS FIND
PEACE AGAIN?

What would Eve's family be thinking as they prepared to attend her wedding? Her twins had been in regular contact to check she was okay, ditto her parents. Meanwhile, cousin Peter, who was testing Eve's patience to the limit, had sent a text that morning with two queries from his mother: was it really safe to visit Saxford, and would there be any sweet white wine on offer at the wedding reception or should she bring her own? It had to be said, you could see where Peter got it from.

'Long time no see!' Monica smiled, her wavy dark hair falling forward, and Eve felt guilty for looking her up with ulterior motives. 'How's life in the countryside?'

'More eventful than you might imagine. You heard about Lance Hale's murder?'

The instant she said it, Monica's expression changed a fraction. 'Yes, we covered it of course. And now his doctor's dead, I hear. Interesting. You know something about it?'

Eve realised Monica was planning to grill her, just as she'd been intending to tap Monica for information. 'I was there when his body was found, when everyone thought it was natural causes. Or at least, almost everyone.'

'Can I quote anything you tell me?'

Eve grimaced. 'Probably better not. I'm still in and out of the Hales' Suffolk house at the moment, writing Lance's obituary. I don't think they'd like me speaking to the press about the murder.'

'I hear you. Off the record then.'

'I was actually hoping you'd tell me something, because you've written about members of the household recently.'

'Hmm. And will you help me later, when the crime is solved?'

'I'll try my very best to.'

Monica nodded at last. 'All right then. What do you want to know?'

'I wondered why you were writing so many positive things about Maynard Hale. The coverage doesn't quite fit the paper's politics.'

'Eve, Eve!' She leaned forward. 'We represent all views, remember? Renowned for it.' She gave a wicked smile.

'I also wondered why two of your articles mention both Maynard and Erica Paxton. I know they're each linked to Lance, but Maynard's an MP and Erica's an academic. The mix felt a little forced.'

Monica sat back and gave a light sigh. 'And there was I, thinking I'd managed it beautifully! I happened to be interviewing Maynard about his work and he started to talk about Erica. He said he thought our readers would be interested in her and explained the importance of her research, so I let her share the limelight in those two articles.'

All well and good, but they still seemed overtly flattering. Eve didn't want to offend Monica, but she knew it would be water off a duck's back, so long as she kept her tone light. 'They almost seem like puff pieces, and I know you're not the sort to take backhanders.'

'Not unless I've run out of doughnuts.' Monica grinned. 'You know how it goes, Eve. Sometimes you have to give a little to gain a lot.'

'Maynard was feeding you information on someone else? Lance?'

'Getting cooler. Look, I can't say any more. You know how it is. You'll find out soon enough.'

Eve sighed inwardly, but she'd expected Monica to be tight-lipped. This was just the opening salvo. She'd keep nudging her,

trying to prick her conscience, and maybe she'd crack. Just a
hint might be enough to trigger a breakthrough. 'Okay, I get that
there was some kind of trade-off going on between you and
Maynard, but where does Erica fit in? Why was he bigging
her up?'

Monica stared out at the cold winter sky. 'I wondered the
same thing. All I can tell you is that I saw them together several
times a couple of months ago. They looked thick as thieves,
heads down. Once, they were holed up in some bar, and it
looked as though Maynard was telling Erica a lot more than he
ever told me. Does that help?'

'I'm not sure. What about Jenna? Did you know her?'

Monica nodded. 'Well enough. I admired her as a professional – mostly. She was passionate and she'd do anything to get
at an important story, and I mean anything. Sometimes I felt she
was out of control: hooked on the buzz, even if it meant she
went too far. I'd love to know what she was doing the night she
died. She wasn't one for soulful solo walks.'

As Eve left Monica Sutton's office she wondered if Erica could
have been having an affair with Maynard, instead of Lance. It
would fit with Maynard using his power to get Erica some good
publicity and it might explain Lance's accusations of betrayal.
Eve imagined he'd have hated Erica palling up with his son.
Even if he didn't want her himself, her moving on to Maynard
would have been a blow. Lance had regarded Erica and his children as rivals; them joining forces would have been the last
thing he'd want. It was hard to imagine Maynard being Erica's
type, but maybe he'd kept his true character hidden.

Eve also wondered what Monica hoped to get out of
Maynard. She'd made it clear Eve was on the wrong track when
she'd suggested it was information on Lance. She might have
sniffed out Maynard's old secret, of course, but Eve doubted it.

She couldn't see Lance or Lucy letting that information slip to a journalist.

Eve switched her focus to Lance's film-director friend, whom she was due to have lunch with. She walked across town to the restaurant Felix Masters had suggested and found him waiting for her at their table.

He stood as she approached and took her hand, shaking it and smiling at her warmly. 'I'm glad you looked me up. It's so odd to know I'll never see Lance again – it was only chance that kept me away from his party. I'd have managed it if the event had been in London, but his plans changed, so I was stuck.'

Eve bet it was he who'd caused Lance to change the venue at the last minute. *Good.* Now she needed to work out why. She sat down as Felix did and glanced at the menu. She normally treated her interviewees and winced at the prices.

'My shout!' Felix laughed.

She couldn't believe she'd given herself away and felt a blush rush up her neck. 'Let's go Dutch, if you're sure.'

At last, he sighed and gave in. 'All right. Something tells me you won't be happy unless I agree.'

She found herself liking him. She'd have felt far more awkward if he'd insisted.

After they'd ordered and the waiter had retreated, Eve turned to Felix. 'So, how did you and Lance meet?'

He smiled. 'We were at university together, he, Jacqueline, Lucy and I. Never in a million years did I imagine what the future held for each of us. Everyone's had to deal with tragedy except me. It left me looking over my shoulder for a while, feeling I must be due my share of bad luck.'

'Did you talk about Jacqueline's death much with Lance?'

Felix shook his head. 'He wasn't one for opening up, and soon after she died he got his posting abroad, which made communicating harder. I got Lucy to confide in the end, but it took a long time.'

Eve felt lucky that Lucy had been so forthcoming with her. It was down to Lance's death perhaps, bringing back old memories with fresh trauma. 'We talked earlier in the week. You know her well?'

'Probably best out of the three of them. We dated for a while at university. Parted on good terms. She can't get over the way she fell for Bruno. I think it put her off relationships for good. She was devoted to Lance, of course, but like a very protective nanny.'

'And Lance?'

'I think her support allowed him to pick up the pieces and move on. She looked after him in a way that Jacqueline never had. Nor should she have. She had her own life to lead, whereas Lucy abandoned hers after what Bruno did. I still worry about her. I'm not sure what she'll do now. Lance became her reason to keep going.'

It was interesting, but Eve needed to move him on to Sonia if she was going to find out why Lance and Lucy had kept them apart.

'Did you socialise much with Lance and his second wife?'

'Whenever I could. He'd ditched diplomacy for academia by that stage, so we were both mostly in the same country, which helped. I like Sonia and she's talented. She tells a story in every advert she does. People are pulled into her world. Even on the catwalk she has a presence that makes her stand out. That's why I offered her a part.'

'Excuse me?'

'She didn't mention it?' There was something uncomfortable in Felix's look.

'No.'

'Perhaps I shouldn't have either, but it illustrates Lance's character, I'm afraid, and Lucy's loyalty to him.'

Eve frowned. What was coming?

'I sent a message for Sonia via Lucy, asking if she'd be interested in discussing the part. Lucy got back to me to say it was no go. Sonia thought it would mean too much time away from Lance – or so Lucy said.'

Oh no. 'Don't tell me. When you spoke to Sonia later, the message had never got through?'

He nodded. Solemn. 'When she realised what had happened, it was far too late to take the part, unfortunately. Sonia laid the blame firmly at Lance's door. She said she knew exactly what would have happened. Lucy would have taken the offer to him, and he'd have decided he didn't want to spare her. Or worse, that he didn't think she'd be equal to the shift in career.' He shook his head. 'I was dumbfounded, honestly. Or at least, I was initially, but not by the end of our conversation. She was so upset that a lot of other things came out about their relationship. It seems Lance had multiple affairs and undermined her at every step.' He shook his head. 'Sonia told me his older kids hadn't wanted her and Lance to marry. At the time, when he stood up to them, she'd thought of him as heroic. Later, she realised Lance regarded her as stupid too, but in his view, it was a benefit. She'd never be a threat to him.'

Eve closed her eyes for a moment. It was too appalling.

'I know.' Felix grimaced as she met his gaze again. 'I'm sorry, because one shouldn't speak ill of the dead, and Lance could be fun, but the stories Sonia told me were horrific. We were still friendly on the surface, but I never thought of him in the same way again.

'Apparently, he flew out to join her once, when she was taking part in a private fashion show in Milan. When she'd finished her set, she found him talking to a group of senior Italian politicians and she was the topic. He was repeating a series of gaffes she'd supposedly made, and they were all hooting with laughter. When she challenged him, he admitted he'd made them up for comedic effect. He didn't seem to understand why she was upset. He was drunk, of course.'

Eve's breath caught at the thought of it. What a monumentally dense and cruel man.

Felix nodded, as though she'd spoken the words aloud. 'Lance was entertaining and charismatic, but as I eventually discovered, entirely self-centred. It's why I worried about Lucy's complete loyalty to him. It wasn't healthy.'

Eve continued to worry about it too, but Sonia was also coming to the fore. What had happened in Milan would have filled Eve with a desire to pay Lance back, and it didn't sound like a one-off. As for the film part, it had been a huge missed opportunity. Yet rather than rush home and have it out with him and Lucy, she must have kept quiet. There would be no point in Lucy and Lance relocating the party if they knew she'd found out.

So why had Sonia bottled it up? And why had she stayed married to Lance after being snubbed, over and over again? Eve couldn't think of any reason but that she was planning her revenge.

34

Eve thanked Felix Masters for making time for her, then crossed town to meet Leonard Clarke at the university where he and Lance had worked. It was time to find out what he and Jenna had been up to before Jenna died. A softly, softly approach was called for. He was a natural interviewee for Lance's obituary; he shouldn't be on his guard. When she announced herself at reception, a man in jeans and a polo shirt overheard and laughed.

'Len'll be an interesting person to grill for Lance's obituary.'

Eve turned to him and smiled. If he had gossip, she wanted to hear it. 'I know they were rivals to an extent. If there's more to it, then I'd appreciate a heads up.'

He leaned on the front desk as the receptionist looked on disapprovingly. She was probably a lot more discreet than the academics. Eve avoided her eye and waited.

The man was still grinning. 'They were *not* friends. I used to dread being in a meeting with them. Academia's a competitive environment, of course, but this was something else and I always wondered what was behind it. All I can say is, Len wasn't happy when he discovered Lance was coming to work here. I caught him looking for other professorships just after the news broke, though he stayed in the end.'

Eve was even more curious to meet Leonard. When she finally walked into his office, she found he was a tall, slender man with fair hair and blue eyes. He greeted her with a warm handshake and offered her coffee, making it for her himself from a machine in a side room. His office was untidy, crammed with books, papers and keepsakes.

He motioned her to a seat, put her coffee down in front of her, then sat on the opposite side of the desk. 'So, what can I tell you?'

'I'm keen to hear from someone who worked with Lance, and I gather you knew each other a long while.' Jenna's friend Judith had said as much; their connection must date back to well before Lance joined the university. 'Don't worry. All viewpoints count, good and bad.' She waited.

'You think my opinion will be bad?'

She told him what the man in reception had said and Leonard looked annoyed. 'I can imagine who that will have been. I'll be having words later. As he said, there are always rivalries between academics, but our connection is an old one. We were at Cambridge together.' Another one. 'If we were tetchy, it was just work.'

But Eve wondered. He was running a nail up and down the grain of the wood on his desk, over and over, and it was leaving a mark. It wasn't the first one, and she guessed it was a stress habit. 'So you were happy when he retired from the civil service and got a job here?'

'Of course.' Clarke's smile didn't reach his eyes. 'I thought it would be just like old times.'

Either he or the man in reception were lying, and Eve was betting on Clarke. 'Were you at Lance's party in Suffolk?'

He winced. 'No. But I didn't expect him to invite me. It wasn't a slight.'

That was interesting. Not being there put him in the clear, yet he seemed worried to admit it. He must want to hide their poor relationship for other reasons. Eve just couldn't fathom them yet.

'You must have known Jacqueline as well as Lance if you were at university together. She was a contemporary too, wasn't she?'

He shifted in his seat. 'Yes.'

'Perhaps you could tell me about your friendship group and how Lance and Jacqueline fell in love.'

His shoulders were still tense, and he sat forward in his seat. 'It's funny to think back. We were all very close, the three of us as well as Lucy Garton and Felix Masters, the film director. We came from different backgrounds, but somehow we gelled. Lance never had to work to earn extra money, of course, whereas Lucy and I slaved away as delivery drivers and Jacqueline and Felix flipped burgers.'

Felix had gone out with Lucy back then, for a while anyway, and Jacqueline had been with Lance. Clarke must have been the fifth wheel. He hadn't mentioned anyone else in their gang. 'Just you five?'

Clarke nodded, looking down for a moment. He told her about Lance's wild parties, the way Jacqueline had tried to curb his worst excesses, and the skits Felix used to direct as part of the Footlights comedy troupe.

'And did you keep in touch with them later on, when Lance was working for the Foreign and Commonwealth Office?'

He nodded. 'On and off, you know. Of course they were both busy.'

Like ships that passed in the night, Eve imagined. 'It must have been a terrible shock when you heard Jacqueline had been killed.'

He put a hand over his eyes. 'Appalling.'

A tiny suspicion crossed Eve's mind. 'A friend of mine mentioned she saw you with Jenna not long before she died.'

He was looking down at his hands. 'Ah yes, we bumped into each other.'

'Just outside the entrance to her place of work.' *Very convenient.*

Clarke met her gaze now. 'What is all this? What do you know? Has Maynard said something?'

'Maynard?' She shouldn't have shown her confusion – it was bad tactics – but he'd taken her by surprise.

'Nothing. Forgive me. I thought for a moment...'

Eve remained silent, hoping he'd stumble on and say something he shouldn't. He didn't but he did offer her another cup of coffee and that was almost as good.

He disappeared into the side room – presumably to avoid her gaze for a minute or two – and Eve rose quietly from her seat, glancing over her shoulder to check he wasn't watching. He was acting oddly, and he clearly had a secret. It wasn't just Jenna who'd known about it, but Maynard too. Eve was desperate to find out what it was; the stakes were high.

She found he had a desk diary – an excellent result in this day and age – and flipped through it, going back to the days before Jenna was killed. There it was: 'Meet J, 6pm, outside TDR offices'. Definitely no chance encounter. They'd been together just three days before she'd died. Eve turned the pages back and there, four weeks earlier, she found they'd met a previous time. And it wasn't just the appointment she discovered. There was a photo too. Eve recognised the little girl in the image. Remembered the distinctive imperious look, the hair swept back from her forehead. It was Jenna, and she wasn't the only person in the photo. To either side of her sat Jacqueline Hale and Clarke himself. Jacqueline was smiling, but Clarke looked sad.

'What are you doing?' There was panic in Clarke's tone.

'Something unforgiveable, and I'm sorry.' Eve wondered how much to say. 'The truth is, I'm worried about Jenna's death as well as Lance's. There's no proof there's something amiss but I couldn't just leave it.'

He rushed forward. 'You think she was killed?'

Eve could see the raw emotion in his eyes. 'She was your daughter?'

His chest rose and fell. 'Yes. I only admitted it to her shortly before she died. I spent ages debating what to do. I think Jacqueline would have told her in the end, only she never got the chance. I thought it would be wrong to go to my grave without letting Jenna know. But also' – he hung his head – 'I yearned to talk to her. Now I'm worried I stirred things up. Caused her death, even.'

'Do you want to tell me why?' Eve sensed he was desperate to share his worries.

'It took a while to get Jenna to talk to me. When we did finally meet, she naturally wanted proof that I was her father. That last time we got together, she'd had the DNA results. She seemed pleased, but not quite in the way I'd imagined.' There were tears in his eyes. 'She wasn't emotional and fond, more gleeful and delighted. I was worried she'd tell Lance. I knew they didn't get on and I suspected she'd do anything to get back at him. The thought of his reaction scared me. It wasn't just that he'd be jealous. That was fair enough. Jacqueline and I had wronged him. It was that she'd chosen to have an affair with *me*. At the time that wouldn't have made much odds. An affair with anyone would have been terrible. But if it came out now, it would be far worse.'

'Because you were his greatest rival? And people who talked about how clever Jenna was would realise it was your genes she'd inherited, not Lance's?' It was horrific, but she bet it was how Lance would have viewed it.

Clarke nodded. 'The worst of it was, Jacqueline admitted to

me that Lance wasn't Maynard's dad, either. She'd had an affair with the man who did the maintenance at the chambers where she worked. She said he was so much kinder and more perceptive than Lance. I asked Jenna's advice about whether to tell Maynard. She said not to, but I know she did.'

From what Eve had heard about her, she would. She and Maynard had clearly been intellectual and social snobs who hated each other. 'What makes you think Jenna told him?'

Clarke sighed. 'Maynard contacted me. He told me the story about his parentage was rubbish and warned me not to spread it around.'

'Warned?'

'He said people might assume Jenna had approached me, not the other way round, and that I'd pushed her off the cliff to protect my marriage.' His head was in his hands. 'I'm still with the same woman as I was when Jacqueline and I had the affair. It was so stupid of me. Of us. I'd been in love with Jacquie back in university, but she only had eyes for Lance. When chance threw us together, and I realised she was unhappy, I felt it was fate, but of course it wasn't. Jacquie was never going to leave Lance. They rowed like crazy, but they created a spark I could never match.' His watery eyes met Eve's. 'And now I suppose you'll write about all this.'

Eve shook her head. 'That's not the way I work, I promise you.' It was painful to imagine his hurt. He'd wanted to build a relationship with his biological daughter, but all Jenna had cared about was hurting Lance and Maynard. 'I'm so sorry for everything you've been through.'

She sensed he'd like her to leave, so she thanked him and slipped out of his office.

She wouldn't publicise his revelation, but she could imagine Jenna might have, had she lived. Her dad had been picking her work and reputation to pieces, according to Judith, just as he had Naomi's and Erica's. The only time he'd seemed to champion his children was when he wanted to claim credit for their achievements.

And then, Jenna had found a way to humiliate him utterly by revealing the truth about her biological father. The same went for making Maynard's heritage public. Her brother had been putting her down since she was a small child; before she died, she'd had the perfect chance to get her own back. It wouldn't have worked on a well-balanced person. There was nothing wrong with having a maintenance professional for a dad, rather than a respected diplomat and academic. But for an idiot like Maynard, it would have been a powerful blow.

Were it not for Lance's alibi, she'd have looked at him very closely for Jenna's death too. Because of his personality, his motive was huge. But she just couldn't see Naomi helping. Eve sensed she'd have been horrified by his motivation.

And she couldn't imagine Lance collaborating with Maynard either. But Eve was sure Maynard would have been just as desperate to shut Jenna up. And he had no one to vouch for him.

But then, once again, her thoughts turned to Lucy. What if she'd killed Jenna to protect Lance's feelings? Felix Masters had worried over her complete dedication, and Eve felt the same.

35

When Eve had finished talking to Clarke, she went to meet her adult twins and their other halves for a quick drink before coming home. It was so good to see them, but it took her a while to put the day's revelations out of her mind and relax enough to enjoy it properly.

Her daughter Ellen put a hand on her arm. 'Difficult day?'

Eve nodded. 'Sorry. I'd love to tell you all about it but some of it's very personal and not public. Or not yet.'

Her son gave her a hug as his wife Fiona looked on sympathetically. 'We forgive you. So long as you fill us in once it's out in the open.' He went on to tell her about the woman who'd visited his arts centre that afternoon and fallen asleep in a chair that was part of an installation. It cheered her up.

Back in Suffolk, she was less guarded with the gang. They were involved already and without the extra knowledge they'd be working blind.

'I think you should encourage Clarke to tell the police what he told you,' Robin said when they'd left. 'I appreciate he doesn't want to destroy his marriage, but he must see that justice for Jenna is paramount.'

Eve nodded. 'I'll send him an email now. And I'll point out that it could tie in with Lance's death too, though in all honesty, I don't see how. But Maynard could have killed the pair of them for unrelated reasons. I can certainly imagine him being desperate to keep his mum's affairs secret. He threatened Clarke over it, after all. And there's Lucy to consider for Jenna, too.'

She woke the following morning feeling keyed up. At last, it was the day of Maynard's appointment with the person who'd agreed to lend him money. Eve strongly suspected that it had been Acland who'd been blackmailing him, and that Maynard would have cancelled the meeting, but they still needed to be outside Lockley Grange ready to follow him in case.

The day before had made her depressed, and she decided to try to improve her mood by going to church. She wasn't truly a believer, but Jim Thackeray, the vicar, encouraged attendees of all faiths and none and was one of her favourite people. He even welcomed Gus with open arms, despite the dachshund's discordant 'singing'.

She was crossing the village green towards St Peter's, worrying over the enormity of Lance and Lucy depriving Sonia of an acting part, when she saw Sonia herself, just ahead of her, Naomi by her side.

Eve watched them enter the church as Viv rushed up to join her. 'Had any more thoughts since last night?'

Eve shook her head.

'I went into Moira's this morning and she thinks it's Naomi.'

Eve turned to her as they followed the two Hales into the building. 'What on earth gave her that idea?'

'She says it's always the least likely ones.'

Eve suspected Moira watched a lot of television.

They shuffled into a pew and Gus got snarled up with Deirdre Lennox's handbag strap. The bag tipped over and a tube of haemorrhoid cream fell out. Eve stuffed it back hastily and apologised.

The service was a bit raucous. Gus 'sang' his way enthusiastically through 'O come, O come, Emmanuel', but had thankfully calmed down for 'I was Glad', and the other advent hymns. After it was over, Eve and Viv went to the back of St Peter's for coffee. Jim was talking to Sonia and Naomi, expressing his sympathy, no doubt. He was seldom solemn, but when he was, you knew he genuinely felt it. Eventually, it looked as though they were winding up, and Eve turned to Viv. 'I wouldn't mind a quiet word with Sonia.' It was essential after what she'd discovered the day before. The way Lance had belittled her so publicly was horrendous, and losing the film part was huge too. She needed to judge how angry Lance had made her. 'Is there any chance you could distract Naomi?'

Viv nodded. 'It's a deal. So long as you tell me exactly what Sonia says immediately afterwards.'

'As if I'd get any choice.'

Viv stuck her tongue out. 'Want me to ask Naomi some incisive questions in case Moira's right?'

Eve had grave misgivings but gave the project her blessing. 'You will be tactful, won't you?'

Viv raised an eyebrow. 'Of course.'

Eve went over to Sonia and asked if she'd like her coffee topped up.

'That sounds good. The church isn't as cold as the Grange, but nowhere's warm at this time of year.'

Eve did the honours as Sonia patted Gus.

'Sonia, I spoke to Felix Masters yesterday.'

Their eyes met as Sonia straightened up. 'Good old Felix.' She gave Eve a penetrating look.

'He let something slip that was perhaps a bit personal.' Eve waited but Sonia didn't meet her halfway, so she carried on. 'I couldn't believe it when he told me that Lucy didn't pass on his offer of a film part. I'm so sorry.' She wouldn't mention the incident in Milan and the affairs. It was too private and she didn't want Sonia to think she was listing her motives for Lance's murder.

'It was wrong of her.' Sonia's fists were clenched tight. 'But it's water under the bridge.'

'Do you think Lance knew?'

'Not so far as I'm aware.'

Sonia couldn't know for sure, of course, if she hadn't confronted the pair, but Masters had definitely said she'd blamed him. Now, she was covering that up, which she would if she'd killed him. Alarm bells were ringing.

'I hope Felix approaches you again now that he knows you didn't turn him down.'

Sonia's poker face slipped slightly to reveal her emotion. 'What are the chances he'll have another significant role that's just right for me?'

Significant? Eve had assumed it had been a walk-on part or something minor. Not that she didn't have confidence in Sonia's abilities, but she would have been a newcomer. 'I'm sorry. It must have been an awful blow.'

Sonia took a deep breath and shook her head. 'I'm not sure I'd have gone for it anyway. It would have been a lot of stress and travel and I love my regular work.'

But Eve didn't believe her.

'I wanted to talk to you as well,' Sonia said, drawing her further away from Viv and Naomi, though the church was noisy. 'Look what I found.'

She took out a piece of crumpled A4 paper and handed it to Eve, who scanned the first few lines.

'Wait, this is the missing page from Lance's speech?'

Sonia nodded.

'Where was it?'

'Stuffed behind the radiator just to the left of the French windows in the reception room where we held the party. So it wasn't mislaid. Someone did it on purpose.'

36

When Eve left St Peter's, she spotted Lucy across the village green. She was shuffling a series of letters into the post box. Stuff to do with Lance's death, perhaps. Eve raised her hand in greeting and Lucy returned the gesture.

'So? What joy with Sonia?' Viv had dashed to catch Eve up.

'*Please* keep your voice down.' Eve nodded in Lucy's direction, then filled Viv in, in a whisper.

'So you think she's lying about not blaming Lance?'

Eve nodded. 'Perhaps she stayed in the marriage to get her revenge on him. It's not as though the lost role is the only reason she's got to be angry. The way he treated her was clearly appalling. I can imagine her resentment reaching fever pitch. What did Naomi say?'

'She told me all about the production her partner's directing. The move to a major theatre is a real breakthrough for her, apparently. Naomi sounded emotional about it, but it wasn't to do with the case, so you'll be proud of me – I moved the conversation on. Once she got talking about the crate you saw her take from the mystery guy, things got more interesting.'

'You asked her about that?' Eve's response was loud enough to make Gus jump.

'No need to fuss.' Viv waved a hand airily. 'She brought it up. I just said it must be frustrating to be stuck in Suffolk when she had so much to be getting on with. Then she said a friend of hers had brought her some paperwork related to her research – a whole crateful and it arrived on Friday. So what does that tell you?'

Eve felt even more uneasy. 'That she knows I was spying on her, and she wanted to provide an explanation, via you. Only it won't wash. Her friend wouldn't have to burgle a house to access Naomi's work files. I wonder what she's up to that's so secret?'

Eve was due to work a shift at Monty's that afternoon, which was a blessing. It would help pass the time until she and Robin went to lie in wait for Maynard. She still worried he'd have cancelled his appointment, but despite that, a tiny bubble of anticipation sat in the pit of her stomach. What if he hadn't? Where would he take the money afterwards?

Before she left Elizabeth's Cottage, she called Sylvia to ask if they could meet the following morning for a communal breakfast before she headed to Lockley Grange. She wanted to go through the photos from Lance's party. They might hint at who'd stuffed part of Lance's speech behind the radiator.

In the teashop, Eve and Viv made winter cakes, and Eve darted to and fro, wiping up kitchen spillages. Viv tended to lose focus when Eve talked about a case, though she still never got eggshell in her mix, Eve noted. It was puzzling and slightly annoying.

When they paused for tea, Eve's thoughts were still full of the planned adventure that night. She googled 'Maynard Oscar Simon Hale' on her phone for the umpteenth time, wishing for a lead, because even if she and Robin caught sight of a second blackmailer, she was worried they'd never work out Maynard's secret. Without that knowledge, it would be hard to guess if he might have killed over it.

There were no useful results, so she tried 'Mosh' again. 'The one oddity I've picked up on is those missing stories I told you about from the *Tales of the Unexpected* website, but that's hardly promising.' Mosh on its own produced no useful results, and in a fit of desperation, she entered the nickname a second time, coupled with the names of people who'd followed his account on the writing site. One by one she turned up nothing. She'd abandoned hope so thoroughly that she almost dropped her phone when she finally got a result. 'Wait, look at this!'

Viv rushed to her side. 'What is it?'

'A screenshot of one of Maynard's stories on this person's blog.' They read the story together. It was about a man lost in the hills who killed each passerby he met, rather than returning to a 'humdrum' life.

'Grim,' Viv said. 'And not well written. It makes me worry for the person who thought it was worth sharing.'

Eve nodded. She could see why Maynard had deleted it. 'Let's see if there are any more screenshots attributed to Mosh on this guy's blog.'

There were. Each was as unpleasant as the last. They were on their fourth and behind with the baking when Eve's scalp began to tingle.

The story was told from the viewpoint of a thirteen-year-old boy and featured his two younger sisters, both of whom were 'above themselves'. The youngest one in particular thought herself very clever, and wrapped her father and her child-minder round her little finger. The narrator's hatred of her was clear. The supposedly brilliant brother was constantly over-looked despite being so much more talented than his sisters. The children's names were Jenny, Natalie and Mansfield. Their minder was Lotty and their father was Lawrence. There was no clever twist, just straightforward nastiness. Mansfield ended up poisoning Natalie with belladonna berries. Deadly nightshade. The plant that someone had researched in the *Poison Garden* book at Lockley Grange.

In the story, 'Mansfield' gave his sister the belladonna berries mixed with blueberry conserve inside some sandwiches with the crusts cut off. His sister ate the treat eagerly.

Eve felt cold to her very core.

The words Lance had muttered during his row with Maynard came back to her. She'd caught the word 'conserve', and imagined he was talking about guarding their reputations. Now, she thought differently.

'Oh my goodness, Viv, I think this is it.' Eve had never felt so sick. She could feel her eyes filling with tears.

'What?' Viv put an arm around her and gave her a squeeze. 'Tell me.'

'I think the story is wish fulfilment. It never happened. But the girl who eats the berries is Naomi, I'm sure, and the boy who puts them into a sandwich is Maynard. Naomi didn't die.' Thank heavens. 'But I don't think Maynard putting the berries in her food is fantasy.' Lance's comment, Maynard's jealousy of Naomi's abilities and the book on poison all made sense. There had even been fragments of plant matter between its pages. She imagined Maynard hunched over it, plotting. 'And here's the worst of it: if I'm right, Lance and Lucy knew what he'd tried to do and they covered it up.'

If Maynard had attempted murder as a child, he could definitely have killed to protect his secret. Eve guessed his father and Lucy had realised what he'd done just in time. Or maybe Naomi had eaten a tiny bit of the sandwich and got sick. That way, Acland could have found out too, which would explain the blackmail.

Perhaps Lance and Lucy had thought Maynard was too

young to know what he was doing and if he'd been thirteen like the child in the story, it had been shortly after his mother was killed. That could have sent him off the rails. But even so, what he'd attempted was appalling. And it wasn't something he'd done in a moment of madness, only to be consumed by guilt later. He'd written about it – fantasised about it having come true.

Eve was horrified. Lance and Lucy might not have known how he'd dwelt on his attempt afterwards, but hushing it up seemed utterly cavalier. They should have got him counselling or something. How could they be sure he wouldn't try to kill again? And now, perhaps, he had.

Poor Naomi. They'd prioritised Maynard and the family name over her safety. Eve wondered if she knew. And what she'd felt about Lance if she did.

37

That evening at six, Eve and Robin were sitting in Robin's van, tucked into the gated entrance to a farm field, just up the lane from Lockley Grange. They had a view of the Grange's driveway through the trees and the moon was bright enough to show any movement. Eve was still preoccupied over what she'd guessed about Maynard. She'd known he wasn't a nice man, but this was something else – it was impossible not to replay each conversation they'd had with a new sense of horror.

She and Robin had talked it over. If Naomi knew Lance had prioritised Maynard's reputation over her safety, she had another motive for Lance's murder, especially if she'd discovered the truth recently. Though what were the chances of that? And she still had no believable motive for Jenna. Whereas Maynard would have wanted to stop Jenna revealing his true parentage, and he'd attempted murder before. He could easily have killed Lance to stop him talking too. His future would be in ruins if his attempt on Naomi's life got out, and someone had already been blackmailing him over it.

Lucy's position looked all the more precarious. The secret she held was huge.

It was enough to fill Eve's head as they waited near the Grange. The meeting Maynard had scheduled was at 9 p.m. but of course, they had no idea where it would take place, hence being three hours early. Even that had felt riskily late to Eve, but Robin had pointed out that disreputable moneylenders weren't *that* hard to find. It was unlikely Maynard was planning to drive to Scotland to get what he needed.

'My best bet's London,' Robin said. 'It's home turf for Maynard and nice and anonymous.' If so, they might not have long to wait.

Eve was cosied up under a blanket in the passenger seat, her eyes fixed on the Grange's driveway, feeling tense, when she saw something shifting in the shadows. A car was moving along the drive at a snail's pace. Robin had stiffened too, his eyes focused on the distance.

'That's him. Has to be.'

His headlights weren't on; he must be sneaking out. Eve wondered what he'd told the others. That he wasn't feeling well, perhaps, and wanted to be left in peace. She imagined they'd be happy to oblige. He wasn't pleasant company.

'Off he goes,' Robin said.

'And he's not in his own car.' Eve had got a rough idea of which belonged to who over the last few days. 'I think he's driving Lance's.'

They watched as he exited the drive and turned right, inland towards the main road. It was another few seconds before he turned on his lights. Robin gave him a little longer, then set off too, a good distance behind but close enough to keep tabs. The trouble with Suffolk was that the land was so flat. You could see into the distance, but you would *be* seen too.

Eve breathed a sigh of relief once they reached the A12. There were many more vehicles and Robin's van felt less conspicuous. It looked as though he was right, and Maynard might be heading for the capital.

'It doesn't mean he's still being blackmailed,' Eve said. 'If he's careless with money and paid Acland odds and bits, he might just want funds to tide him over until he gets his inheritance.'

Robin nodded. 'True.'

He was tense as well. She could feel it. They wanted justice of course, but the wedding was less than two weeks away now too. And relatives would start arriving sooner than that. A breakthrough was essential and simply seeing Maynard borrow from a loan shark wouldn't reveal anything.

The journey to the capital was straightforward, but things got more difficult when they got into London proper. The backstreets were quiet and the danger of Maynard guessing he was being followed increased. At least they were in a run-of-the-mill vehicle, not Eve's Mini Clubman, which he might recognise.

'I think he's nearing his goal,' Robin said, as they turned a corner, just in time to see Maynard well down the road they'd entered. 'Look at the way he's slowing down. His satnav's probably telling him he's reached his destination and he's looking for the right building.'

It was a run-down area, full of boarded-up shops covered with torn posters and alleyways daubed with graffiti. Robin was right. Maynard had stopped. The posh car he drove stuck out like a sore thumb and Eve wondered if it would still be in mint condition when he got back.

As he exited it, he was barely recognisable. His overcoat collar was turned up and he wore a cap pulled down over his eyes. If they got as far as reporting what they'd seen to the police, Eve wouldn't be able to swear that it was him. But it had to be. The figure was the wrong height and build for anyone else in the house and it was he who'd had a clandestine appointment set up. She sighed. It wouldn't be enough for Palmer. He'd talk about Sonia hiding her hair under the cap or something.

Maynard opened his boot, took out a suitcase and

approached a doorway between one boarded up shop and another.

'He's taking a big risk, picking up cash somewhere like this,' Robin said. 'The local gangs will be well aware of what goes on. I'm guessing the loan shark has pals who look out for his clients. It wouldn't do his business any good if they got robbed the moment they left his place.'

Eve scanned the street. Sure enough, she saw someone standing in the shadows. She pointed him out to Robin and he nodded. 'I'm glad I parked right behind another van. He won't see us in detail, but he's bound to be aware of our arrival.'

Robin reached to open his door. 'I need to make him think we're here for another reason. Lock up after me, and don't unlock until I come back, please. Don't worry. I'll be fine.'

Eve didn't get the chance to protest. Robin was already out, black beanie pulled low over his face, black jeans and jacket making him look as though he belonged. What if he got into trouble? It would be her fault for getting him involved. She locked up as instructed and felt sick. He went and bashed on the door of an empty-looking flat above a disused shop. What the heck would he say if someone answered? And what would they do?

She glanced at the man in the shadows opposite the building Maynard had entered. His eyes were on Robin for a moment, but as Robin knocked again – loudly – he seemed to lose interest.

And that had been what Robin wanted, of course. Eve had to trust that he knew what he was doing. She still prayed that no one came to the door, and breathed a sigh of relief when he got back. She unlocked to let him in.

'Did you have to try so hard to get a response?'

He grinned as he locked up again. 'Wouldn't have looked genuine if I hadn't, but I was pretty sure the place was empty.'

'What would you have said if someone came?'

'I'd have asked for someone called Dan, then got a bit shirty when they told me I'd got the wrong flat, but backed off before I got into a fight.'

'Very reassuring.'

He laughed. 'Now, let's make ourselves scarce while our guy in the shadows still thinks it's a coincidence we're here.'

Robin edged the van back into a side alley and turned, but he only drove as far as the main road. They'd already agreed they'd follow Maynard wherever he went.

It wasn't long before they saw him emerge, he and his car still intact. The guy in the shadows had served his purpose.

'He's still got his cap on,' Robin said, echoing her thoughts earlier. 'Even if he's picked up on camera, he won't be iden-tifiable.'

They followed him out of the rabbit warren of streets and when he came to a main road he turned north.

'Heading out of London again, I guess,' Eve said. And quite possibly back to Suffolk to stash his cash at Lockley Grange. She tried to quell the disappointment which was building in her chest.

They drove in subdued silence, but when the option came, Maynard took a route north towards Epping Forest, not north-east towards home. Eve and Robin's eyes met for a second and excitement bubbled up again.

38

Eve and Robin continued to follow Lance's car, until Maynard turned off the main road and wove through a quiet, leafy village then out the other side. It was wooded on their left, the trees thick and impenetrable in the darkness. Fields stretched to their right.

Robin continued to keep well back, but Maynard was still in sight. They saw when he turned off and followed him without trouble. They were driving along the border of someone's property now. It must be big; the high, ornate iron railings seemed to go on forever. Beyond them in the distance, Eve could see the outline of a large Queen Anne house. They watched as Maynard came to a stop just after the railings finally ended, close to a village church, its spire dark against the night sky.

'I can't risk getting nearer,' Robin said, taking out his binoculars. Eve had hers to her eyes too.

'Thank goodness for the moonlight.' She saw Maynard exit his car and go to the boot. He was taking out his suitcase. Then he entered the churchyard.

Eve could see him walking between the graves, as though he

was examining them in turn. Then at last, he put the suitcase down somewhere out of sight, returned to his car and drove off.

'Proof positive that Acland wasn't his only blackmailer,' Eve said.

Robin nodded. 'Assuming it was him Acland was blackmailing. I wonder if he knows the identity of this one.'

'If not, he'll probably go and hide somewhere to see who comes for the cash.'

'I certainly would, in his shoes.'

And they planned to do the same. As they watched and waited, Eve scanned their surroundings to see if she could see Maynard, but there was no sign of him. It was two hours later, just before one in the morning, when a motorcyclist raced past Robin's van. Robin photographed it but it would probably be a blur. The rider didn't stop as they entered the graveyard but rode down the path to where Maynard had left his suitcase, grabbed and stowed it in one swift move, then sped off.

There was no way they could have caught them in the van. Eve craned over Robin's phone to see the photo he'd got. It wasn't quite as blurry as she'd feared, but the licence plate was covered in mud. It left no way to identify the rider.

Disappointment washed over Eve again.

'I'm sorry.' Robin turned to her. 'It tells us there's someone still living who's after Maynard's money and if they know he tried to kill Naomi as a child then Lance or Lucy probably talked. Unless Naomi somehow found out. But other than that, we're no further forward and I'm bushed. Shall we take a nap before we drive home?'

Eve nodded. 'Good idea.' Now that there was no adrenaline keeping her going, she found she was fighting sleep. She reclined her seat, curled up under her blanket and dozed off.

It was the sound of a motorbike that woke her again, just minutes later. She'd been a light sleeper ever since she'd had the twins, years earlier. She nudged Robin awake and they watched the bike move slowly along the road. The same one? It had to be, surely. Its licence plate was caked in mud, just like the one earlier.

They watched as the rider reached the iron gates of the large house they'd driven past, then dismounted, keyed in a code and entered the grounds. The gates closed after them automatically.

Eve and Robin had their binoculars out again. The rider went round the back, then all was quiet. 'They live there and drove away to put Maynard off the scent?'

Robin nodded. 'Looks that way. Maybe they figured he'd never guess they'd be so brazen.'

At that moment, Eve saw movement in a road beyond the graveyard. Then Lance's car emerged. So Maynard had stuck around, just as they'd guessed. And now he'd seen the motorcyclist come back to the big house too.

He pulled up outside the iron gates and jabbed a button. A bell presumably. Then again. And again. Then he shook the gates, but they were locked fast. At last, he went back to his car, got into the driver's seat, slammed the door and gunned the engine, disappearing in a puff of exhaust.

'We need to tell the police,' Eve said, 'but I'm not sure if they'll do anything, with Palmer at the helm. We can't swear it was Maynard in the car, or that he was carrying money in that suitcase, and Palmer won't want to challenge an MP without strong evidence. I guess Greg might help, behind the scenes, but we need to act ourselves. Find out who lives there.'

Robin nodded. 'And get to them before Maynard does. They should have waited longer before coming back.'

39

Eve tried not to focus on what time she and Robin made it back to Saxford. Resolutely, she set her alarm early enough to make her breakfast appointment at Sylvia and Daphne's. She needed to see if Sylvia's photos could tell her who'd stolen the sheet from Lance's notes.

She arrived at Hope Cottage at the appointed hour, where Daphne took one look at her and prescribed coffee with extra toast and marmalade. She ushered Eve through to her and Sylvia's tiny, cosy kitchen, the walls painted a deep red, and they sat at the table, the coffee and toast rack between them. Gus was sitting at Eve's feet. Every so often he poked his nose out from his shelter to check for the presence of Sylvia and Daphne's cat, who treated him with the utmost disdain. Eve gave him a reassuring pat. Back at Elizabeth's Cottage, Robin was in the process of contacting Greg Boles about what they'd seen the night before, but neither of them had high hopes of progress.

Sylvia had her laptop open, a group photo of people laughing up on the screen, the familiar windows and wallpaper of Lockley Grange in the background. 'You need to start here, from what you said. Taken around ten minutes before Lance's speech.'

Eve thanked her. The timing sounded about right. Erica swore the notes had been in order at that stage. She needed to work out what had happened next.

'I had a look, of course,' Sylvia said.

'We both did,' Daphne added, topping up Eve's coffee.

'But you know the house better than we do and there are lots of photos with radiators in shot.'

Eve ate her toast, as Sylvia, who didn't seem to be hungry, scrolled through picture after picture. Erica looking nervous. Maynard looking snide. Sonia with her head held high. Naomi looking sad. Then came the first picture of Lance at the lectern. He was full of confidence at that point, as though he was lapping up the audience's attention. There were several more as he continued which captured his character perfectly: his powerful charisma and delight at being in the spotlight.

Then came some shots featuring audience members, many looking on with rapt attention, now serious, now laughing. And then—

'Wait a second!'

Sylvia raised an eyebrow.

'That's the right radiator.' The French windows Sonia had mentioned were visible at the edge of the picture. And standing just in front of the radiator, his hand on the windowsill above it, was Maynard. He was looking in the same direction as everyone else in the sequence of photos – towards his father. And he was smiling, but it wasn't a nice smile. He looked as though he was taking pleasure in someone's discomfort.

'Good Lord,' Sylvia said, 'I should have homed in on that one just from his expression. But I'd already gathered that Maynard and Lance didn't get on, so it didn't strike me as odd. I assumed he was happy to see his father stumble over his words, but it never occurred to me that he might be responsible. Do you think he was?'

Eve nodded slowly. It was the way he had his hand placed just over the top of the radiator that convinced her. It was as though he was protecting something there. Subconsciously keeping everyone else away from it. And that was just where Sonia had found the missing page. The mere fact that he was standing there immediately after it disappeared was suggestive. 'I think it's very likely. What a jerk! He let Erica take all that flak when it was his fault. It's all the worse because I think he and Erica had been friends behind the scenes. I don't know the background, but my journalist colleague Monica saw them drinking together, and it was Maynard who was feeding Monica positive stories about Erica.' It was horrendous to let her take the blame, but totally in character.

Eve shook her head. 'Perhaps he did it to get back at Lance after Lance refused to lend him money.'

'What will you do next?' Sylvia asked. 'You look as though you could do with going back to bed.'

'Sadly, I think catching up on sleep will have to wait. I want to go back to Lockley Grange and talk to Erica again. If it's likely Maynard scuppered Lance's speech, she needs to know, especially if she and Maynard are up to something together. She might not realise how duplicitous he is.' She thought of Naomi and the belladonna berries. She couldn't tell Erica that – she had no proof – but she was sure of what he'd done. She needed to do everything she could to put Erica on her guard.

Eve slipped back to Elizabeth's Cottage to update Robin before heading to Lockley Grange.

'Maynard seems to be up to his neck in this, every which way you look,' he said, once she'd explained.

'And then some. Any news from Greg?'

'He'll do what he can, but he doesn't have any contacts down in Epping and it's outside my old stamping ground too.

All the same, I've sent him the address where Maynard picked up his cash, and the one where the biker entered the grounds. And I've got a name for you. According to Google, the house belongs to a family called Greville. They run village fetes there, so they've appeared in the local press.'

'Thanks, Robin.' The moment she'd spoken to Erica, she'd do some digging herself and find out more. She wanted to know how the Grevilles might have discovered Maynard's secret and that meant finding out what connections they had to his contacts. If Lance or Acland knew them, then it was probably they who'd talked, and Maynard could have killed them as weak links. But if Lucy was the connection, she had to be in danger.

40

It was Naomi who let Eve in. There was an awkward pause after they'd greeted each other and she'd petted Gus. Eve was preoccupied with Naomi's attempts to convince Viv her crate of stolen papers was perfectly innocent.

After a moment, Naomi opened her mouth, as though she wanted to say something, but then Lucy walked through the hall and the moment was lost.

Eve set up her laptop in Lance's study as usual, then went with Gus to find Erica.

Frustratingly, she wasn't in her room. Eve should probably go, but she needed to understand the link between Erica and Maynard, and she was determined to warn Erica.

As she hung around, irresolute, she cast her eyes over Erica's workspace. She had files and papers piled high and reams of notes relating to her research. Eve imagined it was her habit to throw herself into work. It might provide some relief from the current stress too, as well as a way to prove herself, after the dressing down Lance had given her.

With Gus shooting her what felt like accusatory glances,

Eve moved behind Erica's desk, wondering if she could find anything that might explain her connection with Maynard.

She flipped open folder after folder, finding only innocent-looking research notes, until she noticed a very slight unevenness in the rug she was standing on. Curious, she bent down and flipped over its corner.

What she found was a slender file of folded card. She hesitated for a moment. If Erica caught her, she'd have no explanation to give. But in the end, she went for it. Erica would have to forgive her or not, because the goal was worth it. She left the rug flipped back so she could replace the folder quickly.

The contents were more than interesting. A dossier on Maynard. Photos of him close to parliament. Pictures of him with a group of men and women Eve didn't recognise. And then a photo of Maynard with Lance's rival and Jenna's biological father, Leonard Clarke. On top of the group photo was a Post-it note, written on in Lance's writing.

You see? He's betraying me. I wouldn't ask you to do this without good reason.

Heck, this put things in a new light. Eve took photos of the pictures in the folder and slipped it back under the rug, then left a note for Erica, saying they needed to talk.

Back in Lance's study, Eve let the new information settle in her head, turning it over, until very gradually, certain facts fell into place. Her thoughts on how to handle the interview with Erica became clearer.

After that, she set to work researching the Grevilles. She couldn't find Facebook accounts for any of them but followed the links Robin had emailed her. She was poring over news stories about the respectable-sounding charity fetes they'd held when she heard footsteps in the corridor. In the split second before Erica entered the room, Eve saw a face she recognised in one of the Greville photos.

'You wanted to see me?' Erica sounded tired as Gus pottered over to greet her. The previous conversation they'd had hung in the air. 'You're not going to ask me more about what we discussed, are you?'

Eve shook her head.

'I can't hate myself any more than I do already.' Erica looked at the floor. 'I wish to goodness Maynard hadn't spread all those rumours about me and Lance having an affair.'

To Eve, that now formed part of a pattern, along with the dossier on Maynard, the good publicity he'd got Erica through Monica Sutton, and the way he'd sabotaged Lance's speech. 'I wanted to talk because I've uncovered something unexpected. It happens sometimes when I'm writing an obituary. In this case, it sheds light on Lance's character, which is useful, but I need to confirm it.'

'Go on.' Her long hair fell forward, her eyes steady on Eve's now.

'I think I understand the unreasonable demands Lance made of you. He asked you to spy on Maynard, didn't he?'

Erica flinched and it took her a moment to reply. 'How did you know?'

Eve didn't want to admit to looking at the dossier. 'I've spoken to various people who saw you together. What did Lance think you'd find?'

'Evidence that Maynard was secretly trying to undermine his career. Maynard's just as competitive as Lance was, so I could believe it. I don't think he's risen as quickly as he'd like in parliament. He's the sort who expects to be plucked from obscurity immediately.' She gave Eve a weary look. 'Lance was still getting more publicity than he was, but instead of being pleased, Lance got paranoid because it would give Maynard extra incentive to bring him down. He spotted Maynard with an academic rival of his – someone he had no business with – and it made him suspicious. After that, he started watching Maynard secretly. It made him anxious each time he met with someone from Lance's circle. He wanted me to get proof of what he was planning.'

'I'm guessing Maynard worked out what you were up to. It would explain the revenge he took on you.'

'Revenge?'

Eve explained her theory about the stolen page from the speech. 'I don't have proof, but I'm pretty certain he took it, thanks to my friend Sylvia's photos. But it's not just that, is it? He got back at you by spreading rumours that you and Lance were having an affair, too. That would damage your reputation. And he got a journalist contact of his to big you up in her newspaper.'

'Why would she agree to do that?'

'It's a very good question. The journalist must be getting something out of it.' Eve needed to push Monica harder to find out what. 'I'd been thinking Maynard was doing you a favour. That maybe he'd fallen for you. But now I believe his motive was more complicated. He wanted to drive a wedge between you and Lance – to make Lance think you'd swapped sides, probably, given the articles mentioned Maynard as well. And I guess it worked. Lance accused you of betrayal at the party.'

Erica nodded and slumped into the chair opposite Eve. 'He was furious: convinced I was the source of the stories. He decided that Maynard and I were lovers, and working against him.'

Eve could imagine it making Lance angry enough to change his will. Perhaps Maynard had killed him to avoid that happening. Once again, she imagined him asking his dad for money on the off-chance he'd get an advance on his inheritance, knowing full well that Lance would be dead by morning. Perhaps he'd been arrogant enough to assume Lance would give in to avoid a scandal.

Erica put her head in her hands. 'It went against my better judgement to spy, and Maynard spent the whole time trying to prise information on his dad out of me. In the end, he got suspicious, and I backed off. The whole thing's been a disaster.'

Eve felt for Erica. 'It's horrible to say it, after I minded him as a child, but I don't trust Maynard. I'm glad you've distanced yourself.'

As Erica left the room to get on with her work, Eve turned her attention to the news report she'd been studying just before she'd come in. The face in the crowd she'd recognised at the Grevilles' fete was Lucy Garton.

Lucy had told the police she didn't know anything about a damaging secret of Maynard's, but Eve had always doubted that was true. Now she was all but certain it wasn't. It was hard to believe Lucy had told anyone that Maynard had tried to poison his sister – it would have involved admitting she'd protected him – but seeing her at the Grevilles' fete was too much of a coincidence. If she knew them well, perhaps she'd let the details slip in spite of herself. It was time to find out.

Eve went to knock at Lucy's door and found her wrapping up an ornament at her desk. It was the carved wooden statue which had been on the mantelpiece when she'd visited last.

'You're passing it on?' She indicated the half-wrapped artwork.

Lucy nodded. 'As a Christmas present. It's not really my cup of tea but one of my relations admired it once, so...'

She let the sentence trail off. Eve decided she'd have to wade straight in. 'Lucy, do you know a family called the Grevilles who live down by Epping Forest?'

She sat back in her chair. 'Yes, of course. They're my

cousins. Not that they're there at the moment. They spend winter in the south of France. But why? How do you know them?'

'Through a friend.'

Lucy nodded. She looked satisfied, though Eve had expected her to ask more. 'It's a small world.'

Eve hoped she wasn't blushing. 'So none of the family are around? They don't come home for Christmas or anything? Only this friend thought she'd seen one of them.'

Lucy had gone back to her wrapping. 'No, I don't think it's likely. They normally stay abroad until spring.'

'That's concerning. I hope it wasn't an intruder that my friend saw. Though what about staff? Would there be any gardeners or cleaners coming and going?' The biker could be a Greville employee, though the possibility of Lucy telling them Maynard's secret seemed remote.

Lucy paused in her work and frowned. 'There's a team of gardeners who come in once a month while they're away, I believe. A new lot this year because the last ones were unreliable. I hope the new team aren't up to no good.'

'Probably not.' Eve couldn't see the biker being one of them for a minute. She could just about imagine Lucy forming a close bond with an old family retainer and confiding in them about Maynard, but certainly not spilling the beans to a new firm. Why would she? Even telling her cousins would be risky, though it must have been a hard secret to carry for so many years.

Eve wasn't sure what to say, but she couldn't leave without issuing a warning. 'Lucy, I don't want to speak out of turn, but I'm worried about Maynard. I overheard him talking to Lance about a secret. He thought you or his dad might have passed it on to someone and it sounded serious. I'm actually a little frightened of him.' That small-boy-turned-man who she'd scolded as a four-year-old.

Lucy turned to face her. 'Don't worry. I've known Maynard very well, for a long time. I think I can predict his behaviour.'

'What about his secret?'

Lucy shook her head. 'I've never passed on anything significant about Maynard, nor would I.'

She was no longer denying there was something to tell, Eve noted.

41

Eve messaged to update Greg and the gang after she got back to Lance's study. If only Lucy's connection with the Grevilles would push the police to ask Maynard more questions, but with the family apparently away and Lucy refusing to admit she'd shared his secret, it didn't seem promising.

She was busy agonising over Lucy's safety and what Maynard might do, when she saw Sonia leave the house. She seemed nervous, glancing over her shoulder and looking at her watch repeatedly as she dashed to her car.

Eve needed to be clear-sighted about this. She now knew that Sonia believed Lance had prevented her from taking an acting job that could have changed her life. Eve could only begin to imagine her fury. Yet she'd taken no action about that, or about Lance's past slights, and it didn't fit with her character. Why had she meekly stayed by his side, acting as his hostess and apparently cheering him from the sidelines? Eve wasn't sure she'd have killed to get her revenge, but she couldn't dismiss the idea.

She hesitated for a moment, then rose from her seat, causing Gus to leap up too, tail wagging. 'Let's get going,' she said to him. She only hoped she could catch Sonia in time to follow her.

Eve was all fingers and thumbs as she adjusted Gus's harness when they reached the car. She made it to the bottom of the drive just in time to see Sonia in the distance, heading inland, just as Maynard had the night before. Eve hoped she wasn't driving all the way to London too.

But it soon became clear she was making for Blyworth. Eve kept well back, but she could still see Sonia ahead of her, joining a queue for one of the town's car parks. At this rate, Sonia would escape while Eve was still waiting for a space. What to do? Eve left the queue, hoping against hope she'd find on-street parking in time to see Sonia leave the car park. In the end, she parked with at least a foot of her Mini over double yellow lines. It was the first time she'd ever done it. She'd always half wished she was a rule-breaker and had wondered how it would feel. Now she knew: deeply uncomfortable. She could do without being fined too, but she really wanted to see where Sonia went. She was back at the car park's entrance within two minutes, just in time to see her emerge and head up one of the town's beautiful half-timbered streets and enter one of Blyworth's more upmarket inns, the Blue Duck.

Eve walked round the side of the building, where she could peer through a window to assess the situation. At last, she managed to spot her, sitting at a table. The empty chair opposite her had a coat hanging over it. Eve looked at the bar, and spotted the man she might be meeting. A smooth-looking guy with black-rimmed glasses and thick dark hair. He took a while, talking to the barmaid. Eve guessed he was ordering food as well as drink.

'We need to get in there,' she said to Gus, 'and we need to do it quietly.' She put her finger to her lips and he gave her a doleful look. 'Promise I'll make it up to you.'

Eve needed to choose her approach carefully. Go too close

and she risked being seen, but too far and she'd never hear what they said.

In the end, she found a spot where she and Sonia were back to back, bought herself a drink and against every protocol the Blue Duck probably had, kept her beanie on. It wasn't much of a disguise, but at least her pixie crop was hidden, and Sonia wouldn't have to pass her if she went to the loo or the bar. It left Eve just about calm enough to settle down to listen.

'So,' Sonia's companion was saying, 'is everything going according to plan? You've addressed all the details we discussed? It's essential that your version of events is convincing.'

'Some of your suggestions worry me.'

There was a pause. 'I know, you said. But I've done this before. You have to trust me.'

'I just think it's too soon.'

'No!' Sonia's companion's voice was sharp. 'It's exactly the right time. You're a good actress – you know that. Just keep behaving as though you loved him and everything was sweet-ness and light.' There was a pause. 'Not much longer to wait now. You're going to make so much money! And so am I!' He gave a low laugh. 'I just need your dedication. Can you let me have it?'

At last, Sonia said: 'All right. Yes.'

Eve had been wrong about the food. The kerfuffle behind her told her Sonia and the man she'd met were reaching for their coats. Next came the scraping of chairs.

As they left, Eve considered what she'd learned. It seemed that Sonia had been panicking about something and the man had come to talk her down. But what were they up to? Eve considered one of the pub's exorbitantly priced sandwiches. She'd be safe to stay and eat now they'd gone, but she was too anxious about getting a parking ticket. She'd buy a sandwich on her way out of Blyworth instead.

As she walked Gus back to her car, her mind roved over what she'd heard. What was the source of the money Sonia's visitor had referred to? Could it relate to Maynard's blackmail? After all, Lance was supposed to talk when he was drunk, and in his sleep. Sonia might know all about Naomi and the belladonna. But it didn't fit with Lucy and the Grevilles, and the man had held up the money as something to look forward to, not something they'd already got.

Eve breathed a sigh of relief as she peered at her car's windscreen. No ticket. Luck was on her side. She opened a rear door and secured Gus in his harness. 'No, I know you don't like it but it's for your own safety. Because I love you.'

As they left Blyworth, she peered at her beloved dachshund in the rear-view mirror. 'What we heard proves one thing: I was right. Sonia sticking with Lance *was* artificial. Her continued fondness for him was an act and she was keeping it up with a goal in mind.'

She was just getting out of her car, back at Lockley Grange, when a text came through. It was from Felix Masters.

> *Just thought you might like to know that Lucy Garton has been in touch. Give her her due, she says she thinks things have changed and Sonia would be interested in any future acting parts that come up.*

That was interesting. It implied that Lucy was starting to think independently now Lance was dead. And maybe that she regretted scuppering Sonia's chances previously. But of course, if she'd discovered that Sonia knew, she might be acting out of fear too.

42

Sonia let Eve back inside Lockley Grange, leaving her feeling anxious and shifty.

'You nipped out for lunch?' She looked uneasy and Eve guessed the meeting in Blyworth was preying on her mind.

Eve nodded. 'I had a few bits and pieces I needed to do in town.' Best to stick to something like the truth in case Sonia had seen her.

Naomi appeared on the opposite side of the hall, raised her hand to Eve in a brief greeting then turned to Sonia. 'Madeline's run finishes tonight. She's coming down tomorrow afternoon.'

'Good, good,' Sonia said, after a moment. 'She'll be happy, won't she? It's all gone so well.'

Naomi nodded, though nothing seemed to lift her spirits. 'Yes, it's all gone brilliantly.'

Sonia turned to Eve. 'Naomi's partner, Madeline Stone, directs plays. She's just had her first real hit. An absolute coup.'

'I remember hearing about it. That's fantastic.' Eve thought of the burglary and the person Naomi had hired to do an illicit job for her and wondered if Madeline knew about it. If not, keeping up the lies would be a strain.

'How's the obituary coming along?' Sonia said. She probably wished Eve would finish up and leave them to it, especially as she was keeping secrets, just like Naomi, Maynard and Lucy.

'Good, thanks. I should be out of your hair very soon. I'm just making use of Lance's books in the library and one or two more papers and then I'll be sorted.'

Eve fancied Sonia looked relieved, but Naomi's expression didn't change, and she fiddled with the bangle she wore.

Back in the study, Eve messaged the WhatsApp group to suggest a catch-up that evening, then worked on an outline of the obituary. She found it almost impossible to concentrate, the clock ticking down to her wedding was getting so loud. She couldn't wait to share ideas with the gang. Surely something had to give.

Viv, Sylvia and Daphne came to join her and Robin for pasta with a creamy mushroom sauce. They sat round the dining table with glasses of white wine and focused on the different strands of the case.

'Can we rule anyone out of involvement in Lance's or Acland's murder?' Sylvia said.

'I'm inclined to give Erica a pass.' Eve had already explained about Lance sending her to spy on Maynard. 'Every question I had about her has been answered. I think she's convinced Acland did all he could to save Lance's life too, though that still strikes me as odd, given Acland's obsession with Sonia. He might not have poisoned Lance, but he was clearly a nasty, unprincipled man. I can't imagine he'd have been sorry to see Lance gone.'

'So you think Erica was wrong, and Acland was just going through the motions?' Sylvia was frowning.

Eve savoured a mouthful of mushroom sauce as she pondered the question. 'I suppose so. Except I'm not quite satisfied with that answer either. Erica's no fool. My gut tells me she'd have sensed it if Acland was faking.'

'Perhaps the oath he swore when he became a doctor came back to him when he saw an old friend in trouble,' said Daphne, who found it very hard to believe ill of anybody.

'Or the situation could have been more complicated than we realise,' said Sylvia, who didn't.

'So let's take it that Erica's out of it,' Viv said, scribbling on a loose sheet of paper.

'I've heard that it's possible to buy new notebooks,' Eve said at last. 'Apparently they sell them at the stationers in Blyworth.'

Viv raised an eyebrow. 'Very funny.'

'Here, have one of mine.' Eve reached one from a drawer in the sideboard. She had lots, though she still found it strangely hard to give one away.

Viv stroked it as though it were a new pet. 'Thank you. What about Naomi? She seems less likely?'

Eve shrugged. 'Character-wise, I agree. I'd just feel happier if I knew why she's taken delivery of stolen paperwork, hired someone to do something secret and talked about destroying someone the day of Lance's party. I can't write her off until I understand all that. Motive-wise, she could have killed Lance because he rubbished her paper, or if she found out he'd kept quiet about Maynard trying to poison her. It would be terribly hurtful. And it's possible she targeted Acland because he'd found her out, or she knew he was in on Maynard's secret too. But she's not top of my list. She's got an alibi for Jenna's death, if she was killed, albeit provided by her dad. And I still find it hard to imagine her murdering anyone, let alone a sister.'

'And Sonia?'

'She's newly interesting.' Eve filled them in on what she'd overheard that day. 'She and this unknown guy are down to make money, and he wants Sonia to keep up the pretence that she loved Lance. The guy pleaded with her to dedicate herself for just a little longer. I've no idea what it means, but Lance lost her an acting part, had multiple affairs and publicly humiliated her. She had a motive to kill him. And if she did, it's not impossible Acland somehow guessed. He was dogging both their heels after all. Sonia hated Jenna too, though that dates back years, so the case against her feels less compelling there. And she didn't cry at the party, so the chilli-oil hanky must have belonged to someone else.'

'I guess we're on to Lucy,' Robin said.

'Now we know the secret Jenna was about to reveal and its likely effect on Lance, I had a wild idea about her heading down to Cornwall to kill Jenna. She devoted her life to Lance after Jacqueline died. I imagine she could have persuaded Jenna to walk along the cliffs with her late at night and although she's clearly very fond of Naomi, I don't think the same goes for Jenna or Maynard. Then if Acland killed Lance, I could see Lucy poisoning him in revenge, but I really doubt that's how things played out. If Acland was guilty, he must have decided to go and watch Lance die. I could believe that, but then to be careless enough to reveal his presence to Erica? It feels unlikely when he'd have had so much at stake.'

Viv nodded. 'So Acland's looking less likely then?'

'I think so. I can't see why he'd kill Jenna either.'

Robin topped up everyone's drinks. 'If we accept that, then Lucy becomes less likely for Acland's murder. I can't see her motive unless she was avenging Lance's death.'

'Yes.' Eve thought back to her previous theories. 'I'd wondered if she could still have killed him in the belief that he was guilty, but on reflection, I think she'd have wanted proof.' She looked down at her own notebook. 'So as ever, Maynard comes to the fore.'

'He had a motive for killing Jenna, if she was pushed,' Sylvia said.

Eve nodded. 'Jenna knew Lance wasn't his biological dad

and we know Maynard's a despicable snob. I think he'd have been horrified at the idea of his true parentage coming out and he always hated his sisters anyway. Then he could have killed Lance for a combination of money, revenge and a determination to shut down his secret, which apparently only Lance and Lucy knew.' Eve turned to Robin. 'I'm still scared for her. I tried to warn her again, but she won't talk openly about Maynard's secret, let alone admit she's passed it on.'

'You've done what you can.' Robin took her hand and gave it a squeeze. 'Then we come on to Maynard's motive for Acland. It looks possible Acland was blackmailing him, just like the unknown individual on the bike. That would be quite enough to put him in danger.'

Eve nodded. 'Everywhere we look it's Maynard, but we've no proof.' And her parents were arriving in Saxford in little over a week. It was a far lesser worry than getting justice, but she was still finding it hard not to panic. She'd banked on having this time to get sorted.

It wasn't long before the group disbanded. 'You must be exhausted after last night,' Daphne said, patting Eve on the shoulder as she, Sylvia and Viv made their way out into the crisp, cold night.

Eve was certainly desperate to get to bed, but despite the trip to London the night before, she lay there wide awake. Robin slung an arm around her but before long, he was sound asleep.

Eve lay there feeling tense. She was so worried for Lucy and dreaded dreaming of thudding feet in Haunted Lane. At some point, despite her fears, reality faded away.

For once, waking to the sound of the footfalls and Gus whining didn't send her heart racing. She just felt a terrible sense of foreboding. She longed to ring Lockley Grange and ask someone to check on Lucy, but she had no way of knowing what was really going on or making her request sound sensible or compelling.

When she went to the village store to pick up some milk the following morning, Moira already had the news – heaven only knew how.

'Oh yes, Eve, I can't believe someone hasn't already told you, what with you working at the Grange. Lucy Garton was attacked in the night. Hit over the head and left for dead, so I hear. She's in hospital now and I understand it's touch and go. Such a very terrible thing to happen.'

43

Soon after Eve got back to Elizabeth's Cottage, she got a call from Sonia, warning her to steer clear of the Grange that morning. '*Poor Naomi's had to put Madeline off visiting until tomorrow too. The place is crawling with police.*'

Eve understood it was a shame to postpone Naomi's partner's visit, but saying 'poor Naomi' when someone had tried to murder Lucy felt like odd priorities. She wondered just how angry Sonia had been with her over the lost film part and if she was panicking inside. If she'd failed to kill Lucy, she must be terrified.

'What happened exactly?'

'*None of us know.*' Eve could hear the fear in Sonia's voice, as though her breathing was tight. '*It's frightening. Poor Lucy.*' It was so hard to tell if she was being genuine. '*Someone walked into her suite and hit her over the head. We only found her this morning. Naomi noticed her door was ajar, got the mother of all frights when she saw her, and called an ambulance. She came round half an hour ago apparently.*'

Robin was busy on his phone, Eve noticed. The note he put

in front of her told her he was already getting updates from Greg.

Attacker approached from behind. Lucy can't identify them.

'If I were Lucy, I'd have locked my door at night,' Eve said. She hadn't been firm enough. She should have made her realise the danger was real.

'*I've been locking mine.*' Sonia's deep breath was audible. '*The trouble is, Lucy's such an old, established part of the family I don't think she can believe any of the household would do her harm.*'

It certainly hadn't worked when Eve had tried to warn her about Maynard. She'd been confident she could predict his behaviour. The question was, had she been right, and someone else was to blame? Or had she misjudged him?

Eve visualised him lacing his sister's conserve with poisoned berries. To be capable of that, as a teenager...

Sonia promised to let Eve know when she could come back to finish off and Eve expressed her sympathy and let her get on with it. It was frustrating to be stuck at arm's length.

Once she was off the phone, she turned to Robin. 'There's no question that the attack was genuine?'

He shook his head. 'None whatsoever. She's very lucky to be alive, apparently. From the medical evidence, the team guess she might have heard her attacker and shifted slightly so the blow didn't land as cleanly as it could have. Either that, or her intruder's aim was off. She hadn't gone to bed. Naomi Hale found her collapsed on the sofa, facing away from the main door to her suite.'

Perhaps she would have locked up when she'd finally turned in. 'They haven't managed to question Lucy herself yet, beyond asking if she saw her attacker?'

Robin shook his head. 'It's too soon, but they'll be on to it the moment she's well enough.'

Eve updated the gang on WhatsApp, then paced the sitting room as she and Robin tossed out ideas.

'Sonia sounded scared, but whether she's frightened of the killer or worried Lucy will identify her is hard to say. Her motive's there. She must have been livid with Lucy after she kept Felix's offer from her.'

Robin looked thoughtful. 'Any thoughts on how to find out more?'

'I'd like to go back to Lockley Grange as soon as possible. I might be able to get a look at Sonia's private papers. Perhaps they'll hold a clue as to what she's up to.'

Robin took her hand. 'It's too risky. We're about to get married. Think of the cost if I had to cancel everything because someone bumped you over the head too.' He grinned but his eyes gave a different message.

'I wasn't thinking of anything daring. I could ask to discuss the draft of the obituary, then have a snoop while she makes me coffee. She's bound to offer.' Eve didn't discuss draft obituaries as a rule. Relatives always wanted to rewrite everything from their own point of view. But all the same, Eve needed an excuse to talk. 'Perhaps I'll leave Gus with you, to make any snooping I do that bit easier.'

Robin's eyes still held hers. 'All right, but please be careful. What about the other suspects? Does the attack on Lucy alter your thinking for Erica or Naomi?'

Eve shook her head. 'I'm convinced the couple she saw were Acland and Erica, but I'm all but certain Erica's innocent. If she thought she'd been identified, I think she'd finally give in and admit what happened to the police. As for Naomi, I suppose she could have tried to kill Lucy for keeping Maynard's attempt on her life a secret, or if Lucy found out she'd killed Lance. The former would be a big coincidence. It's not as though Naomi had any reason to suddenly go googling "Mosh" like I did, or rootling around in the library. The latter's not impossible, I guess, but that's also the only motive I can see for her killing Acland. It would be unlucky if two separate people saw her commit murder. And she doesn't fit for Jenna: no motive and an alibi.

'But the questions about her remain. Snooping at her stolen papers might solve everything, but I'm sure she'll have hidden them away. She certainly didn't want Maynard to see them.' She turned her mind back to the latest developments. 'Do you think the change in murder method is significant?'

Robin frowned. 'It's possible one person killed Lance and Acland and another attacked Lucy.'

'And then Jenna was pushed.'

'Perhaps. We still don't know for certain that it was murder.'

'True.' But Eve was sure that it had been.

Robin was sitting on one of the couches as Eve continued to pace. Gus looked from one of them to the other and shifted uneasily. It made Eve stop and sit down too.

'The other possibility,' Robin said, giving the dachshund a soothing pat, 'is that the killer switched methods to put us off the scent. Or just because it was hard to poison something that only Lucy would eat or drink.'

'So it doesn't tell us anything for certain. If we're looking at one person attacking all four victims, then Maynard just trumps Sonia in my book. I'll bet he's done the same research you did and knows his remaining blackmailer is connected to Lucy's cousins. That would make them and her obvious targets. I wonder what made Lucy tell them his secret, assuming she did.'

'Maybe she was with them soon afterwards and it was too big to keep to herself.'

Eve could imagine it being a burden, but Lucy must have agreed to cover it up. Making that momentous decision then telling a third party would have reflected badly on her. Then again, people didn't always act rationally when they were under pressure, and perhaps she was especially close to one of the Grevilles. She was certainly up to date about their movements. The fact that one of their number had waited until now to blackmail Maynard was interesting. Perhaps it had never occurred to them until he became an MP and they saw how much he had to lose. Or maybe the blackmailer suddenly needed money, which had driven them to it.

'Any idea how to catch Maynard out?' Robin asked, breaking into her thoughts.

'I'd rather hoped the police might do that, especially now Lucy's been attacked. Surely they can ask him about his trip to London and Lucy's cousins' house?'

'I imagine they might now.'

'I'll go back to my journalist colleague, Monica Sutton, too. For some reason, she's agreed to publish stories that play into Maynard's hands. She as good as admitted it was a case of "I'll scratch your back if you scratch mine". Either Maynard's feeding her information about something else, or she's keeping him close because he's the story. After the latest attack, perhaps I can lean on her to tell me more.' She sighed. Monica would be a tough nut to crack, but she was human just like everyone else. Emotional blackmail might work.

Eve called Monica the moment she and Robin had finished talking.

'*Ah, come on, Eve,*' Monica said. '*You know I can't tell you. It would jeopardise something I've been working on for months.*' But she sounded uncomfortable.

'There's a woman barely alive in hospital and she's still in danger. Off the record, I think Maynard might be responsible. Knowing more could save her life.'

'*I doubt it.*' She sounded more trenchant now.

'Look, what if I send you all my thoughts on everything that's happened – in the strictest confidence – and you reply with anything you can say that might help me?' It was a risk. If any of what Eve guessed turned out to be true it would make a huge story. But Eve trusted Monica.

'*All right, deal!*' Monica sounded relieved. Her conscience must be troubling her at least a little.

Eve wrote a long email, detailing everything from her thoughts on Jenna's death up to her latest hunches following the attack on Lucy and sent it off, praying that she was doing the right thing.

After that, she pondered the following day. If she was allowed back into Lockley Grange, she might be there when Naomi's partner Madeline came to visit. That could be interesting. If Naomi was going to share her secrets with anyone, a partner seemed the most likely candidate. She googled Madeline Stone and found rave reviews of the play she'd been directing. It had run from 9 September until now, first in the smaller Edinburgh venue, then in the larger one, and had sold out every night after the first three performances.

After that, Eve worked more on Lance's obituary and as the day wore on, bits of news came through. She relayed everything to the WhatsApp group.

The police *had* asked Maynard about his London and Epping trip. He'd denied everything. His father's car had been picked up on a couple of cameras, but there was no proof that he was driving it. The rest of the household denied all knowledge too. If anyone had seen him go they weren't admitting it. Unfortunately, they hadn't stuck together that evening, so no one could alibi anyone else.

The good news was that Lucy was doing better than they'd hoped. She might be allowed home the following day. The police had suggested she stay somewhere else, but she was determined to go back to Lockley Grange. She'd told them she believed her attacker had come in from the grounds and that none of the Hales would dream of harming her. Her assailant had entered her suite so quietly that she hadn't known she'd had company until she felt the blow. It had happened at around one in the morning. She said she'd never needed much sleep, and in her shoes, Eve wouldn't have felt relaxed enough to go to bed early either. But Eve would have locked the door.

'Why on earth won't she go and stay somewhere safer?' Eve said to Viv, when she went to do her shift at Monty's that afternoon.

'I know I would.' Viv popped some sticky ginger buns into the oven. 'Unless she knows she's not in danger and the attack was a put-up job.'

Eve shook her head. 'I wondered the same thing, but the medics are convinced. She's very lucky to be alive. And there was one more bit of information that came through just before I left Elizabeth's Cottage. The attacker hit her a second time after the bump on the head. Her shoulder's broken. Whoever did it must have been seriously angry with her. It's lucky they thought they'd killed her with that first blow.'

44

The following day, Eve went back to Lockley Grange. She hadn't been there long when she got an email from Monica Sutton in response to the sensitive information she'd sent the day before.

> *Blimey!* Monica had written, *What a nest of vipers! But your theories have reassured me that what we're investigating has nothing to do with the murders in Suffolk. As for Jenna Hale's death, I can contribute something useful. You can cross Maynard off your list. We know for a fact that he was breaking the law that night, but right here in London, not down in the West Country, and the crime wasn't quite as egregious as murder. I was keeping him close because he talks too much. I managed to create a bond by publishing those articles, and he let things slip that helped me home in on the truth. You'll have to wait for the details, but I hope that helps. And if you fancy pushing any information my way once you've got your ducks in a row, I'll be eternally grateful.*

The news pulled Eve up short. She sat there re-reading the message, but it was quite clear. Maynard hadn't killed Jenna.

She felt a huge sense of anticlimax, though she wasn't out of suspects. Sonia immediately rose up the list, but she didn't fit the bill as convincingly as Maynard. Perhaps they were dealing with more than one killer after all, or Eve had misunderstood the meaning of the chilli-oil hanky. Eve messaged the WhatsApp group to update them, feeling anxious.

After that, she turned to pick up the flowers she'd bought for Lucy from the village store. She was just about to take them to the woman's suite when she spotted Naomi out of the window. She was walking slowly up to a battered old VW Beetle where a slight woman with thick, dark hair was emerging. This must be Madeline, the theatre director, whose visit had been put off yesterday. She exited the car, dashed towards Naomi and held her tight. It must be a big relief for the pair to reunite, now that Madeline's first major production had finished. Eve imagined she'd have itched to come to Suffolk to be with Naomi after Lance's death, but the production sounded make-or-break, careerwise. Naomi had made it clear she didn't want to scupper Madeline's chances, and it wasn't as though Edinburgh was on the doorstep.

The pair turned towards the house. Madeline had an arm around Naomi's waist, but Naomi looked unhappy and distant. Eve couldn't help wondering if it was because of the secrets she'd been keeping since her father's death. Perhaps it would change her relationship with Madeline forever.

Eve fought with her conscience, and however intrusive it was, concluded that it was morally excusable to try to hear what the pair said. It was the first chance they'd had to talk face to face since Lance's murder, which was a prime time to share dark secrets. Eve was glad she'd left Gus at home for once. He knew how to keep quiet, but it would be that bit easier to be subtle without him. She went to stand in the corridor and listened, picking up distant voices. Sonia greeting Madeline, she thought, but she'd probably give the pair some space after saying hello. Sure enough, Sonia said something about having to go out soon, and Eve caught a glimpse of her ascending the stairs. Moments later, she heard a door closing somewhere on the ground floor. She checked over her shoulder to make sure she wasn't observed, then followed her nose until the murmur of Naomi and Madeline's voices reached her.

They'd gone into one of the smaller rooms, which had two exits, one on to the corridor and one to another room. Guiltily, Eve let herself into the adjoining room, but she still couldn't hear clearly. She was going to have to take risks if she wanted to know more. At last, she put her ear to the panelled door which connected the two rooms.

'Don't let's talk about what's been happening here,' Naomi was saying. Her voice was rather stiff. 'There's nothing to say, beyond what you already know.'

'Really?' Madeline sounded anxious. 'Because I feel like you're holding out on me. And we promised to tell each other everything, remember? Always and forever?'

There was silence and it was Madeline who spoke again. 'Please, Naomi, you're scaring me. Tell me, what is it?'

There was a long pause, and when Naomi replied, Eve could tell she was fighting tears. 'Nothing. Tell me about your run. It sounds like a triumph.'

Madeline gave a deep sigh. 'Boasting apart, it was. Better than I could possibly have hoped for. Everything's opening up for me. Despite the lack of the brass palm tree.' She laughed but the sound was unsteady. An attempt to lighten the mood perhaps. Eve tried to think why the idea of a brass palm tree was familiar.

'Ah, yes.' Naomi tried a laugh too, but it sounded even less convincing than her partner's. 'Sorry about that. Letting you down two days before you opened wasn't ideal. I was convinced Dad would be happy to lend it to you.'

'Me too.' Madeline's laugh was a little more convincing this time. 'I remember you saying he thought it was kitsch.'

Something Madeline had wanted as a prop, presumably. And Eve made the connection now: she'd seen the offending article in a huge photograph displayed on the day of the party. Lance had made disparaging comments about it, but Lucy had put it up in the hall at Sonia's suggestion, to make the entrance look warmer and more inviting.

They went on to talk about Madeline's plans. Naomi was driving the conversation, keeping it on neutral subjects. Surely, she'd crack and share something more personal with Madeline eventually? Eve felt increasingly awkward standing there, listening to stuff that had no bearing on the murders.

At last, Naomi's voice lowered a little. 'Madeline, there's something I need to tell you.'

At last. But at that same moment, Eve heard her name being called. *Heck.* It was Sonia. It was the worst possible timing, but there was nothing for it. Eve crept away from the door and let herself out of the room. It would have been very hard to explain if Sonia had seen her emerge, but she wasn't in sight. Eve could hear her voice from somewhere near Lance's study.

'Ah, there you are!' She smiled as Eve approached. 'I just wanted to let you know that I'm going out. You said you'd nearly finished, so I wanted to say goodbye if I'm likely to miss you.'

If Eve wanted to snoop at her papers, she might have to do it in her absence. She pasted on a smile and thanked her for all her help. It felt as though Sonia was dismissing her. How would she find out the truth if she lost access to the Grange?

Eve needed to make every second count. She'd lost the chance to hear what Naomi was going to tell Madeline, but she could at least reason with Lucy. It was time to deliver her flowers. Surely someone could persuade her to move out until the killer was caught.

Eve traipsed upstairs, where she knocked gently on the door to Lucy's suite.

'Come in.' Lucy's voice was sad and weary, but when Eve entered, she wasn't in bed. She sat on her sofa facing away from the door, her arm in a sling, head bandaged. She turned as Eve entered and winced as though it hurt her to move. She still wasn't locking her door.

'I hope I'm not disturbing you,' Eve said. 'I can see I'm not being very original.' There were multiple bunches of flowers in the room.

'You shouldn't have,' Lucy replied, 'but it was a kind thought. There's a vase in the display case there if you wouldn't mind.'

'Of course,' Eve approached the glass-fronted cabinets she'd admired on her previous visit.

After she'd filled the vase with water, cut the ends off the stems and arranged the flowers, she hovered in the doorway. Lucy hadn't invited her to sit down.

'Lucy, I'm so sorry about what's happened. You know you'd be welcome to stay with me and my fiancé if you'd like?' Until her twins arrived for the wedding, obviously... 'Or there are rooms at the Cross Keys if you'd prefer more privacy.'

But Lucy just shook her head. 'It's kind of you, but I'd rather stay here. I've made my home with the Hales for more than twenty years. I can't turn my back now.'

Eve nodded, then said goodbye and left the suite. Frustration was going to be the order of the day, clearly. As she walked down the stairs, she looked out of the window to the forecourt. Madeline was leaving already. She had her head down, her arms gripped tightly around her torso, hugging herself. Instead of driving straight off, she sat in her car, slumped over her steering wheel. Inside, Eve could hear the faint sound of crying.

45

Eve went back to Lance's study and fumed with frustration. Whatever Naomi had confessed to Madeline, it seemed to have left them both devastated. Outside, Madeline still hadn't driven off. She looked utterly destroyed.

The thought brought Eve up short, reminding her of what she'd overheard Naomi say on that phone call to her friend.

She sat down at the desk and went through her notes. Here it was.

You know what it's like when you know something needs doing, even if it involves destroying someone you love? Before Friday I'd never have imagined I was even capable of it.

Naomi had told the police she'd been talking about destroying Lance's reputation, but Eve had always suspected it was a lie.

And then, at another juncture, she'd said: *I can't tell her. Not yet.*

Eve had imagined she'd been talking about confessing something to someone in the house – Sonia, or perhaps Lucy. But what if there was another explanation behind the snippets of conversation? Something that had nothing to do with the murders. Because however awful and dramatic things were, people still had their ordinary, everyday concerns, which could feel every bit as heart-wrenching as the news that made the papers.

Eve thought of Naomi's first phone call again. Whatever the truth behind her words, they related to a decision made on Friday, and if she'd lied about them relating to her dad, there had to be a reason for that. It suggested she hadn't wanted to tell the truth at that point. *I can't tell her. Not yet.*

Eve was starting to suspect that the 'her' was Madeline, and that the destruction Naomi knew she'd wreak related to ending their relationship. She wouldn't want to do it during Madeline's successful theatre run. As to what had brought that to a head on the day of the party, there was another event Eve could think of which appeared to have affected Naomi, on top of the row with her father: her conversation with Erica. She'd rushed to her immediately after Lance had shown her up in front of the guests and they'd huddled together, turning their backs on the roomful of people.

Eve had a new theory and she needed to put it to the test. She stood up and went to the gap behind Lance's glove drawer, where she eased out the note Erica had written.

Forgive me writing. I couldn't bring myself to ask you directly, but am I right? Are you feeling the same way I am? I spend all my time thinking about you but if I've misread the signs, please let me know – gently! – and I promise I'll banish these thoughts from my mind. It feels wrong to even ask given you're already attached. xxx

The hairs on Eve's scalp lifted – the thrill of feeling she was close to the truth. The note would fit just as well with Naomi as the recipient as it would for Lance. And Naomi had been fiddling with the zip on her bag just after she and Erica had talked so intensely, the night of Lance's murder. Maybe she was zipping it closed after stowing the note. If Erica had been handing something over secretly, it would explain the pair turning their backs. Lance had been watching, but from a different angle. Perhaps he'd glimpsed the exchange, and of course if there was a note, he'd want to know what was in it. He'd got paranoid – convinced Erica was betraying him. Any sign that she was ganging up with one of his children would anger him. Eve imagined him pinching the note from Naomi's bag. She bet that's what had happened. She'd even seen Naomi searching for something soon after the party. She'd told Eve it was missing paperwork.

But Eve needed to prove she was right. She picked up the note and left the study. Minutes later she was listening to Naomi crying inside her room as she placed the note on top of a bookcase just outside her door. After that, she prepared herself for a long wait. She needed to see Naomi's reaction when she found it. She hid herself just up the corridor in a doorway.

Half an hour of hovering was worth it. Naomi appeared, red-eyed, and stopped in her tracks to examine the note. After that she looked up and down the corridor, then tucked it into the pocket of the corduroy jacket she was wearing. She kept her hand over it and Eve was sure she had the answer. It was close to her heart.

At that moment, Eve marched up the corridor, ready with her excuse for being there. 'Hello. I've just taken some flowers to Lucy.' She leaned forward now. It wasn't just play-acting; she was genuinely concerned. 'Are you all right?'

Naomi closed her eyes for a moment, then faced Eve and nodded. 'Just found that missing paperwork I was looking for the other day.'

It was a boost to know she'd been correct. 'Sorry,' Eve said. 'To be honest, it was me who put it on the bookcase. I found it in your dad's study, and I had a hunch it had been sent to you. I thought you might miss it.' It all made sense now. Naomi did feel the same. She and Erica had fallen in love, but Naomi didn't want to break up with Madeline until her play had finished. It backed up what Eve had always felt about Naomi: she was thoughtful, felt things deeply, didn't want to cause hurt. In this instance, she couldn't avoid it, but she'd done the right thing. She hadn't even wanted to tell the police the truth about the conversation Eve had overheard about destroying someone. Eve could see her point of view. It should be Madeline who heard the news first.

Naomi seemed lost for words. 'I can't believe Dad stole it,' she said at last.

Eve nodded, though she could – all too easily.

She headed back towards the stairs to give Naomi some space. Talk about a period of emotional upheaval.

Back in Lance's study, she let her thoughts settle. The latest developments explained a lot but there was more she wasn't getting. It was to do with Naomi's reaction when Erica gave her the note. Eve remembered it well because she'd looked poleaxed. Of course, realising she'd fallen for Erica and knowing she'd have to break up with Madeline would be huge, but her feelings would be mixed. She'd be experiencing happiness and excitement alongside deep sorrow at what must be sacrificed. Yet Naomi had looked floored, and that had overridden everything. What was it about the note that had triggered that third emotion, and made it so strong?

Eve thought back. Immediately afterwards, Naomi had asked Erica something. Eve hadn't heard her words, but Erica's reply had rung out. She'd been vehement. *No. Of course not. No way.* Perhaps Naomi had thought Erica had been having an affair with Lance, just like everyone else did. She might have been hankering after her but felt it was no good, because of that. Or have been disappointed in Erica for her behaviour.

Either way, Naomi wasn't the sort to listen to tittle-tattle. If she believed it, she must have good reason, but she couldn't have seen them together. She wouldn't need to ask Erica if it was true, if she had. So maybe someone she trusted had told her it was the case.

Once again, Eve turned her mind back to the night of the party. Just after Naomi had questioned Erica, she'd accosted her father. Eve remembered how quick he'd been to usher her out of the room. After that, they'd had that furious argument. What if Lance had told her he and Erica were having an affair and she'd caught him out in a lie? But why would he lie about it when Naomi was fond of Sonia, and he knew it would upset her?

Eve paused a moment and paced the room, thoughts whirling in her head. Naomi had implied she and her dad had been close before he'd rubbished her research, and that had only been within the last month. A tiny pang of doubt attacked her somewhere deep inside. Was it possible...?

A moment later, she was sitting down again, scanning her notebook at speed, looking for the information she needed.

Two dates. 7 September – the night Jenna died – and 9 September – the day Madeline's production opened.

And then that one, odd, fact: Lance's unwillingness to lend Madeline the brass palm tree as a prop for her play. Why refuse? It was sitting there in his London house from what Eve had heard, and everyone knew he hated it. Naomi had been so sure he'd agree that she'd promised it to Madeline, only to let her down – presumably the night before she'd travelled up to Edinburgh.

The same night Jenna had died.

What if it wasn't Lance's unwillingness to lend it that had thrown a spanner in the works? Perhaps Naomi had gone round to ask for it, but Lance had been out. When she'd heard Jenna was dead, she'd have wanted to know where he'd been. Maybe he'd taken advantage of the rumours Maynard was spreading and told Naomi he and Erica had been together. Eve could see her agreeing to keep that quiet. If everyone thought Jenna had fallen, it would have felt harmless – a way to protect Sonia from hurt.

Eve took a deep, unsteady breath. It would certainly explain Naomi's reaction to Erica's note. And her row with Lance just afterwards.

Eve could see Naomi outside, walking across the lawn. She probably wanted some peace to come to terms with the break-up with Madeline, but Eve badly needed answers. She followed her out of the house.

It was still bitter outside. High in a Scots pine Eve could hear a crow cawing. She increased her speed to catch Naomi up.

'I'm sorry to disturb you again, but something's just clicked.' Eve explained her thoughts on Naomi's reaction to Erica's note. 'You were worried your father might have killed Jenna, weren't you?'

Pain shot through Naomi's face.

Eve felt horrible for adding to an already difficult day, but it couldn't be helped. 'I was worried someone at the party wasn't as upset by her death as they seemed.' She explained about the hanky she'd found. 'I think it was Lance who was using it to bring on tears.'

'It backs up my own theories,' Naomi said after a long pause. 'I saw him with a cotton hanky to his eyes. It's just so unbelievable but I think I've found Dad's motive. I managed to get hold of some of Jenna's papers and they mentioned Leonard Clarke.'

Ah. 'Those were the papers your friend delivered?'

Naomi nodded. 'He had to break into Jenna's flat to get them. I didn't have a key.'

'I talked to Leonard Clarke for your dad's obituary. Did Jenna's notes reveal why she was interested in him?'

Naomi nodded. 'She kept a diary which told me everything. You know already?'

Eve bit her lip. 'I'm afraid so.'

'Her diary explained the truth about Maynard's biological father too,' Naomi went on. 'It would fit if Maynard had killed Jenna: he's so hardened and ruthless. But it was Dad who asked me to alibi him and lied about where he was.'

'He said he was with Erica?'

She nodded. 'He asked me to vouch for him to save his marriage to Sonia. I've always liked her, so I helped because I didn't want to see her hurt. It surprised me about Erica, because I'd thought there was a spark between us, but of course, that wouldn't stop her being keen on Dad too. I was a bit hurt, but I put a lid on my feelings. I'd got no room to talk, given I was still with Madeline. I loved her – I still do – but not in the same way. My feelings have changed.'

Eve nodded. 'Life really throws some curveballs sometimes, doesn't it?'

Naomi gave the glimmer of a smile. 'It certainly is at the moment, but I confided in Sonia about Erica. Talking it over helped.'

It explained why Sonia was so sure Lance hadn't been having an affair with Erica. She knew Erica and Naomi had fallen in love. 'I've heard from a contact of mine that Maynard was definitely in London the night Jenna was killed.' It was only fair to pass on what she knew, but it wouldn't bring any comfort.

Quiet tears ran down Naomi's cheeks. 'I'm sure it was Dad now. He looked so scared when I told him I knew he'd lied about being with Erica. He insisted he'd told me the truth, but his panic was obvious. I should have told the police the moment I realised it wasn't true, but I still couldn't believe he'd killed Jenna. I wanted to find out more myself, first.'

They walked on in silence and Eve thought of Lance's half-finished note she'd found along with Erica's letter to Naomi.

Darling, come and meet me tonight at the pool. I'll head down there once things have quietened down. Let's talk, I

She couldn't help wondering if Naomi was the intended recipient. Presumably he'd been interrupted and never finished it. She wondered what he'd have done if Naomi had turned up at the pool. Tried to talk her round, or attacked her? She very much hoped for the former, but she couldn't be sure. And all the while, his own life had been hanging by a thread, entering its final hours.

It seemed all but certain that Lance had killed Jenna, but who had killed him and Acland and attacked Lucy? If Naomi knew they'd covered up Maynard's attempt to kill her, she had a potential motive for each of them and her brother might be next. But Eve baulked at openly asking what Naomi knew. If she hadn't found out, Eve hoped she never would, unless Maynard was a danger to her now. She'd say something oblique instead.

'Naomi, do you like blueberry conserve?'

Naomi wiped away the tears which were still falling and looked at her oddly. 'Yes, I like it. But why on earth do you ask?'

'Sorry, marketing question. We're thinking of introducing blueberry conserve cakes at the teashop next summer and it just drifted into my mind.'

'Oh, I see, sounds nice.' Naomi looked perplexed. 'Lucy used to make it for us with whole berries, years ago.' Eve watched Naomi closely, but she only looked surprised and confused for a moment longer – as well she might – before blinking the seemingly bizarre conversational pivot away. Eve was sure she didn't know the truth.

Naomi was off the suspect list and Eve was glad.

As they parted, she was confident Naomi wouldn't mention her odd question to Maynard. She hadn't seen them exchange more than a word or two the entire time she'd been at the Grange. Eve would have to work out whether she needed to warn Naomi about him, long-term.

46

Eve went back inside, shivering from the cold, and took out the sandwich and water bottle she'd brought with her. She ate quickly without registering the taste of the food. She was making progress, but time was running out. She was about to lose access to Lockley Grange and she couldn't still be chivvying away at this on her wedding day. It wouldn't be fair on anyone. She needed to work out how the heck the facts she'd amassed fitted together.

She went through her notes as she ate. When she got to the page on the way Terence Acland had followed Lance – probably hoping to prove he was being unfaithful to Sonia – a fresh thought struck her. What if he'd been blackmailing Lance, not Maynard? If he was sticking to Lance like glue, he might know he'd been down to Cornwall the weekend Jenna died. He'd sold the Tibetan cabinet after Lance was killed, but it could still have been Lance who'd handed it over. Perhaps Acland's efforts to revive him at the pool *had* been genuine after all. Once he was dead, the payments would dry up. And of course, if he'd had that enormous hold over Lance, he could have pressured him to divorce Sonia. There'd be no need to see him dead.

Acland probably still hoped to prove Lance was being unfaithful, though, to try to get Sonia onside. Eve shuddered. If she was right, Acland had been even more appalling than she'd thought – and she'd already decided he was awful. She thought of the scene Sonia had witnessed back in London – all that back-slapping between Lance and Acland, and a feeling of false bonhomie. She bet that was when the blackmail arrangement had been agreed.

Then another memory came to her. Moira at the village store said that Acland had been happy just before he died. When she'd quizzed him about it, he'd told her he 'thought the income from a scheme he was involved in had dried up, but it turned out there was more.' What had that been about? More income from his blackmail? If so, then Lance couldn't be the source after all. He'd been dead by then.

So maybe it had been Maynard who Acland had blackmailed. Acland and this cousin of Lucy's as well.

It focused her on Maynard again. Although Sonia also had motives, it was he who Eve imagined entering Lucy's suite. She visualised him stealthily opening the door and creeping up behind her as she faced the opposite wall. It would have been dark, curtains drawn, lamps glowing.

It was then that Eve realised.

When she'd visited Lucy, she'd loved how her entire sitting room felt full of light and movement. The effect was caused by the way the room's lights shone in the glass cabinets that covered the wall opposite the door to the suite. Eve had seen her reflection in them too and used it to tidy her hair.

If Lucy had been sitting where she said she was, she'd have seen her attacker when they entered the room, reflected in the glass. She couldn't have avoided it unless she'd had her eyes closed.

Heck. Eve felt cold all over. Lucy knew who'd attacked her, she was sure of it. Was she still protecting Maynard after all these years? Had he taken the place of his father in her mind now Lance was gone? But surely she wouldn't lie to the police if he'd tried to kill her. Her mind flitted to Naomi, Sonia and Erica, but produced the same result. It just couldn't be. And yet it must be. It had to be one of them and Lucy had to know who. They'd almost killed her, yet she'd come back, and she wasn't talking.

Eve must speak to her again. This was stupidly dangerous. She had to make Lucy see sense.

She grabbed her handbag in case she needed her phone and bounded up to the third floor.

Once again, Lucy's door was unlocked. In her haste, Eve knocked and walked in without waiting to be invited. Lucy was sitting on the same sofa she'd occupied when she was attacked. This time she didn't look round as Eve entered but when Eve appeared in front of her Lucy looked frustrated.

'I'm sorry,' Eve said. 'I know I'm trying your patience.'

Lucy just shook her head, perhaps in denial, perhaps in despair.

'Can I please make you some tea? We really need to talk.'

'I don't think there's much to say,' Lucy said, 'but thank you. I'd like some tea.'

Eve went through to the kitchenette. Outside, she could see Naomi and Erica crossing the garden, walking away from the house, holding hands. Some of the heaviness that seemed to have pressed down on Naomi had lifted. Or maybe Eve was being fanciful. She put water in the kettle and set it to boil, looking back out of the window again. The view from Lucy's suite was magnificent and a loving couple crossing it only improved matters. Not like the night Lance had died and Lucy had seen—

Eve's thoughts were thrown. When Lucy had seen a couple by the pool. She'd seen Erica and Acland, Eve was sure. But though Lucy's claim held water, she couldn't have seen them from her suite. Why hadn't Eve thought of it before? She'd noted the view when she'd first visited – thought how it probably hadn't changed for a hundred years. All her windows faced the garden and the woods. From this angle, you couldn't see the pool.

As the water came to the boil, Eve felt suspicion creep through her like icy water gradually filling her veins. Lucy must have gone to some lengths to see Erica and Acland in the middle of the night. But unlike them, she'd watched from afar. The way a cautious killer might if they wanted to check the overdose they'd administered had worked.

Every bone in Eve's body wanted to reject the thought. Lucy had just survived a brutal attack herself and she'd been Lance's right-hand woman for years. She'd howled in pain when she saw his body. But then wouldn't that be natural, a small voice whispered, if she'd held him in high regard for more than two decades, yet finally decided she must kill him?

That was all very well, but what would trigger her change of heart now? If Eve was right, she'd agreed to help Lance cover up Maynard's attempted murder of Naomi years ago. Her conscience probably troubled her. She might blame Lance for putting her loyalty to the test when she was so vulnerable, but why act on it after so many years?

She poured water into the mugs. What if Lucy had found out that Lance had killed Jenna? That could have opened her eyes to his sense of right and wrong. To what he'd made her do for him, and how appalling it was. The question was, how could Lucy have discovered the truth? But then she remembered the conversation she and Lucy had heard from the room next door to her suite: Sonia talking to Molly Walker about clearing it of Lance's things. And there'd been no sign of a male presence in Sonia's room. Perhaps they'd slept separately and Lance had occupied the room next to Lucy's bedroom. She could have heard him through the wall. He drank too much and talked in his sleep. She bet he'd had disturbed dreams if he'd pushed Jenna off a cliff.

A picture was building. One of Lucy waking up to reality after all these years. There was Acland to consider too. But who was more likely than Lucy to know the doctor had discovered what Lance had done and was blackmailing him because of it? Heck, she could even have told Acland she'd found a note from Lance identifying another item that was to go to him. Acland would have invited her in with open arms, only for her to spike his tea with more digoxin. Eve couldn't prove it, but it would fit.

Lucy could have killed Acland because he was as bad as Lance, happy to cover up the murder of an innocent woman in exchange for the promise of cold, hard cash. But that was dangerously close to what Lucy had done herself. The circumstances had been different when she'd lied to protect Maynard, and by extension Lance, all those years ago. It was during the aftermath of the most horrific experience. She'd have been clinging on to security, not graspingly demanding money, but still...

And then at last Eve saw it, and the thoughts going through her mind were horrific. Eve doubted Lucy thought there was anything to choose between herself and Dr Acland. In her eyes, they were both guilty of terrible wrongs, just as Lance and Maynard were. And if Lucy thought that, then it was logical to assume she thought she deserved to die too.

The unlocked door, her refusal to leave Lockley Grange and her comment about being able to predict exactly what Maynard would do finally made sense. As did the fact that she'd lied to the police about not seeing her attacker. And her plea to Eve to make sure she uncovered the truth. Even her actions in the run-up to the attack fitted. The way she'd been looking up wills on the computer and sending presents to relatives. The envelopes she'd been clutching when Eve had seen her in

Saxford. She'd been setting her own affairs in order, Eve was sure of it, not tidying up after Lance's death.

She hadn't even looked round when Eve had entered her suite just now, and she'd looked disappointed when she saw who it was. She'd been hoping it was Maynard, come back to have another go.

Lucy's planned punishment for him had been to make him a murderer for real, only she'd survived. Maynard had attempted murder twice over.

Eve's job was to make sure justice was done afterwards.

'You're taking a long time.' Lucy had hobbled into the kitchenette and was standing just behind Eve's left shoulder.

47

Eve wasn't scared. If she was right, Lucy had been killing to right wrongs. In her eyes, she was stopping a rot she'd first noticed long ago, but had failed to tackle at the time. Her worldview might be totally out of kilter, but she hadn't expected to live or have her freedom. Eve didn't think she'd kill to escape now.

'I suddenly realised that you can't see the pool from any of your windows.' Eve sat on one of the kitchen chairs and Lucy took the other, looking defeated. 'You must have left your suite to watch Lance, the night of the party. That meant you saw the couple who were nearby at the time. No wonder you mentioned it. They hadn't been part of your plan. You wanted to understand what they were doing and if you'd been found out.'

With her good hand, Lucy took the cup of tea Eve had made. 'I didn't want anything to jeopardise my work.'

'You knew Lance had killed Jenna?'

Lucy nodded. 'And that the case would never succeed if I accused him. He slept next door – in his father's old room. He and Sonia found they needed their own space as time wore on.

It meant I heard him talking in his sleep, as soon as we came down to Suffolk. I stay up late, whereas he'd collapse in a drunken stupor. He kept saying, "It was an accident. I didn't push her. We struggled and she fell. I only wanted her to stay quiet. I didn't want her dead." So I knew, and it made sense. Lance had suggested I go away that night to see a friend of mine in Surrey, so I was out of the way, and Sonia was working. I didn't know why Naomi had alibied him, but I was sure she was lying and that he'd tricked her somehow. Lance's guilty conscience was obvious.'

'You knew Dr Acland was blackmailing him too?'

Lucy sighed. 'Yes, I'd seen him following Lance around and Maynard had commented on it. Terence was obsessed with poor Sonia, of course. Then he came to the London house shortly before we left for Suffolk and he and Lance argued. I had no idea of the cause, but it was very unusual. Yet despite the row, they were smiling when they emerged from Lance's study – each fawning over the other. I could see that they'd settled their differences in a way that somehow benefited them both, but it didn't leave Lance happy. Then when we came down here, I heard Lance talking about blackmail in his sleep, within a day of seeing him sneak that Tibetan cabinet out of the Grange. He'd put it in the boot of Dr Acland's car, so then I guessed, of course.'

Eve could see it all. 'I saw Acland take the cabinet to a dealer. I photographed it and left the photo in the kitchen to see if anyone reacted. You talked about it as though you hadn't seen it in years.'

Lucy nodded. 'I was acting, but I wanted you to know who it had belonged to. I had to make sure you'd work it all out – and realise who'd killed me – even if the police didn't get that far.'

Eve was kicking herself. 'I was still wondering if it was Maynard who Acland was blackmailing. But it wasn't, of course, and in the end, there was never an outside blackmailer, was there? It was you who told Maynard to take his payment down to Epping Forest, and you who made sure he saw an unknown motorcyclist ride up to the house belonging to your cousins.' She closed her eyes for a moment. She'd never imagined it might be Lucy on the motorbike, but Leonard Clarke had told her he and Lucy earned extra money at uni, working as delivery drivers. 'Where did you get the bike from?'

She sighed. 'One of my cousins owns one – they taught me to ride, long ago. They're in France, as I said, so I knew they wouldn't realise I'd borrowed it – and that they'd be safe.'

'So you fooled Maynard. You wanted him to think it was you who'd let his secret out of the bag. After that, you guessed he'd kill you and be tried for murder, just as he should have faced justice all those years ago when he tried to poison Naomi.'

Pain gripped Lucy's face. 'You know about that? You're right.

'I could have let Maynard know I was the blackmailer – the result should have been the same – but I didn't think he'd believe it. He knows I'm not the sort, and there was a danger he'd work out I was simply goading him.'

But Eve doubted he'd have guessed. How could someone like Maynard possibly understand that Lucy was prepared to sacrifice herself because of her feelings of guilt and a desire for justice?

'I knew I wouldn't get to keep the money,' Lucy went on. 'Asking for so much was just a means to an end – a way of getting Maynard to see what a very hazardous liability I was.' Her head was in her hands. 'I've regretted not saying something about his attempted murder of Naomi so many times. Lance said Maynard was just a child, but deep down, I knew he was responsible for his actions. I was scared he'd try again, but I felt for Lance, so I kept watch and didn't speak out. As it was, I think Maynard dismissed Naomi as a threat once he understood her character. I heard him say do-gooders never have any power. It was pretty much what Lance thought too. But Jenna was another matter. I wondered if Maynard had pushed her, until Lance's night-time confessions. Maynard was innocent of that at least.'

'But once you realised Lance was a killer, you felt you had to act?'

Lucy nodded. 'Suddenly, the guilt over protecting Maynard and risking Naomi's safety became unbearable. Naomi's a dear. I should never have prioritised Lance's feelings and my secure bolthole over her wellbeing. Once I saw Lance for what he was, it threw a harsh light on other, smaller decisions I'd made too. I kept an invitation to act in one of Felix Masters' films from Sonia because Lance didn't think she'd be up to it. I realised I'd affected her whole life for a violent, ruthless man who would always prioritise himself.'

Eve sighed. 'I found out about that. For one wild moment I thought Sonia might be the killer. I knew Jenna had treated her badly, and the same seemed to apply to you, Lance and Acland.'

Lucy's look was bleak. 'Poor Sonia. I'd always trusted Lance up until then. I made it my mission to support him in any way I could after Jacqueline died. I hated myself, and I suppose I almost worshipped him by comparison. He seemed so strong and clear-sighted. I was humbled when he forgave me for choosing to leave with Bruno and it made me desperate to atone.' Her eyes were full of tears. 'It's hard to explain, but finding out Lance could be as evil as Bruno changed everything.'

'What made you leave him the note with the black border? It was a risk.'

She hung her head. 'I know, but I'd hoped I could remove it again without anyone seeing it. And if not, I didn't really care if people discovered Lance had been murdered. I just needed enough time to complete my plan, and I wanted him to feel scared. He deserved to be punished.'

'I can see that, I suppose. And why didn't you tell the police it was Maynard who attacked you? You knew he'd come for you, and you must have seen him reflected in your glass cabinets.'

'It's true, I did see him, though I pretended I hadn't. My plan was to sit there with my back to him and let him get on with it, but I failed.' She was sobbing now. 'I flinched when he came for me. Switched positions slightly. Maybe that's why I survived.'

'The police would have tried him for attempted murder if you'd reported him. Palmer would probably have decided he'd killed his dad and the doctor too.'

'But it was justice and the truth that I wanted, not that!' Lucy's tone was vehement. 'I needed Maynard to pay for the murder he'd tried to commit years ago. And for you to find out the truth about Lance and Terence and tell everyone why I'd done what I did. I could have confessed after Maynard's attack went wrong, of course, gone to jail, faced the publicity. Seen him get out before me.' She took a juddering breath. 'But the thought was too awful. No, I knew sooner or later Maynard would try again, and my original plan would come to pass.'

It was at that moment that Eve was distracted by a tiny click from the next room. Thoughts of Maynard made her chest tighten.

She got up from her chair and Lucy stopped crying. Eve peered round the kitchenette door, but the sitting room was quiet and deserted. She tiptoed to the door of the suite and listened. Nothing.

'I think we should lock your door and call the police,' she said, turning to Lucy, who'd followed her into the sitting room. 'I know you didn't want it this way, and I'm sorry, but we're out of options.'

At last, Lucy nodded, and went to a drawer in her desk. A second later, she was facing Eve again, frowning. 'The key's not there.'

Panic twitched Eve's stomach as she dashed to the armchair where she'd left her bag, but her mobile was missing too. A second later she was at the door of the suite, turning the handle, already guessing what she'd find.

It was locked.

'Maynard must have done this. Have you got your mobile?'

Lucy reached for her bag to one side of the sofa, her burst of energy evaporating the moment she looked. 'It's gone.'

Useless regrets flooded Eve's mind. Maynard must have sneaked into Lucy's living room and listened as they'd talked. Why on earth hadn't she acted more quickly? She'd been spell-bound by Lucy's story. Blind to what might happen next.

'I don't think there's anyone left in the house to help us,' Eve said. 'Sonia told me she was going out and I saw Naomi and Erica cross the garden when I went to make tea.'

Eve could hear sounds on the landing now. Heavy footsteps pacing to and fro. And then a smell worked its way under the door.

Petrol.

Eve felt sick with fear. She could see Maynard's plan now. It was a long way down from Lucy's rooms.

'Maynard, you won't get away with this.' She was shouting through the door. 'The fire investigators will see an accelerant's been used and you're the only one here. They'll know you're responsible.'

'No, they won't.' His voice was muffled. 'They'll blame Sonia. As you so helpfully pointed out, she had a motive for every victim.'

This was appalling.

'This isn't right.' Lucy's voice was a whisper. 'Maynard

must get the blame. And you must survive to make sure the truth comes out.'

'You too,' Eve said, but Lucy shook her head.

How the heck could they communicate with the outside world? 'Is your computer booted up?'

Lucy nodded, rushing towards it, but when Eve launched a web browser to send a message, she saw there was no internet connection. Maynard must have unplugged the router.

Her hands were shaking. The smell of petrol was intense now. Sickening. She was sure Maynard would put a light to it within seconds. He had no reason to wait.

Her heart going like the clappers, she browsed for available Wi-Fi connections on Lucy's laptop. With Maynard just outside the door, there was the briefest of chances...

There it was. The Wi-Fi hotspot connection on her own phone. Maynard must have it on him and the phone had data. She needed the password. It was crazy. She knew it so well, but her mind went blank. Precious seconds ticked past. The moment Maynard walked away, the hot spot would be out of range.

At last, it came to her. SylviaDaphne416. Her neighbours and part of an old phone number.

She had a connection, but it would be gone in moments. Maynard would run for it once he'd lit the petrol. Think, think. There was no time to try for a Skype call and she couldn't remember her password anyway. She wasn't sure WhatsApp would work either, without her phone to scan the QR code which would come up on screen.

She went for Facebook instead, bashing in the names of her twins and the year they were born to access her account. Then she was on a group chat she'd once set up with the gang.

Help. At the Grange.

She sent it.

Maynard guilty.

She pressed send again.

Stuck in Lucy's suite. M setting a fire.

She tried to dispatch the third message, but it was no good. The internet was out, and Eve could smell burning.

48

If she and Lucy died, Eve realised the police would probably think Maynard was guilty of all the murders thanks to her message. She didn't have many regrets about that, but she didn't want to die. The door was already burning and she hadn't even managed to tell Robin and the gang that they'd need the fire brigade. She hadn't thought quickly enough.

Eve moved to the sitting room window, looking at the ground far below. She was facing a sheer drop.

But then she thought of how clearly they'd been able to hear Sonia and Molly's voices from next door. Eve knew old houses were bad for soundproofing. Elizabeth's Cottage was terrible. But the sounds that travelled from room to room weren't usually quite so clear. She rushed through to Lucy's bedroom and started tapping at the wall.

'What are you doing?'

'Do you have a hammer? Or something heavy I can hit this wall with? There's a part that sounds hollow.' There was no way it was solid brick. She was betting there'd been a door there at one time, linking the two rooms. There might only be plaster-board over the top.

Lucy returned with a toolbox a moment later.

Eve slammed the bedroom door shut against the fire and pointed at it. 'Block the bottom with the duvet!'

Lucy moved as though in a daze.

If only this worked. If only they weren't trapped.

Eve found a hammer and gave it all she'd got. In an instant, she realised she was right. The hole she'd made showed a hollow cavity with more plasterboard beyond, breaching a gap between solid areas of brick. The smell of smoke was strong, and progress agonisingly slow.

At last, Eve began to attack the board on the far side of the gap, but Lucy's bedroom door was smouldering just behind them.

She managed to enlarge the gap so they could enter Lance's room, but even as she did so, she knew it was futile. The fire must be spreading up the corridor outside. There would be no way out. And Lucy hadn't crossed to Lance's room with her.

'Come on, Lucy! If you don't survive it'll be my word against Maynard's.' Eve had to make her fight.

At last, Lucy stepped through the jagged gap. There was a photograph of Lance and Sonia on the bedside table there, smiling back at her. And there, in the sloping roof, was a Velux window.

As Eve looked at it, wondering if there was any way they could use it to reach safety, Lance's bedroom door caught fire.

Eve turned to Lucy. 'We have to get onto the roof. And we need to be ready to go. The moment I open the window the draught will draw the fire into the room more quickly.' Eve could tell Lucy didn't want to come with her. 'I'm sorry, Lucy, but it's your duty. You have to finish this. I want you to climb out ahead of me.' Eve didn't trust her to follow otherwise. 'Open the window and climb out now, for everyone's sake.'

Eve couldn't let Lucy die.

As the fire spread across the carpet with alarming speed,

Lucy suddenly sprang to life as though Eve had finally got through. She shoved the Velux open, and Eve helped her up. It was hard going with one of Lucy's arms not working and she feared for her once she was on the roof.

'Press yourself flat against the tiles and keep away from the edge.' Thank goodness it wasn't icy.

The fire had reached the bed and the smoke was making Eve cough. This was all taking too long but she couldn't let her panic show. 'That's it. Just ease yourself across.'

At last, there was room for Eve to exit the window too, but how long before the roof went up?

Clinging to the edge of the window, her body tensed against the tiles, Eve visualised the shape of the Grange. The large apex roofline onto which they'd just climbed led to a perilous three-storey drop on the side they were on. But not on the other. Up and over the apex, the roof sloped down to meet a second, adjoining, triangular roofline. There was a dip between the two where there'd be no danger of falling. If the fire spread, they could still die up there, but it would give them some breathing space. If only one of the gang had seen her Facebook message. Sylvia and Daphne weren't as responsive on Messenger as they were on WhatsApp. They didn't have the app installed. And Viv might not hear her phone ping if she was busy in a noisy teashop. As for Viv's brother – he was still on holiday with his wife. He might not even have a phone signal. She was pinning her hopes on Robin. Praying he hadn't been using some noisy bit of garden machinery when the message arrived. In the meantime, they needed to move. It was freezing cold on the roof, but it wouldn't stay that way.

'We have to climb up,' Eve said. 'Over the top. You remember there's a sort of valley on the other side, where this roof meets another one?'

Lucy nodded.

'Can you manage with your arm? You go first and I can act

as a stop if you slip.' Unless she slipped herself and went over the edge.

Lucy was inching up, Eve just behind her, nearly at the top when the first bit of roof caved in behind them, consumed by flames. How quickly would the fire spread inside the house? Eve dreaded getting to the apex and looking down into a valley which had already collapsed to ashes. But they had to keep going.

'That's it. I'm right behind you.' If much more of the roof on this side collapsed, the apex would become unstable, even if the other side survived. They needed to get up and over as soon as ever they could.

It was just as they reached the top that Eve heard sirens. Police cars, ambulances and fire engines. Thank goodness. And there ahead of them was the slope down to the valley between the two roofs, as yet undamaged by the fire. Eve and Lucy looked at each other, then began the gentle descent on their bottoms, Eve yelling all the while to the emergency teams down below. Robin was there too. It was he and Gus who spotted her first.

49

The next few days passed in a blur. After being rescued by the fire brigade, everyone made a huge fuss of Eve, which was lovely in many ways of course, but also slightly inconvenient as her parents' arrival was imminent and she was behind with wedding admin. Meanwhile, cousin Peter had been in touch to ask if the beds at the Cross Keys had memory foam mattresses. Eve ground her teeth and counted to ten before she replied. If anything ought to give her a sense of proportion, it was Lucy Garton's sad story.

Viv had been trying to help with the last-minute stress, but this had somehow resulted in Eve's altered wedding outfit being sent to a small village the other side of Norwich. Robin had gone to fetch it, saying he was anxious about Eve's blood pressure.

Everyone kept saying they could both use a holiday, and shortly after Christmas they'd get it on their honeymoon. In the meantime, and just as joyous from Eve's point of view, they'd have a big family Christmas – a precious thing when her parents were normally so very far away in Seattle.

Alongside the wedding preparations, there were developments relating to the case, of course. Maynard and Lucy had been arrested and the truth was coming out. Eve felt desperately sorry for Naomi, who would finally hear that Maynard had tried to kill her, and that her dad and Lucy had protected him. She felt anxious for Lucy too. What Bruno did had changed her for life. Meting out justice in the way she had was terrible, but Eve felt she was broken. Not responsible in the way that another person might be.

Robin had nodded when she'd voiced the thought. 'She'll get a medical assessment and I'm sure the past will be taken into account when she's sentenced.'

When Eve finally spoke to Naomi, she got more insight into her character. She'd taken the news about Maynard and the attempted poisoning better than Eve had hoped. She said she'd never trusted him, but she could understand why Lucy and Lance had wanted to give him another chance. Her horror was for the way Lance had killed Jenna to avoid public humiliation, and how Maynard's murderous character had revealed itself again. She was sitting next to Erica, who squeezed her hand tight.

'I didn't want to tell anyone I was looking into Jenna's death,' she said shakily. 'I so hoped I was wrong, and Dad was somewhere else that night.'

Eve suspected another mystery was about to come clear. 'I know you got hold of Jenna's papers because you were suspicious, but did you go further? Hire a private detective or something, to do the legwork?'

Naomi nodded. 'It seemed like the only way, when I was stuck at the Grange. I arranged it through a friend and swore them to secrecy. I was so scared it would come out before I was sure of my ground.'

The second overheard phone call made sense now.

Poor woman. She'd had to deal with so much, but Eve could see she was strong. She suspected love and her passion for her work would pull her through. The parliamentary committee which had wanted to discuss her report had given her a fresh appointment. No one was admitting they'd been swayed by Lance's counterarguments, now it was clear he'd been a murderer. Witnesses who'd seen him in Cornwall on the night of Jenna's death had come forward, as soon as they knew what they were looking for.

Erica had been given a slap on the wrist for not admitting she'd seen Lance die, but the police weren't taking it any further. It didn't make a material difference. Erica told Eve she'd been dreading confessing the truth to Naomi, but Naomi being Naomi, she'd understood.

Monica Sutton was somewhat disgruntled. Her scoop on Maynard had been overshadowed by him being charged with attempted murder. All the same, she and her paper had proof he'd received large payments to lobby for an arms company in parliament. They'd got him on camera, thinking he was talking to one of the firm's representatives, the night Jenna died. Eve had promised to give Monica the inside story of her escape from Maynard as soon as she was legally allowed to do so.

She had to make one last trip to Lockley Grange to pick up her things from Lance's study. That side of the building was undamaged, though repairs to the other wing would cost a fortune. Something for Maynard to look forward to when he came out of prison. Naomi would get the London house as planned.

Eve sat opposite Sonia at the kitchen table after she'd got her stuff. It was another part of the house which had been declared safe. 'I'm sorry that everything's been so horrific.'

Sonia sighed. 'At least we know the truth now.'

In front of her was a notepad and Eve read what she'd written upside down.

For Naomi, the best stepdaughter a misfit stepmother could have.

A dedication.

Suddenly, Eve was back in the Blue Duck, listening to Sonia's conversation with the suave-looking man who'd talked about him and Sonia making lots of money. *I just need your dedication*, he'd said. *Can you let me have it?*

Eve almost burst out laughing. She'd thought he meant Sonia needed to be stoical. Keep lying about still loving Lance and the money would roll in. She'd assumed it had to be something semi-criminal at least. How ridiculous.

'You're writing a book?' Eve nodded at the words on the pad. 'Sorry. I couldn't help noticing.'

Sonia bit her lip in mock contrition. 'My publicist would have my guts for garters if he knew you'd seen that. He's firmly of the opinion that publishing to a huge media splash is the best way to go about it, with no advance publicity.

'It's all about the truth behind mine and Lance's marriage – a bit of a shock-and-tell book I'm afraid,' Sonia said, 'but he could be so cruel, Eve. My fury with him built up over the years until all I could think of was revenge.'

Eve remembered the stories Felix Masters had told her: the other women, the way Lance had publicly humiliated Sonia – playing up the ridiculous dumb-blonde stereotype – and turning down a life-changing job offer on her behalf. She got it. 'You planned to leave him just as the book was published? So no one suspected the truth about your marriage until the first reviews hit the newspapers?' Eve guessed the exposé would have far more impact if her true feelings came as a shock. She could see why the publicist had asked her to carry on acting as though everything in the garden had been rosy.

Sonia nodded. 'If he hadn't behaved so badly, I'd have thought it was too cruel. As it was, I was looking forward to pulling the rug from under his feet.' She went pale. 'Now I know what Lance did to Jenna it makes me realise how close to the wind I sailed. If he'd known what I was up to, he'd have done anything to stop me.'

It was a chilling thought.

Sonia took a deep breath. 'The latest developments will help the book sell even better, of course.' She closed her eyes for a moment. 'At least it will be out too soon for anyone to think I wrote it to benefit from the murders.'

Poor Sonia could certainly do without that.

Back in Saxford, time passed in a flurry. What with getting the spare rooms at Elizabeth's Cottage ready for the twins and their other halves, and making sure everything was set for her parents' arrival (they were staying in comfort at the Cross Keys), Eve barely had time to think about her piece for *Icon* magazine, but she had to get it done. She had a deadline, and there was no way she wanted it hanging over her as she walked up the aisle for a blessing at St Peter's.

She stayed up late one night to draft the opening paragraph and after that she was away, but she had to write a lot from scratch. The article was no longer an obituary and it barely featured Lance Hale. Eve had been in touch with *Icon* to explain she couldn't do it.

Part of her longed to show Lance for what he was, but it was complicated. If she wrote about him, she wanted to give the whole truth, not an edited version, and his guilt was part of that.

If she wrote honestly and completely, she'd make it clear that Naomi had lied when she'd alibied Lance. Lucy was going to plead guilty, and with no trial, the information wouldn't come from her. Eve would have to reveal Lance's motive for killing Jenna, too. Her true parentage would come out and Leonard Clarke's marriage would be on the line.

Eve couldn't do it to either of them. They'd been through enough.

She hadn't said all that to *Icon* – knowing she had such explosive details would make them determined to hold her to her contract. Instead, she'd told them she'd been advised that completing the obituary at this stage might be legally difficult, and promised to provide them with an alternative story instead. She'd written about Sonia and Naomi, focusing on their strong stepmother–stepdaughter bond and many achievements. She wished she could tell Lucy's story too, but as with Lance's obituary, there were too many innocent people who'd be hurt by the truth. Lucy wouldn't want that.

Eve looked again at the opening of her article.

The women of Lockley Grange – power, glamour, grit and compassion

She wasn't wild about the title. Power and glamour were too clickbaity and Sonia and Naomi were really the women of North London, but that wouldn't have worked. In any case, *Icon* loved the name of the Suffolk house; they said it sounded like something from a Brontë novel.

Huge and echoey, Lockley Grange is the imposing home of the Hale family, and has lately been the part-time base for two extraordinary women: Sonia Welton and Naomi Hale. Sonia is a household name, the face of some of the UK's most exclusive brands. But have you heard of Naomi, whose pioneering work on child poverty is changing policies as I write? The step-mother–stepdaughter duo are close and though they operate in entirely different fields, they each light up the world with their unique talents. Here is their story.

Thanks to some frantic phone calls and one last meeting with Sonia, Eve had plenty of personal tales to tell.

Three days later, Eve and Robin were married at 3.45 in the afternoon in Blyworth's registry office, a pretty half-timbered Tudor building. They were accompanied by Eve's parents, her twins and their partners, and their witnesses, Viv and Greg Boles. Then they travelled back to Saxford in a 1938 Rolls-Royce Wraith, the headlights picking out the lane ahead, Robin clutching Eve's hand and smiling as though dawn had broken after years of darkness.

Beyond St Peter's lychgate, the path to the church's arched doorway was lined with large white candles, and the church's interior glowed through the windows.

Eve felt a pang that neither of Robin's parents were living, but his cousin, Greg Boles's wife, was waiting at the door of St Peter's, one of three ushers who'd directed the many friends and relatives who'd flooded through the doors. Sylvia and Daphne were the other two, though Moira seemed to have joined in. Eve couldn't help but smile; she was clearly having a lovely time.

The guests were mostly seated in the glow of the candles inside the church. The place was a sea of light, white roses and ivy.

Eve's parents, her twins and their partners hugged her tightly before going ahead of her and Robin to find their seats. They were right at the front, alongside Viv, who was patting a wildly excited Gus. Next to Viv was her brother Simon and his wife, as well as Sylvia and Daphne. The gang had met the twins before, of course, and had hit it off with Eve's parents the moment they'd been introduced.

Eve thanked the fates for waterproof mascara, because she was streaming as she walked down the aisle. Robin seemed to be affected too. As for Jim Thackeray, Eve noticed he had to clear his throat twice before he began the blessing. Eve felt a surge of joy as she stood by Robin's side, and Jim nodded and smiled as though he'd always known this was the way things were meant to turn out.

A LETTER FROM CLARE

Thank you so much for reading *Mystery at Lockley Grange*. I do hope you had fun trying to work out who was guilty! If you'd like to keep up to date with all my latest releases, you can sign up at the following link. Your email address will never be shared, and you can unsubscribe at any time. You'll also receive an exclusive short story, *Mystery at Monty's Teashop*. I hope you enjoy it!

www.bookouture.com/clare-chase

The idea for this book came to me after watching three very competitive siblings and realising how destructive the need to succeed on other people's terms can be. As usual, I played around with possible ramifications until I had the bones of my plot.

If you have time, I'd love it if you were able to write a review of *Mystery at Lockley Grange*. Feedback is really valuable, and it also makes a huge difference in helping new readers discover my books. Alternatively, if you'd like to contact me personally, you can reach me via my website, Facebook page, X (formerly Twitter) or Instagram. It's always great to hear from readers.

Again, thank you so much for deciding to spend some time reading *Mystery at Lockley Grange*. I'm looking forward to sharing my next book with you very soon.

With all best wishes,

Clare x

www.clarechase.com

facebook.com/ClareChaseAuthor

x.com/ClareChase_

instagram.com/clarechaseauthor

ACKNOWLEDGEMENTS

Very much love and thanks as ever to Charlie, George and Ros!

And I can never say it enough, but I'm indebted to my amazing editor Ruth Tross for her clever, clear and insightful input, which makes such a huge difference. Heartfelt thanks too, to the entire Bookouture team who work on my novels. You can see what a phenomenal group effort it is by looking at the following page, where everyone involved is mentioned by name. They are the most wonderful, skilled and friendly group of professionals and it's an honour to work with both them and Ruth.

Love and thanks also to Mum and Dad, Phil and Jenny, David and Pat, Warty, Andrea, Jen, the Westfield gang, Margaret, Shelly, Mark, my Andrewes relations and a whole bunch of family and friends.

I'd also like to thank the lovely Bookouture authors and other writers for their friendship and support. And a hugely appreciative thank you to the generous book bloggers and reviewers who pass on their thoughts about my work, including some who have been with me right from the start. Their support is truly incredible, and it's also a joy when newcomers join in.

And finally, but crucially, thanks to you, the reader, for buying or borrowing this book!

PUBLISHING TEAM

Turning a manuscript into a book requires the efforts of many people. The publishing team at Bookouture would like to acknowledge everyone who contributed to this publication.

Audio
Alba Proko
Sinead O'Connor
Melissa Tran

Commercial
Lauren Morrissette
Hannah Richmond
Imogen Allport

Cover design
Tash Webber

Data and analysis
Mark Alder
Mohamed Bussuri

Editorial
Ruth Tross
Imogen Allport

Copyeditor
Fraser Crichton

Proofreader
Nicky Gyopari

Marketing
Alex Crow
Melanie Price
Occy Carr
Cíara Rosney
Martyna Młynarska

Operations and distribution
Marina Valles
Stephanie Straub

Production
Hannah Snetsinger
Mandy Kullar
Jen Shannon
Ria Clare

Publicity
Kim Nash
Noelle Holten
Jess Readett
Sarah Hardy

Rights and contracts
Peta Nightingale
Richard King
Saidah Graham

Made in United States
North Haven, CT
16 February 2025